THE ONE
KNIGHT STAND

COLLEGE STUDENT BY DAY. POKER PROFESSIONAL BY NIGHT.

MAREK GARCIA

ISBN: 1979252718
ISBN 13: 9781979252713

FOR THE KID WHO HAS FELT ISOLATED.
FOR THE KID WHO HAS SUFFERED WITH
DEPRESSION, ADDICTION, OR ANXIETY.
YOU ARE NOT ALONE.

FOR THE KID WHO HAS **IT**.
THIS ONE'S FOR YOU.

THE ONE
KNIGHT STAND

PROLOGUE

ACE: SHE HAS ME

Here's the thing—I admit I'm walking into a room full of losers. Why are they losers? Because they all come into this room thinking the same thing—they're going to make a lot of money tonight, and they're going to make it with ease! But what poker players don't seem to understand is that for someone to make money here, someone else has to lose it—meaning at least two out of three people are walking away disappointed.

What is it with us humans that we are constantly assuming we're great? Why do we always assume we have a God-given right where the odds are in our favor? And even worse, for some reason, people play soccer, sing, or go to school and admit they're mediocre. But when it comes to having cards in their hands, everybody's ego at the table kicks in, and players swear they're untouchable. Whatever it is, I capitalize off this human flaw.

But here's the other thing—I'm part of the exception. I make money off others' egos. I can look at them from within and distinguish myself. I don't gamble—I work. My strategy is unrivaled. I'm not one of them, at least not anymore. I acknowledged a long time ago that I didn't have a God-given right, so I earned my right. I used to be one of them, and it took me time, much pain, and work to become somebody else, but I did it.

This isn't just fun for me—this is my life. This is my full-time job, my medicine, and my best friend. I eat, sleep, and breathe poker.

Okay, now follow me, and watch as I make some money off these losers. Listen to that noise. Can you hear it? It's the loud sound of a poker room on a Saturday night—a thousand people shuffling their chips. Now, can you smell that? That's the smell of money, the smell of greed. But don't worry, this isn't the 2007 type of greed. This is the good type of greed.

As I sit down at my table, I start immediately. I scan the table. You know—for that one person? In all the movies, there is always that one guy. They call him the "sucker." The sucker is the one person you look for in a cash game to eventually extract all of his or her money. They think they have *it*, and they're characteristically arrogant. Oh yeah, and they usually wear either a hoodie and sunglasses because they just came here from watching the World Cup of Poker on TV, or they have the pretentious look—a nice shirt with an expensive watch they bought on Black Friday. They say if you can't spot the sucker within the first fifteen minutes of sitting down, then *you are the sucker*. This is why the first fifteen minutes after sitting at the table are the most important.

This time it takes me about ten minutes to identify her. She is making oversized bets, calling obvious strong hands, and committing a typical rookie mistake—showing her bluffs after the hand with a half-hidden grin on her face. It is only a matter of time until she makes a mistake against me where I can make her pay.

Now, this is possibly one of the simplest concepts while at the same time one of the hardest in this game—patience. It takes a lot of discipline to not call what can probably be a bluff. But it is all part of the plan— build her confidence, let her think she can keep winning, and just when she thinks she's about to pull her biggest move—*bingo*.

Any of this making sense to you? Don't worry; it's not supposed to—I make the money; you just watch.

After about an hour, it's time. I look down: ace, king; she raises to a hundred dollars, and I call, out of position, four players in the hand. The flop: ace, ace, four with no flush possibilities. It's like the universe wants me to take her money. I have trip aces with the best kicker. So what do I do? I check—I am going to let her get herself into trouble. I am hoping she has an ace and a jack, maybe pocket kings, or something similar so that she can make a heavy continuation bet. The next person checks and then there is a $300 bet, which the sucker raises to $700. This is where I act stupid and take a full minute to make my next move while seeming frustrated until I finally make the obvious call. This is called "slow playing," ladies and gentlemen. It makes the opponent assume your hand is weak, making them think they're ahead. Now, the other two players fold, so it's just me and the sucker. Next card: deuce—changes nothing. I check, and she bets eight hundred and fifty, everything going according to plan. Again, I take my time and try to seem as puzzled as I can in the two minutes until I finally make what I hope looks to be a tough call.

The river comes, and it's...you guessed it, a king. I have a full house now. This was actually not part of the plan; things are going better than what I even needed. I start to bite down on my own teeth with a fist over my mouth as my heart starts pounding through my chest like a prisoner trying to escape. Now I *know* I have the best hand, and I have some options.

I can check again and hope she makes another big bet, I can make a small bet and hope she calls or raises, or I can make a big bet to which she can also call or raise while running the risk of her folding. I choose the riskiest option—I check. I try to act like a scared dog, but inside I'm screaming, *Go all in, you idiot!* And that's exactly what happens. Well, not exactly. She bets $2,000, but that's still great news. Now, I take a couple of seconds, count my chips, and push fifty-three hundred in as I look up to meet her eyes, biting down a bit harder. She snap calls.

I flip over my cards and show my full house, still trying to keep eye contact. *See what happens when you play against me? I think it's time you go home, honey.* I should take a picture of her face right now. She looks like she has just met a quiet vegan. Get it? Surprised? Because that never happens…whatever.

The point is, she seems as if she can't believe what just happened. She flips over her cards: ace, four. My eyes shoot open. You know what that means?

She had me. She had a full house on the flop. She had the better hand, and I got "lucky" on the river. I would've lost that hand, had the king not come out. She was trapping me. The whole time I was behind, until the river.

I made about $15,000 tonight, but she had me.

DEUCE

AFTERMATH

I just made $15,000, now what? You're thinking something extravagant has to happen. I need to celebrate, right?

You know how celebrities or the rich always have these lavish lifestyles on TV, where they're constantly having fun every moment of their lives? Well, that's just not real. Don't buy into that crap. Just because one has the money and good looks doesn't mean their life is easy and they're partying every night.

I'm kidding. Of course we party every night.

I just had a five-figure payday. What am I supposed to do? Go out to dinner? Nope. I'm in South Florida, and I'm going to act like it. So I get ready to go out. Tonight's destination? Downtown Miami. When you work hard and win big, you have to celebrate harder and party even bigger.

I pull out my phone and start dialing.

"How's it going?"

"Great. Leaving the Hard Rock. Get your dick out of your hand, and put on some pants, we're going out tonight."

"Profitable night, I see. I'll be waiting in my apartment."

That was Alejandro.

Fuck. I just used his real name. Uh, let's just call him Alexander. I usually only hang out with poker players. But I fancy Alexander because he enjoys the finer things in life like myself. He's also an asshole, but uh, so am I. Also, he has an apartment downtown, so he's useful.

I make a second call and arrange to go to a club downtown and buy a table (the only proper way to celebrate down here). Listen, I know you're starting to judge me, and if it were up to me, I wouldn't seem like such a douche. You know, going out in Miami, buying tables and everything, but that's the only way it can be done. I don't know how it works where you're from, but the hot girls here are like moths. They're thoughtless and are only attracted to the shiny. Tell a girl you have a table, and she'll follow you like a lost dog that's about to get fed.

I just lost all the feminists, didn't I? Too much? I'll tone it down.

But when it comes to girls and life, here's the truth—you don't have to be good looking, be the starting quarterback, or be a genius. You don't have to be a superhero or drive a nice car. You can get any girl and anything you want in life.

As long as you're rich.

And try to be funny too—don't be boring. The money is all that really matters, but be funny too. Money does buy a lot of things, sadly. Well, sadly for those who don't have it.

The night is starting off how it always does. We order the bottles we want, we say hello to a couple of the other regulars, and talk to the promoters and bouncers for a bit and pretend I care about their latest stories. The usual.

Then, as the club starts getting fuller, it begins to get louder. I have to start drinking at my table now—I'll check back with you later.

♠

It's about the sixth drink of the evening now, and with all the wonders that come with it, I see the girl I want, down on the dancefloor—a tall blonde with a small group of friends. She has the ultimate package—pale European face with blond hair and a Hispanic waist; this is the girl I want tonight. But I decide not to make a move just yet because she'll know who we are eventually, and she might come to me. Don't chase what you want in life, make it chase you.

Alexander and I buy a round of champagne showers to the table. The flashy bottles come accompanied with the *Rocky Balboa* theme song and the attention of everybody in the room. Like I said before, it's only a matter of time until the moth flies to the light.

I look down at my watch, and it's about midnight now. Still nothing has happened. But when I look up, I make eye contact with her. I'll admit, she is a dime, one of kind. Maybe not one of a kind, as there will always be another one like her, but she is managing to capture my curiosity. After she grins, I signal her over to the table with my fingers. At first, she is playing hard to get like the typical Miami girl, and signals me to come down to the dancefloor, but we don't have time for that. I run my fingers through my long Italian dark black hair and decide to wait for the right moment.

More drinks are being passed around, more girls coming to the table, and although most of them are hot enough to be in *Playboy*, my curiosity has turned into attention with the blonde, who still hasn't appeared. But now it's around 1:00 a.m., and I still want her and I haven't made any progress. So I walk down the steps that lead to the dancefloor and make my way over to her and her one friend she's currently with. I introduce myself and comment that they do not have drinks in their hands, and the dancefloor is all too crowded. I say the magic words to them, and they follow me to my table. I'll admit it, I chased this one, which doesn't usually happen, but this girl appears to be anything but usual.

At the table Alexander wings, and we do the typical small talk with the girls. She introduces herself as…uh, I can't hear her. Let's just call her Kat. Alexander and I do our thing and we isolate our girls.

Kat's hot, and she knows it, which makes her even hotter, and I am going to make sure this turns into something. I serve her a drink, and she sits down on the couch surrounding the table. She immediately asks what we are celebrating, as we are clearly not having an ordinary night. I tell her that I am a poker player and had had a great night to which she replies, "Oh my God, I love poker!"

Sure she does. I then ask her what she does for a living to which she replies, "…"

Again it is impossible to hear her, and I honestly don't care. Anyway, she asks me where I play poker and where I am from to which I finally answer, "Okay, relax. How about we dance now and keep playing twenty-one questions when we don't have to scream?"

She gives a convincing smile and then follows. As we start to dance, she turns over and says to me, "Don't waste your time; this isn't going to turn into anything." But as I can feel her body right on mine, I can imagine it telling me otherwise.

I smirk to myself, take a sip of my Bacardi Limón, and reply, "Who said I wanted this to turn into something?"

"I am just saying."

I whisper something witty in her ear; she says one of my favorite lines that girls tend to say to me, "You're very confident."

Bingo.

Fast forward through an hour of dancing, then small talk, more dancing, and then more small talk. I am ready to make my move now. I wait until the right song and whisper into her ear, "You know, for turning into nothing, seems like you're enjoying yourself," to which she just laughs.

As soon as a girl kisses you, you have her. That's the hardest part of the whole night, the rest is just closing. You already sold the stock so stop fucking selling. Now you just have to discuss the terms and conditions of how much she wants to buy. From here, it is just playing your cards right, like I do every single day. After one more song, I turn her around so that we keep dancing, but her head is resting on my shoulder. I step back and look at her light eyes. "Sometimes you got to make an exception."

It's two hours later now, and we're in Alexander's apartment. We stumble in, and I offer her some water like a gentleman. See, I'm not an asshole. Next thing I know we're kissing again. But I stop for a second and roughly place her against the wall. Now just look at her—killer long blond hair, bright-pink lips, and those eyes that are doing all the talking right now. Look at her legs, man. Shit, I am glad I'm a poker player.

Next thing I know we're taking our shoes off. She then says the magic words. "Give me a second; I need to use the bathroom. I'll be right back."

Okay, now stop cockblocking. I'll let you guess what happens next, but you have to get out of here.

PART I
DEPRESSION

TRE

ASKING MY MOM FOR
TWENTY DOLLARS

I wake up and see Kat, or whatever her name is, next to me and can't help but smile. See, that's th—Actually, follow me. Let's go to the balcony; I don't want to wake anyone up. As I walk outside the room to get a drink of water, trying to balance my steps as I walk my hungover self to the kitchen, I see Alexander has already started to make himself some breakfast.

"Where's the girl?"

"She's still sleeping, in the room. What about you? Any luck?"

He looks at me with a blank face. "Hey, we really need to talk," he says as I pass him to open the fridge.

I know where this is going. "Alex, I don't need this right now. Talk to me about this tomorrow. Today, I need to focus," I finally say after taking a sip from the water bottle.

"You always say that."

"No. I mean it. I don't want to hear it today."

I make my way to the balcony, where I open the screen door and step outside. See, Alexander thinks I shouldn't be playing poker anymore. He thinks I'm going crazy and treats me like a drug addict every time I party too hard. I never get into any real trouble. Who cares if I party hard? I realize I was a bit aggressive last night; I'm not usually like that. Things have been speeding up lately and I'm just trying to keep up. I hope you stick with me an—

Wait. I just realized it's been two full chapters, and I haven't even introduced myself yet. How rude of me. My name is Charles Marquez—I'm a twenty-year-old student at the University of Central Florida where I study finance. But who cares about finance when I've already allowed myself to live a lifestyle where I can get anything I want. I make more money in one night than what most Americans make in a month. This is my story.

♠

If you're going to stay here with me, you need to let me focus. Tonight can be the biggest night of my life. It might be the night I have been waiting on for the last year. But before we move on with tonight, let's back up a little. I wasn't always like this, and it's important for you to understand how I arrived here. I used to be a better person. Better yet, I used to be a different person.

There's a memory from my childhood. It was the summer of my tenth year of existence. Interesting way to say I was ten years old, right? I was eating in an outdoor restaurant near the beach with my family one weekend near Fort Lauderdale. While we were eating, a Ferrari pulled up into the parking lot and I, as a kid, was fascinated. I watched this red sports car drive up to where I was, and I couldn't believe my eyes. I immediately ran to the car to see who would come out, as I thought only famous athletes drove those cars. When a young guy stepped out of the car, I instantly approached him and asked if I could sit inside the car for a picture. He gave me a look as if I was the stupidest person in the world. "No, don't touch my car. Being poor doesn't give you the right to bother rich people, kid. Learn that now," he said, locking his car and walking toward another restaurant.

I know it was stupid, but I was a kid, and my heart was broken. I'm not even really sure why I did that. What I do know is, I felt an incredible amount of embarrassment in that moment. I ran to my mom, but I didn't cry. I just let her hold me and tried to analyze what had unfolded.

That moment did something for me. This was a pivotal experience in my life because I told myself that I didn't want to be the type of person who asked others for anything. Whether it was money, or just for a simple favor, I was going to grow up to be somebody who didn't need anybody else. I knew I never wanted to feel that same embarrassment again, and I didn't want anybody to be able to talk to me like that. It was that moment that I knew I wanted to be rich, I wanted to live a life where I could provide for myself and not have to depend on anyone. Feeling such embarrassment that day set the course for who I wanted to become. For who I knew I was going to become.

From what I can remember, after that, I have always had a special admiration for the flow of money. Even when I was a kid, my dad, brother, and I would bet on different soccer games. Eventually, my brother and I started betting on video games. But apart from betting hundreds of dollars on video games, my childhood was a normal one, so let's skip on to my later teen years.

I do remember the first time I played poker. It was with my friends when we were in middle school. We would gather a group of about five of us and play house games. We would even wear sunglasses like the players we saw on TV, thinking we were cool. I loved playing; something about this game attracted me more than it should. It was like a more sophisticated way of gambling. Even then, I saw the hint of the big rewards poker could one day bring.

One night, my friends and I were going to have a big game—nine players, twenty dollars each. This was going to be the biggest game we had had yet. Everybody wanted to win that night, and it was really going to show who was the best. Growing up, every kid wants to know who the toughest kid in the neighborhood is. Well, my group of friends wanted to know who the best card player was. More than that, I wanted the money.

I knew I had to bring my best game for the tournament. And when the tournament began, I was doing it—I was playing well; I was determined to win. I explicitly remember there was a hand where I was trying to find out if it was worth calling a specific bet, considering what future bets would be made. I didn't know it then, but I was already calculating implied pot odds. Nevertheless, I successfully played my way to the final two players.

And then it happened.

I lost.

Big losses have an odd effect on a poker player. It's the big losses we remember; it's the big losses that want to make us play again. It's the times we were so close to winning when we could almost taste the money that really get to us. Like the famous poker movie *Rounders* says, "Few players recall big pots they have won, strange as it seems, but every player can remember with remarkable accuracy the outstanding tough beats of his career."

Maybe it's because I hate losing more than I love winning, maybe it's because I was so close, and maybe I simply wanted a chance of winning my twenty dollars back. But I couldn't leave the matter like that. I needed to play again. In fact, I might have never played again if I had won that night. Who knows?

I admit at times I wonder what my life would be like if I'd never started playing. I wonder what all this stress and greed has done to me. I wonder where I would be in my life and what I would be doing if I wasn't here talking to you. But I assume that's just a waste of time.

Now this is the important part. Even as a kid, I didn't like asking my parents for money. We were a middle-class family, and twenty bucks wouldn't hurt anybody, but I just never liked the feeling of asking my parents for cash. It made me feel guilty in a way—they gave me everything, and all I did was ask for more. But that night, the first thing I did when I got home was ask my mom for twenty bucks. Why? Because I was getting a rematch the next day. I was going to go back and get what was mine. I knew I was a better player than my friends and I had to go back and win.

I'll never forget how I felt that night, asking my mom for twenty dollars to go play cards. It's a feeling that's hard to describe. It kind of felt as if I was asking her for money to buy drugs or something. I felt like a loser asking for money from the only person who would never say no to me.

FOUR

ON TO SOMETHING

"Gambling" was, is, and always will be *my thing*. I developed an admiration for poker as a kid, and just like everybody else, I imagined myself on TV one day, playing against Ivey, Negreanu, and Moneymaker. But eventually, time continued, and dreams have a way of disappearing as life goes on. I never invested much energy into poker after that night, all because I played small games because of my limited funds. Because of this, poker grew old, and I'd never gotten a big enough payday to think it would ever take me anywhere. I forgot about poker and left it behind.

Again, everything after that was pretty typical—spent high school kissing girls, shorting the stock market, and pointing out inconsistencies in religion to my parents.

♠

After high school I made the decision to come to the University of Central Florida. Finance major. School had been going well; it was fun. But that was a while ago now. The summer after my freshman year in college is where the real story starts—the summer between my first year and second year to be exact. All it took was that one summer, one summer of poker to set the course for my life to where I am now. It took that summer for me to fall in love. But don't worry; this isn't your typical love story.

I didn't have many plans for that summer other than getting a summer job. So when I arrived back home, a couple of friends and I began to play limit poker at the Hard Rock during the first week of our vacation, nothing big. The Hard Rock was *the* casino. It had shops, restaurants and all the gambling one can imagine; a twenty-minute drive from my house. I loved it. Having chips in front of me. Betting. The feeling of my heart beating all the way up to my chest. I loved eating at nice places after successful nights. I loved being the quiet kid who could compete against people who were decades older. I loved the stress and the feeling of the dealer pushing chips toward me after I won a hand. But I hated losing more than I loved winning.

I was another ordinary college kid before all of this. Looking back, there was a certain simplicity to the life I lived then, only having to worry about getting good grades. But eventually, one night during the beginning of the summer, my group of friends was invited to play a local weekly tournament for a $40 entry with a $400 first-place payout. My friend's uncle knew a guy who knew a guy who could get us into the game. I know what you're thinking—it's not much. But to a college kid like me, $400 was a lot, trust me. And to a finance major, it was a ten-to-one return. Not bad at all—better than most of the guys in suits and ties over at Wall Street.

That night changed my life forever. Cliché, right?

I agreed to play in the tournament not expecting anything, just to see what could happen. I walked in and remember thinking how I was surrounded by older people, a lot older. I was playing *their* game, but I wasn't intimidated. Not because I expected to win, but because I expected not to; I was playing for fun with no expectations. Up to that point, I had played a lot of poker during the first two weeks of summer but nothing serious, just enough to know the ropes and some basic strategy.

The tournament was in a mansion-like house that had a big room toward the left side where there were two poker tables and a small bar. I was seated in one of the two tables, and the rest of my friends were placed in the other. I sat down and tried to familiarize myself with my surroundings. A bunch of old white men. None of them smoking cigars like in the movies; none of them mean or arrogant either. They all had white hair, were drinking either beer or wine and were wearing expensive sweaters. *Why are old people always cold?* Just like it is now—I was the youngest player there. I handed two twenties to the owner of the house and was given my chips. After a few minutes of courteous small talk, the tournament had begun, and before I knew it, I was playing. I thought I knew what I was doing then, and for some reason, it worked. I bet when I thought I could win a hand and I folded when I didn't. *Simple.* After an hour had passed, I looked around, and I had the biggest stack of chips from both tables. I thought maybe it was just luck but the same thing continued for most of the night. Finally, after a couple of hours of play, I made it to the final table of nine players. Seven oldies, a friend of mine, and me. Then, after another hour at the final table, there were just two of us left, and by this point, I didn't think it was luck anymore.

In the last hand, playing against the owner of the house, I remember I had a king and a jack, and on the river came a king. My opponent pushed all in, and I called. He flipped over king, nine. I flipped over my better king, and in a matter of seconds, I went from being a regular broke college kid, to a college kid with $400.

It's a funny feeling winning a tournament when you're the "new kid," when you're playing against people who've been playing their whole lives. Looking around, I knew they were all suckers. All these oldies who had just lost to a newbie. Beginners luck? I didn't think so. "Luck" is for the losers over at the slot machines. I had *it*. I had the skill—it was in me. I had taken a bite of the fruit, and let me tell you, it was more than delicious. All I could think about that night was the next time I could have another bite and a bigger one for that matter. That tournament made me realize I could make something out of poker. I knew a bigger payday was within reach and tangible. Like a boy who had just experienced his first kiss, I was excited, and I wanted more. Just like anybody who makes decent money in the stock market for the first time, or gets lucky and makes a return anywhere, and wants to do it again, but this time a lot bigger. Little did I know what I was in for.

Speaking of luck, I need to make something clear now—luck doesn't exist. If there's one thing that really gets to me, it is when people say, "You're so lucky" or "Everything happens for a reason." That's just a broke person's mentality for justifying their own mediocrity. There's no such thing as being lucky. Everything is simply mathematical probabilities, and it's up to me to determine what's worth the risk and what's not. It's the same thing as the guys in the hedge funds are doing, except they have to wear an uncomfortable shirt all day. I have trained too hard for anyone to call me lucky. So if you take one thing away from this—there's no such thing as luck.

♠

After that win, I gave poker more attention and realized I had to make another move. Next stop—no-limit cash games. No limit is where the big boys play or, better yet, where the real poker is played. Like the name suggests, there is no limit to the bet sizes, and one can lose all his or her money in seconds, as well as make a lot in seconds. The minimum entry for the smallest game here is usually a hundred dollars. I had never played no limit before. Why? Because I never had the extra hundred dollars to buy in. But now, I had an extra four hundred. And to be quite honest, it looked intimidating, playing with the big boys. But I did it; I took my winnings from the tournament and bought in for a hundred dollars at a no-limit table at the Hard Rock.

Here, I *was* intimidated; this was actually at a casino. People were there to win real money, and they weren't about to have some kid beat them out of their chips. After just a couple of minutes of sitting down, I thought what I was watching was something out of a movie. People here played differently than I had ever imagined, hundreds of dollars exchanging hands within minutes. People gaining so much money from one second to the next. Adults acting like children, or children acting like adults, I didn't know which one it was. It was a gamblers paradise, though, or hell. So much money was circulating around the table, and I knew I was home. I knew this was the world I wanted to be part of. I was captivated, hypnotized at watching this Wall Street–like behavior.

This is when I decided that I was going to do whatever it took to become a bull in this world. I remember the first hand I played when I sat down. An older player raised preflop to thirty dollars, and I thought that was absolutely crazy. How could you risk thirty dollars before even seeing the flop? But that was real poker, and soon, I would be crazy too.

That night I won immediately.

Okay, I lied, again. It wasn't so easy. The first time I played a no-limit cash game at the casino, I lost. And then I lost again and then again. I'll admit it; I became overly confident from the initial tournament, and I didn't really know what I was doing yet. So after I ran out of money, I started to think that maybe it *was* beginner's luck that won me that initial tournament. When I didn't have enough to buy in again, I was back at the mansion with the old fellas the next Friday to see if I had the same outcome. I tried to do the same thing I did last time, paying close attention to each move. And again, I won the tournament. It wasn't just luck that made me win, I had a talent; all I had to do was figure out how to translate the talent into cash games.

♠

It was around this time that Macoa came to Mexton for the summer. Mexton is where I was raised (more on this later), and Macoa was the girl I had my eyes on growing up. I met her in elementary school when she was in my class, and, to keep it short, Macoa was my childhood crush. The only problem was that she moved to France when we were in middle school. But this girl always managed to come back into my life just when I was about ready to forget her.

I think she didn't like me the way I liked her because I was too nice; I would always remind her of how beautiful I thought she was. Surprisingly, or not, this doesn't work with girls. I learned that the hard way. I had chased her my whole life, but she had always seen me as just a friend. Her "best friend" to be exact. She had constantly been a presence, and I thought she was near perfect, since the day I met her. I try to really think what it was about her that captured me, but I'm not sure. It was just *her*, everything about her. Many guys had a crush on her growing up, but for some reason, mine didn't disappear.

Point is, she had moved away but she still managed to stay on my mind. I would see her some summers when she would visit or when I was in Europe with my family but not much other than that. I hadn't seen her in a while, but she was in Miami, close to Mexton, for the summer. I was going to use this summer to make her mine. She would finally fall in love with me. I was going to tell her how I had felt since the day we met. I had at times told her before—she had an idea of how I thought of her, but it had always been a joke to her. This was partially my own fault, as I never really grabbed her, sat her down, and seriously told her how I felt. It was hard, sometimes not believing it myself, because she was the type of girl who I thought I could only be with in my mind.

It's not that I thought she was too good for me or anything. But I just thought about her too much. And when you have a conversation with someone in your head a million times, you never imagine it to ever be real. She also always seemed to have a boyfriend, so it was never easy to tell her how I felt. And when I heard myself try to articulate how I felt to her, I couldn't help but saying it in a joking manner. It was my fault, as my own intensity has always led people to not take me seriously. But I would tell her how I had always thought of her, this time, and then get her to be mine. I needed to finally get my childhood crush. That summer would be different. I'm rambling now.

Anyway...let's not get too distracted.

FIVE

DEVELOPMENT

After analyzing my mistakes and understanding the difference between tournament play and cash games, I gave it another go, and, finally, I won. I realized I needed to play more conservatively for cash games, as cash games were long hauls of using the same strategy rather than long hauls of changing strategy in tournament poker. After I won for the first time, I was at the Hard Rock again the next night. And I won again and then again. I hit a winning streak where I won at least fifty dollars five times in a row. Again, this amount of money isn't mind blowing, I understand. But winning fifty dollars in just two hours repeatedly, I knew I was on to something. So I started playing more, reading more, learning more, and watching more poker. I was hooked. Soon enough, the bigger money started rolling in.

It wasn't long until I began to average winning more than a hundred dollars on the nights I went to go play. This was awesome to me and the most beautiful part of my long experience if I think about it. I sometimes even have nostalgia for this time because I had the best of both worlds— my poker life and my old life. I thought I was the best in the game and unstoppable. See, when you have no expectations, no fear, and are pretty much ignorant, poker is different. When I was making a hundred dollars, it was a huge reward to me, and I would feel incredibly content. I was genuinely happy and excited to win that money. But when you start making goals of winning more, when you start to have expectations, a hundred dollars goes from being the jackpot to being the entry ticket. Those days of first playing were the times that any amount would make me happy; I was having genuine fun with the game, I was going to the poker room with my friends, and we would see it as a hobby where we could just make easy money, nothing more. But I always saw it differently than my friends: I was always focused on the next move.

I was new in the game, and my naïveté was my biggest strength. It's hard to explain this phenomenon, but being new and naïve in the game, at times, can help you immensely. Once you know the game too well and have gone through countless bad beats, your strategy changes. See, when you're fresh in the game, you always think you have the best hands. You never suspect somebody to be slow playing you, and your oversized bets can be seen as more than they are. But once you really learn poker, once you've been beaten too many times, once you can't lose the money you're playing with, your game grows cautious; you come to be more paranoid and play tighter. You start to make goals and expectations, and a fun hobby turns into a stress-filled lifestyle.

Ignorance is bliss, I've heard.

♠

After a month of riding this wave, I came to a point where I needed to up my game again. Similar to anything else, whether it's business, sports, or writing—your strategy gets saturated—you always have to keep developing your edge. You have to find something you're the best at, milk the crap out of it, and then when it stops working, find something new. A rewarding feeling nowadays is when I can see somebody else who was like me a couple of months ago at the poker table, making the same mistakes I was making, and now me being able to detect them.

So when I saw myself struggling and not making the same money after some weeks, my bluffs not working, and me calling the wrong bets, I knew it was time to take a step back. I was back to studying my mistakes and getting ready to come back stronger.

I want to take some time out to actually explain what poker is to me. At least, what it *was* to me. Poker is something special. It's my escape from reality—I need to do this. Poker allows me to lose myself and transcend. I can go somewhere else when I'm playing. I'm no longer within but part of something more beautiful. I'm not a prisoner of the pain of my past or the anxiety of my future; that's how potent the *now* is. It's in the mercilessness of the jungle that I find my tranquility—my mind is cleared, and I can finally breathe fully. In a way, it is very medicinal: my anxiety is calmed, my pain is numbed, and my worries disappear.

Eventually, poker turned into an addictive form of a drug where I became somebody I thought I never would.

But once, it was beautiful.

SIX
MEXTON

know what you're thinking. How did I go from hundred dollars a night to having hundreds of thousands of dollars' worth of chips in front of me? How did I go from worrying about Macoa to waking up next to girls who can have their own calendars? Don't worry, we'll get there.

♠

It was the end of May, and I was playing poker almost every night. I drove to work in the morning, then to the gym or whatever in the afternoon, got a bite to eat, and then drove to the poker room to do the real labor. I'll admit that the first time I went to the poker room alone was a bit odd. In the past, poker had been entertainment where I'd go play with a friend or a group of us for an hour or two. Naturally, the first time I played alone for more than a whole night didn't feel right.

Now, I'll address the "problem" I have. When my friends were still talking to me, they kept telling me I had a gambling problem. And, maybe I do, but what else was I going to do? I already went to the gym five times a week. Listen, I was in Mexton for the whole summer, and all you need to know about this place is that it's a small town in South Florida full of wealthy people, where the whole city lives in a suburbia. There's never anything noteworthy happening, not even a robbery here or there to spice things up a bit. All there is to do other than playing soccer is getting frozen yogurt with a group of friends and gossiping. And I promise you, I didn't care about the fight Claire and Jack had last week or what Alberto was doing to his car nowadays. Not complaining; just rationalizing. And I don't mean to sound like a high-school girl's bio on social media, but what that town had to offer wasn't for me. I'm conscious of the fact that I sound lame by saying I'm not lame, but I'd simply rather have played poker than be around Mexton all summer.

The only thing in Mexton for me that summer was Macoa, so I'll try to describe exactly what she was for me a little bit more smoothly. I had chased her my whole life up to that point. There were times as a kid, where I would go to parties hoping she was there, or would do things thinking I would get her attention like listen to the same music she did. Yeah, it was bad, I know. She isn't even that pretty, or hot. You know, most people don't see her the way I saw her. She was just uh, well, something else. In my mind I put her inside this fantasy, and I imagined myself with her, being so happy and living a perfect life. I don't know if I ever really wanted her. It's hard to explain.

I just thought, what if I actually hung out with her romantically? What if I actually talked to her and heard her talk about me the same way I talked about her? What if I actually saw the reality of her, and she didn't turn out to be perfect? I didn't want that. Maybe deep down, I wanted her to be abstract. Maybe the only reason I was in love with her was because she lived far from me, and I knew she could never actually hurt me. It's easy to like someone from a distance. I thought about all this the nights I was alone in the casino.

I decided not to see her that summer; I decided to let her remain in the back of my mind. Not only was I focused on other things, but she also had a boyfriend and was only here for a few months. Because I was concentrating on poker now, I was over her by that point and didn't really think it would be a bad idea to forget about her. She wasn't worth it anymore. Poker was worth it.

Some people are in a relationship and focus on their partner. Some people resort to partying. Others do drugs. Me? I have thousands of dollars in chips in front of me every night. This whole poker thing started as something to do because of a lack of entertainment. But before I knew it, I was making real money, and I had to keep my eye on the prize.

I'll admit that it did get lonely sometimes, you know? Going to the poker room alone and not really having somebody to do it with, but I had accepted that the road to success was a quiet and lonely one.

SEVEN

TIME TO GET SERIOUS

I try to acknowledge my mistakes in life. I make a mental note of them and then analyze them later. Looking back, taking the game as more than a harmless hobby might have been a mistake. I mean, last night was fun and all, but as we stand here in Alexander's apartment, I can't help but think of how lonely I am, and how I wasn't before I started playing. It's so hard to think about. I fucking love the thrill of having anything I want, but truth is, it sucks to wake up every morning and look around and not see anybody worth it. I could've just had fun and made a little money. I can only notice this now as so many things have changed—I couldn't have possibly known it then. Maybe if the universe hadn't led me to where I will be tonight, my story would have been different. Who knows?

But before you come with me tonight, there's still some more catching up to do.

♠

One night I was in the poker room, and I made around a thousand dollars. That was a highly developed thought, right?

I honestly don't know how it happened—I wasn't even playing that eloquently. But after a couple of hours, my chip stack was bigger than it had ever been before, and I cashed out at over a thousand dollars in profit. It was the first time I had had a payday of four figures in my life. This was the night that made me change my mind-set. I knew I had to get serious now. This money wasn't just extra cash anymore; it was real dough that could change the way I lived.

I even thought of quitting my summer job. I didn't talk about that yet? Okay, so that summer I was working at a high-end hair salon. My job was mainly washing hair. Funny, right? I know, it's true though. My friend's parents owned a hair salon, I asked for a job in the beginning of the summer, and they hired me as a hair assistant. It was a pretty comfortable gig, and I would get great tips from all the rich MILFS who would come in.

So why didn't I quit after that night?

My parents didn't know I was making that much money from poker; even my friends didn't really know. Even I didn't know! Whenever I would win, I'd take the money and put it in an envelope labeled "poker" and never kept track of how much money was coming from it. I was a college kid on break in South Florida, so I would spend a good amount of the money I made by the weekend.

My mom never liked me gambling, so, I rarely told her about it whenever I played. This was something I understood I couldn't tell people just yet. I wanted to prove myself before I told my family, compared to other things, as I used to tell my mom everything. I would at times go to the poker room but tell my parents I was playing cards at a friend's house; I'm guessing my mom imagined us playing for twenty dollars. If my mom knew I was gambling hundreds of dollars, she would've had a heart attack. I couldn't quit my job because of this and the fact that I had been hired only weeks prior. Honestly, I didn't mind. My job ensured I would wake up early and not waste my days sleeping or being unproductive. The salon was also right next to the gym where I worked out, and I would get to touch hot women when I washed their hair during the day. Creepy, but true. Being that it was only a summer job, I only had a month and a half left to work anyway.

Talk to any gambler or investor, and they'll tell you all about the money they've made. They'll tell you all the big plays they've been a part of and provide a vocal showcase of their most brilliant returns. Obviously, they won't be so happy to tell you about the times they've failed and the tough days when they lost it all. Before you think this story is too good to be true, it might be. I haven't mentioned that I have lost, a lot. I've gone completely broke too many times, lost several more, and have contemplated quitting more than that. I should've stopped playing weeks prior to that night where I hit the home run. But I thought I was on to something, I thought I had *it*, and when I finally hit the home run that night, I knew all the strikes had all been worth it.

The thing is all gamblers, and really all humans, are alike. We all think we're better than everybody else, and we all have a deep and secret belief that we are different. This idea is quickly reversed when somebody gambles and loses it all. But the difference between successful people like me and

33

the rest of us is that I never blamed luck or other people for my failures. After my losses, all I did was keep practicing and analyzing so that I could come back better. I never lose and approach a game the same way again.

Like the stock market has been described before, "It's foolish to think that you can withdraw from the Exchange after you have tasted the sweetness of the honey." I don't care how much money you've lost; if you could know what it feels like to win a huge pot, if you could just feel that warm sensation where your heart is pounding like a drum as you've made the money in a tournament, if you knew how your ego responds to that feeling of cashing in your chips, you would understand why I'm still here. Maybe I should've stopped, but I didn't. I was in it for the big money now. So like I said, I did hit a big streak of winning, and I knew I could get somewhere now. I finally decided it was time to play my first real tournament at a poker room.

After about a week of trying to decide where I would play my first tournament, I finally found one, after searching online, with a $50 entry and a $5,000 guaranteed payout at a local poker room. I decided this was going to be the one. I remember walking into the room with my backpack, which held the gear I always wear when I play: earphones, my black UCF hoodie, and gum. Don't worry, I'm not one of those who wear sunglasses.

I have to admit, I liked being the only kid at a table. I'm not sure how to describe the feeling, but I liked being the underdog. It's funny because even when another young player is at another table, I think to myself, *What is a kid doing here?* as if only I can hold this title at a young age. Poker rooms are usually filled with the sound of hundreds of people shuffling their chips. There are anywhere from twenty to a hundred tables. They are large green oval shaped tables, sitting up to nine people. Usually filled with only males. The ages usually ranged from 30 to 60 if I had to guess.

Most dressed in T-shirts. The dealer sits in the middle. Dressed in a black buttoned-up shirt, always.

I arrived for the tournament and was assigned my table. I sat down to begin, and everything was going according to plan at first—I won some hands in the first level, and then I stayed quiet.

Time passed, and after a good number of hands, I wasn't being dealt anything I could work with. After a few levels went by, I started to realize that I hadn't won a hand in a while. I was getting cold cards, and my chip stack was disappearing. I needed to make a move soon to get back in the game. Then, finally, I was dealt pocket sevens, I raised to two hundred, and I received a few callers—I only had two thousand behind me at that point.

Side note: In a tournament, chips do not have any monetary value. There's only a payout if you make it to a position that gets paid. But until then, having chips means nothing in terms of money, essentially. Two thousand chips does not mean $2000 in any way (in tournament). Okay, now back to the action.

The flop came three, four, and a six with two diamonds. I liked that flop, because I had a bigger pair than anything on the board, and I even had a straight draw. So after a check from the person behind me, I bet three fifty and I got two callers. The next card: ten of clubs. Didn't change much, but it did slow me down a little. Normally, I wouldn't check there because when I do, it tells my opponents the ten scares me, and I have an under pair. But I was short stacked and had to protect the remainder of my chips. I checked, and they did too. The last card was another diamond—the four of diamonds, and there was a six hundred and fifty bet. I called. They hit the flush on the river. Shit.

Now I only had a thousand. So what do I do now? I had to wait until the next decent hand and go all in before the flop. So after three hands, I got ace, jack of spades and went all in for a thousand; I got two callers. I could tell you what the cards were, but it doesn't matter. I lost.

There I was, out of the tournament before the break.

I checked the cards another time to make sure it was definite, and it was. I took a deep breath in and stood up; I was done. I looked around, thought about buying in again, but knew it was time to leave—I wasn't ready for these types of tournaments. I walked toward the door with my head and shoulders down when right near the end of the poker room I noticed certain tables that had a barrier. I looked around and studied the guarded tables. I realized that there was a bigger more professional-looking tournament being played. I asked one of the floor managers what was going on, and he told me there was a special event—a thousand-dollar buy-in with the chance to play with one of the best poker players in the world. His name is Phil Lally, one of the best, if not the best poker player in history, and he dominates the big games around the world these days. I had no idea he was there. I had seen him countless times on TV and YouTube, so I was excited at the chance to see him in person and maybe ask him for an autograph or something. I asked the manager when the next break was, and he replied it was anywhere from an hour to two.

More than an hour passed with me sitting next to the railings where they would walk along. Finally, the break was announced, and I saw Phil walking toward me. There was another person in front of me who took a quick picture with him and then finally I stopped him and introduced myself. I jumped right into it.

"Phil! My name is Chuck. It's a pleasure to meet you. I just started to play poker. Can you give me some advice?"

He looks at me. "Do you want a picture?"

"Yes, that'd be awesome," I replied. "But can you give me any advice to how to be like you? What are your secrets on the success you've had with poker?"

"The secret is the poor stay poor. Might as well accept that now. You don't have *it*, kid. You wouldn't be here if you did. You're just one of many lying to themselves. Give up now and don't waste your time," he said looking at my phone, anticipating a picture.

I thought he might be joking. But after a few seconds of silence he finally said, "Still want a picture?"

"No. Thanks."

EIGHT

MY PLAN

Like I said before, it's the losses in this game that have a lasting impact. But what this particular loss did for me was give me a wake-up call—I needed a plan. If I was going to make a career out of poker, I couldn't continue playing without keeping track of my numbers. I knew I was making money in the long run because I still had cash, but I wasn't keeping track of how I was making it. Keeping a record of my gains and losses was necessary. I needed a budget. I also needed a goal; I needed to have a purpose. How would I use all this money? I needed to have a number I aspired to reach, rather than just spending the money I made every night. With that said, I would look for a target and a written map of how I would attain it. I started thinking; I began asking myself how much was going to satisfy me and why I even began playing. What did I want? What was all this for?

I thought back to when money had limited me in the past and what

I could do with it once I had it. A lot of ideas came to me. I could use this money to travel, buy a car, or help my parents out with expenses. All these ideas were worth considering, but they weren't enough. I wanted something bigger. I needed to have a goal that made everything worth it.

And then it hit me.

I remembered back when I was in high school and wanted to apply to a plethora of schools but was limited to only in-state universities because of the price of out-of-state tuition. I even had to pursue a different major than what I intended because the only schools that had the major I desired were out of state. As you can probably tell by now, I've always been fond of mathematics and the idea of making calculated bets with projected returns, so I wanted to study applied mathematics in college, but no university in Florida offered it, resulting in me studying finance at UCF.

I knew what I was going to do. I would apply to the best universities in the country that had my major. I would make enough money to pay my way through my last two or three years at a new school, and then once I had that money, which is around a hundred thousand dollars, I would stop, completely. This goal was quite distant at the time, as I had only won a couple of thousand dollars until then. But I had more than a full school year to do it and knew that I'd be playing bigger games, I knew it was somewhat within reach. What's the point of making a realistic goal anyway?

So here was my plan—I was going to keep playing. I was going to write down every time I even entered a poker room and keep detailed notes on how much I made or lost, along with why and how I made or lost it. Every time I won some money, I would save 20 percent and start my education fund. I would reinvest 70 percent back into the game, and use the remaining 10 percent for personal expenses (i.e., girls and alcohol). I would do this until I had enough money to pay my way through college.

Then, once I had enough for school, I promised myself I would stop.

NINE

HAIR ASSISTANT BY DAY, POKER PLAYER BY NIGHT

END OF SUMMER

By routine, I was pretty much living the same way, every day, the last month of summer. I would go to work in the morning, get out around three, and then go to the gym. After the gym, I drove home for dinner, and then toward 7:00 p.m., I would head out to the Hard Rock where the real fun would take place. By mid-August, I was only going to ride the wave for a couple of more days as summer was coming to an end, and I would have to go back to school in Orlando.

When one makes a goal, similar to a New Year's resolution, it's easy to keep up with it at first. Your motivation and discipline is impeccable when you first start. Similarly, this was the same for me when I first made my goal. I'd go to the poker room every other night and make around $900 weekly, on average. Everything was running smoothly, and I was sticking to the plan.

One of the downsides of the goal is the fact that anytime you play a cash game, greed gets the best of you. You'll be up $300 after a couple of hours, which is more than your nightly goal, but you want more. You tell yourself you'll only stay until the tip of the hour, but you end up staying longer, and then you lose some. Then you win again, and again, you stay longer. You tell yourself you'll play one more hand. This cycle continues. But I couldn't do that anymore. I had to remain disciplined; I wasn't playing for fun anymore. So whenever I was up by at least three hundred, I made it a rule to leave immediately. I didn't play anymore hands, I'd simply stand up, collect my chips and walk away.

One of the not-so-fun sides of making a rule was what happened every now and then, and it happened on the last night of summer. It was Saturday night; I got off early on my last day of work and left the gym by 6:00 p.m., drove home, ate, and then relaxed a bit. After I showered and put on some clothes, at around nine, I drove all the way to the poker room, which is about a thirty-minute drive. I was hoping to have a fun, long night ahead where I could make some money and enjoy my last night in South Florida. You know, finish the summer with a bang. I sat down and had a good start quickly as I spotted the sucker in the table.

Here's the rule with suckers—you keep playing until you've taken full advantage of them. Once they lose all their money, you need to identify another one. There always needs to be a sucker whom you're focused on because you know what happens if there isn't one.

Do not stay if there is no sucker.

After a bit less than an hour, I had won a couple of big hands, and after forty-five minutes, I hit my goal for the night of $300 as the sucker left the table. Why was this unfortunate? Because now I was done; I had to go home. I had driven thirty minutes to only be there forty-five? I did make the money I wanted to, but damn, who wants to go home that early?

It was around eleven, and it was my last night of summer, and surprisingly, I didn't feel like going out. I had done my fair share of partying the whole summer and didn't want to spend the last night getting drunk. I didn't want to party, but I didn't want to go home either. So I did something I normally wouldn't do—I texted Macoa. Remember her?

Truth is, I secretly was waiting for us to run into each other during the summer, but we never did, and summer would soon be over. I pulled out my phone as I walked toward the casino garage.

I haven't seen you all summer. Late dinner?

I continued walking toward my car, and as I opened the door, I felt my phone vibrate.

Hey! I'm not hungry, but we can do something else! Pick me up?

I then found myself on my way back to Mexton from the Hard Rock to pick her up, and I couldn't believe it. And like I always used to do, I started to overthink things. I really wanted to use the opportunity for closure. I wanted that night to serve as the moment where I would realize that she's just a person, nothing more. I would realize that my whole childhood I was simply romanticizing her, and I was only in love with the idea of her, not her. By hanging out with her, I would see that she was just an ordinary girl, and I would soon enough forget about her.

I picked her up and took her to the park we would go to when we were kids. We had a nice time catching up, but most of the time I just looked at her. Being with a girl like Macoa was like meeting a celebrity, you can't help but be fascinated rather than simply living the moment. Something about her, something about her smile, about the way she smelled, about her skin, her hands, and something about the way she walked. I guess I was in awe—there was just something to her. I could never really put my finger on it.

Think about it like this: imagine your celebrity crush; now put them right in front of you, physically. Not on TV, not in your imagination, not in a picture, but right there in front of you. In my eyes, at the time, this girl was standing right in front of me. About five feet tall, long black hair. A face that provokes feelings I'm too embarrassed to admit, dark-brown eyes, and a small birthmark above her eyebrow that only she could make attractive.

I was thinking about all this when I suddenly snapped out of my thoughts. *What am I doing?* Why was I mesmerized by her again? I had told myself that this summer would be different, yet there I was, doing the same thing I had always done. I had to stop; I couldn't live my life like that anymore. I was a different person now. I forced myself to change my mentality in that moment. Although she had this effect on me, this time had to be different, because even though I could acknowledge how much in awe I was, I didn't really care. I didn't let it affect me to a point where I was not myself. I wasn't being a fan anymore, I was just being, you know, me. Yeah, she was great, but so am I.

When we left the park, we started talking about all the times we shared as kids. How we were best friends, how so much had changed, and what had managed to stay the same. It was nice, sharing these intimate moments with her on my last day in town.

On the way to drop her off, we continued talking about our childhood and how everything had changed between our circle of friends. How we were so sure of ourselves years ago and how everybody ended up where we didn't imagine.

In the sudden silence, I realized that we had spent almost an hour outside her house in my car, parked, just talking. It had been a while since we just talked like this, and I realized in that last hour I wasn't overthinking; I was just doing. I was no longer hypnotized.

I stepped out of the car, and she followed, and then proceeded to walk toward her driveway, where I gave her a long hug. But when I let go of her and saw the look in her eyes, I needed to tell her; I needed her to finally know how I felt. Or had felt—I don't know if I still felt it, but I needed her to hear it. I didn't want to continue my life with her not knowing the reality of my feelings toward her. I didn't have much to gain from telling her this, but I wasn't really looking to gain anything.

I obviously wished at those times that we would somehow end up together, but if we didn't, I wanted her to know what it was like for somebody to truly care for her. I didn't want her to continue her life accepting the same bullshit she always had without knowing that I had adored her.

"Macoa…You know you have always been my dream girl, and you know I have really meant everything I have always 'jokingly' told you. I have a hard time articulating my thoughts sometimes. And I know I should be less sarcastic and talk more but if you just knew what I thought about you…" I told her that she was beyond beautiful to me, that whenever I would see her, my heart would literally race, that when we spent extended periods of times together, I was in another world, that simply looking at her was enough, how I was lucky to have met her, and that just being with her made me happy. I told her that even though she admitted to me at times that she felt small and was insecure, I thought she was more than that. I also told her that I could keep trying to describe how I saw her in my eyes, but it wouldn't be enough and that I didn't want her to say anything,

I simply wanted her to know.

When I was finished, she paused and just looked at me for what seemed to be an eternity. It had caught her by surprise, and now she was the one in awe. As I was waiting for her to say something, she leaned in toward me, gradually rising up on her toes. She leaned in as I stood frozen, and the next thing I knew her lips were warm.

After eleven years of chasing her and always wanting to kiss her, I never imagined it would be like that. And in that moment, which lasted for an infinitesimal amount of time, I felt infinite. I had imagined one moment my whole life, and it was gone before I could even acknowledge it was happening.

I looked at her, realizing I didn't know when the next time I would see her would be, so before I let her go, I kissed her again, this time making sure I didn't forget it. We hugged a last time, and right before she left, I reached into my pocket to grab my wallet.

In my wallet I always keep a king of hearts and a queen of hearts. I grabbed the queen card and handed it to her. "Hey, before you go. I want to give you this card. It's the queen of hearts."

She looked at it for a second. "What's it for?"

"Keep it in your wallet. Sometimes you'll forget who you are, but this is to remind you what you are to me. I don't know when will be the next time I see you, but maybe I'll ask you to show me it so that I know you still have it."

She hugged me again, looked me in the eyes, turned around, and walked toward her house. Next thing I knew I was in my car driving home. *Did that just happen? Was that real?*

To this day I wonder if that kiss was a pity kiss, or real.

TEN

THE ONE KNIGHT STAND

Whatever that kiss meant, I didn't care. Well I did, but I was back in school now, and I had to forget about everything in Mexton. Except for my dog, of course. He's a Boston terrier; his name is Bruce, and I love him.

As you can probably tell, I think more about the things in my life that I never had than the ones I did. I could probably write a whole book about Macoa, and maybe one day I will. But this book isn't about her—this book is about what's going to happen to me tonight, and what got me here, so let's keep going.

Monday morning, I drove back to UCF in Orlando. I was back in school, and I had other things to do and focus on so that I could keep playing poker. But the first weekend back in UCF, I made a terrifying discovery, one that could have altered my whole plan—there were no poker rooms in Orlando. The closest casinos were a bit more than an hour away, and I couldn't make that trip often, let alone daily, maybe not even weekly. It was a harsh wake-up call, but summer was over.

♠

I spent the first couple of weeks without playing poker, and I started to think that maybe it was in the past. I pushed the game to the back of my mind and focused on school. I had accepted that it was just something that had been temporary, and I could do it every once in a while, but not a main focus.

Then one night I found myself in the room of one of my professors, discussing an exam. The room smelled like most universities smell—like old wood. Everybody who scored above an eighty-five was asked to be interviewed by the professor so that we could provide study tips for other students. But when I was in the room, I saw the professor had a couple of books on poker and probability on an elevated bookshelf.

"You play poker?"

He followed my eyes to where I saw the books. Then he chuckled. "Ha. I used to play a lot back when I was a graduate student in California. I don't have the time for it now. And I learned it's not worth it."

"What do you mean?"

"Well, me and a bunch of other math kids used to be 'rounders' back in California, but after years in the game, I learned that you can love the cards all you want, but they'll never love you back."

"Did you read that in a Tyler Nals book or something?"

"Something like that. Anyway, there's nowhere to play here other than the State Tour."

"What are you talking about? What is that?"

"You've never heard of it? It's a yearlong charity tournament held by the state of Florida. You have to qualify by city, then by county, and then the finalists play a big tournament that's broadcasted live on TV. It's mostly a bunch of old guys, but if you actually make it deep into the tournament, it's a cool experience."

How come I have never heard of this before? I quickly pulled out my phone and searched for the tournament. After a few clicks, I found the website. All I had to do was qualify by playing a local tournament in Orlando. I had found a way to play poker again. It was far from what I needed, but it was a start. "Are we finished here?" I asked before quickly packing up and leaving to my apartment.

When I got back to my place, I researched, confirming what I had been told earlier that the State Tour is a statewide annual tournament with two qualification rounds. First, I had to win in my local city to eventually play against the whole county. If I made it past those two rounds, I would play in the finals of the state. There were no payouts, unless you won the whole thing. Huge turnoff. But I liked the competition aspect of it, and it would keep my skills sharpened until I figured out what I would do about cash games. That same night, before I went to sleep, I signed up. All I needed was my name, some basic information, and my school e-mail. Soon I could play.

I know by now you're wondering what the hell the One Knight Stand is. Here's the answer—about three weeks later, the first tournament of the season was a local qualifier held near my school. I considered not showing up due to the lack of money. Why would I play poker without any possibility of being paid unless I won the whole thing? But the first-place payout was a hundred thousand dollars, exactly my goal, so I showed up for the first round. And, of course, I won. This secured me a spot in the next weekly qualifier the following Wednesday. I was excited, and this now had my full attention. I arrived at the weekly qualifier, which was in Downtown Orlando and sat down in the hotel it was being hosted at to start playing. The hotel had an antique feel to it, but it was definitely fancy. We played in a wide ballroom. There was a cameraman filming the whole room, moving from table to table; he made me feel like I was a professional. During this event, which was streamed online, there were two commentators. At the beginning of the tournament, they each placed their bets on their favorite players out of the more than twenty players there to win. One commentator chose me.

Because many players played various local city tournaments in their attempt to qualify, and I only needed one, and because I was a knight (the UCF mascot), one commentator called me *The One Knight Stand.*

Here is the exact quote from an article written about me on the tour website prior to that livestream: "Up next we have a man whom men idolize, women hate, and poker players adore. Around the office we call him 'Mr. One Knight Stand.' I am of course talking about the University of Central Florida Knight *Charles Marquez.* Mr. OKS doesn't like to waste his time; he takes out the competition with one swift move and doesn't like to call them back. This week he only played in one event and earned a first-place finish. I can confidently say Charles will be a top competitor this season…"

And I know you bought this book in the *fiction* section, but I can't make this stuff up. That *really* happened.

This was the beginning of my other half. And this is where a new chapter of my life really began. The chapter you're here to see.

The One Knight Stand would soon become my alter ego, my best friend, and my evil twin. This would be the start of my transfor—never mind. You'll see what happens.

JACK

WHEN THE SUN GOES DOWN
AND THE LIGHTS TURN ON

Two months of being in school had flown by, and the only poker I had played were the two nights I played qualifications rounds for the tour. I missed playing cash games, but more than missing playing, I missed the money. My spending money was running out, and if I wanted to have enough by the end of the school year, I needed to constantly add to my college fund, which was currently only at $9,000. I had forgotten what it was like to play cash games and again thought my time with poker was over; I felt like I hadn't seen my girlfriend in months.

But, finally, my prayers were answered. In the last qualification round of the tour before the finals, I met a guy by the name of Lance while playing in the final table. We started talking because I noticed he was a good player and also a student at UCF, as he was wearing a Knights T-shirt.

"What's your major?"

"I'm doing accounting. What about you?"

"Finance."

Eventually, I asked him if he ever went to Daytona or Melbourne to play cash games, as those two were the closest poker rooms to us. He told me he barely made the trip, as he preferred to play locally. I thought he was referring to just playing tournaments with his friends or at the lame bars. But to my surprise, he started talking about some cash games in the area. I asked him to elaborate, as I was completely sure there weren't local cash games.

"Take down my number, man. We can chat after this tournament is done."

Once I messaged him after I had arrived home, I asked him about the cash games he mentioned. "Yeah man, I didn't want to talk about it in person during the tournament, but there's local underground cash games I've played a couple of times."

"What do you mean? Who runs those games?"

When he answered, it was music to my ears (or eyes). I didn't exactly know what he was talking about, but I kept asking questions. I was like a middle schooler discovering sex. He told me all about the Orlando scene and told me there were games every night where anybody could play. Now, you can call me naïve, but I thought these games were strictly in movies. I didn't know what to expect, but without a doubt, I was in.

That weekend, Lance picked me up and drove us to an apartment that was about twenty minutes away.

"Just be cool; don't act like it's your first time."

But it was my first time playing underground, and I had no idea what to expect. What was I doing there? I was a *regular* kid from Mexton. What was

I doing in a house full of strangers playing poker? This is how all murder stories start out. But I didn't have time to question my surroundings because cards were soon in my hands after we entered the house. The first couple of hands I folded, as I was a bit careful in this new atmosphere. But then I was the big blind, and when the action came to me, I looked at my cards: Cowboys. For all of you who still haven't gotten with the program, "cowboys" means pocket kings. For those who have no hope, "pocket kings" means having two kings.

I raised the bet to forty-five dollars and had a few callers. On the flop came king, five, and a jack, two of them being spades—my heart rate accelerated. I bet a hundred and forty and had two callers. On the turn came a three—changed nothing; I bet two hundred and got one caller, and finally on the river came another spade—a ten. I didn't have much money behind me so I just checked, and my opponent went all in, I had to call. He flipped over a flush.

I couldn't believe it; these were the things I hated about poker. I had an amazing starting hand, and I got sucked out on the river. I couldn't ever catch a break, every time I tried to jump bigger, I would be faced with gravity. Was there some force in the universe that simply didn't want me to win?

Close to broke, I thought maybe I didn't have it when I arrived home and sat down on my bed. I wasn't good enough to play with these guys. Anybody could win small games, but this was another level where I needed a bit more than naïve luck. Whether I was good enough or not, I knew I would be back soon. I didn't want to be done playing; I simply wanted to be done losing.

Depression is a cold dark hole you just can't climb your way out of, regardless of how much you try. It's not that you're necessarily living a miserable life or bad things are happening to you; it's just, you seem to live with this dark cloud that follows you wherever you go. It's being tired when you wake up and not being able to sleep. It's isolating yourself from the ones you love and doing things you know will make you unhappy later on. It's nothingness. You don't want to be sad, but you gravitate toward being sad and even find comfort in unhappiness.

PART II
ADDICTION

QUEEN

IN THIS FOR GOOD

had to make a decision whether I wanted to stay in this world or not. Losing wasn't fun, and winning wouldn't be easy. It's hard to make a decision knowing that sometimes even giving something your all won't bring success. Which was stronger? My fear of being average, or my craving to be superior. It was decision time.

♠

On a Tuesday, Lance picked me up around 7:00 p.m. All I was told was that we were going to play a bigger game in a similar area. I knew I couldn't afford to lose again, so I spent the car ride mentally preparing to make a killing. We drove about twenty minutes and parked near a nice suburban house. We waited inside the car for about another twenty minutes, as we were one of the first people there and were waiting for Lance's guy to get us in. As we waited, we saw people pull up to the house and go in. Eventually, I saw a lanky dark man walking toward the car, and I was told to step out. We all walked toward the house. I had no idea what to expect. I could only imagine what was past that door—I could've been on my way to getting kidnapped for all I knew. Lance's guy rang the doorbell, and a middle-aged bald black man, with sweatpants on, answered seconds later. I expected there'd be some type of secret password to get in like in the movies, but I could tell the guy we were with was a regular.

"Welcome, guys," said the older man in a gruff voice as the door closed behind me.

I walked in and was directed to the poker table. The place seemed like a regular nice house, but after taking about fifteen steps inward, I reached the table. The deeper into the house I stepped, the more it seemed like a mini Hard Rock in there. It had nice pieces of art, some sculptures, and right in the middle, a nicer-than-most poker table.

The game tonight? 2-5.

By the way, when I say a game is x-x, it just signifies the blinds. Larger numbers, larger games. Larger games, more money. Simple.

Until then, I had only played 1-2, where players usually buy in with no more than $300, but this is where the real big boys sat, where buy-ins are usually around $600. I needed a win desperately to get me back into my groove. I'll admit it, I was more than a bit frightened. I hadn't been playing regularly and wasn't on a good run; and I was about to sit down at my biggest game yet knowing that a loss would kill me. Now I was playing underground with people who were gambling with real money. No more *worst-case scenario I lost $200* mentality. But I couldn't show I was intimidated. It was time to play some cards.

As soon as I sat down, I looked around the table, you know, the usual.

Directly to my right was a guy who looked like a total nerd. He was probably around twenty-six years old, came in wearing a gray T-shirt and jeans—type of guy who looked like he worked for Microsoft and pulled off a perfect score on his SAT. In front of me were some Hispanic guys I couldn't get much information on from looking at them; they struck me as the type who worked as salesmen for whatever and spent their money on gambling or strip clubs. Diagonal from me was a white guy who was probably forty years old; he looked like the typical bookie, wearing a snapback, a lot of jewelry, sweatpants, and Nike sneakers. Then, a lady in only lingerie walked in; I had no idea what was going on, and I thought maybe she was in the wrong place. Only later did I realize that she was the masseuse/waitress. Interesting. Then, the most perfect thing happened to confirm the stereotype. The bookie handed the nerd two $100 bills, the nerd grabbed the money and handed him back a huge Ziploc bag full of weed. The only thing missing that night were cigars to make it a movie.

A couple of more guys sat down, and it was time to get the cards going. The first person to buy in was the Microsoft nerd; he bought in for four hundred. Next were the Hispanic guys who bought in each for five hundred. The host of the game then looked over to the bookie who said, "I'll take eight." He then looked around his wallet and looked back up. "You know what? Fuck it. Give me a grand."

Shit was getting serious.

Lance and I bought in around three fifty each, which was all I took.

I played pretty tight toward the beginning, as I didn't have enough chips to be playing mediocre hands. But, finally, after about half an hour, I was dealt pocket sevens and called a seventy-dollar raise. On the flop came another seven, and I knew I had the best hand. But would it happen to me again? Would I not bet enough and get sucked out on the next two cards? I had to make sure I won that hand, so I bet a hundred dollars, and I got two callers. The next card: the last seven. I closed my eyes and let out a deep sigh of relief.

This right here, ladies and gentlemen, my good friends, is *the* feeling. I had the "nuts" now, the best possible hand, and I knew no other hand could beat me. *This* feeling is the best in the world. It's beautiful because you know you're good, and all the money will come to you at the end of the hand regardless of what happens. You no longer have to worry about bluffs, the river, nor any other action. You're good. You're sure you will win this hand, and you only have to worry about getting the most money you can now. When you know you have your opponents, it feels magical. For thirty seconds, or a minute or two, there's nothing in the world to worry about.

I went all in and only got one caller, and I won the hand with my quads. I was back.

♠

The importance of that night was that I really had to be careful now, in every aspect of the word. I was playing with a lot of money, and I was now underground. That night made me grow up. The game was strictly business. I was working in a serious environment now, no friends. I thought it could've potentially gotten dangerous at that point, and I had to adjust accordingly. I had to consciously be able to turn the switch on and off for who I was. Normally, I was Chuck Marquez, but when I played, I now needed to fully be the One Knight Stand.

When I got home, I put my earnings in my college fund, which was now up to $11,000.

KING

DON'T ASK ME WHY I BECAME COLD

So what makes me different? I've told you all about how I'm not part of this inner circle of losers. What makes me superior? How do I distinguish myself from everybody else at the table? For starters, I use simple math. I see ratios and percentages where others just see chips. I know the actual theory behind this game and can run simple algorithms in my head while these dogs can barely understand the rules. More importantly, I don't have any emotional ties with me at the table. These players lose a lot of their money because they're tied to their stupid feelings—they personalize every bet they make. You can't be emotional when you have fifty grand in front of you, and that's the number one reason I lose money a lot less than everyone else. I am not emotional.

The next weekend, I returned underground. That night, we were going to another game; another guy at another house was hosting that night's event. See, the thing is the underground scene is like a mafia—rather than competing for players, the hosts of the games collude and take turns each night hosting games, to maximize profits and minimize conflicts.

Lance and I drove to the house around 8:00 p.m., and the cards flew. No interesting characters this time, just a bunch of old guys playing poker. The whole night was up and down for me, mostly up but with no real action. These underground games are particular, as they hold some distinction from regular cash games. First, odds are you play with the same circle of fifty guys; somebody new shows up here and there, but like fight club, it's pretty much the same every week. This affects the game in obvious ways. Second, it's more a relaxed environment, as the hosts provide free food and drinks, and all the snacks one can imagine, adding to the light atmosphere. I don't forget that I'm gambling thousands of dollars, but it feels like I'm gambling them in a spa. The hosts don't create this atmosphere by accident.

What I liked about those games was that people were particularly dumb. For some reason the fact that they knew each other and that they were playing in a home versus a casino made players act differently. They were going all in with any decent hand, so I figured all I had to do was wait until the right spot and shove. And after I was about sixteen hundred up, I was in the right spot. I was on the button and landed a hand I could do some damage with. There had been two raises, one to fifty and the next to a hundred. When it got to me, I made it two hundred. The first raiser called, and the second raiser took a while but eventually made the call. On the flop came ace, four, six. Oh yeah, I didn't tell you what my cards were; I'll let you practice your reading skills this time.

The ace slowed me down a bit, but after two checks, I bet two twenty. The first player thought about it for a minute, and after debating with himself a couple of times, he folded. The next player immediately raised it to five hundred. Didn't see that one coming. Seemed like he definitely had an ace, but my implied odds were good, and I was in position, so I called. The next card came—a king. It was like the universe wanted me to be rich. He checked, and I suspected he was slow-playing his ace, but I also checked, knowing there'd be plenty of action on the river. The river came, another six. He bet four hundred, and I checked my cards to make sure I have it. I doubted he made aces full, and I wanted to raise and try to get some value but I had no more money. I just called and showed my cards. He immediately flustered and angrily turned over an ace and a king and mucked them. I had him.

You think you know what I had?

That night was my biggest payout to date. I left with thirty-three hundred in profit. When I arrived home that night, I walked straight to my envelope to put away my earnings. I was close to having $15,000; I was not only excited to see my progress, but since it had been my biggest payout, I also felt like hugging somebody. I could see that I was really turning into a good player. I was ecstatic. Three weeks prior I had contemplated quitting, and now I was on a winning streak. I wanted to go out and celebrate or at least see somebody. I had just won more than three grand and was filled with adrenaline. The last thing I wanted to do was go to sleep, but all my roommates and friends were already in bed, as it was late in the night on a weekday.

But you know where it wasn't late? France.

Truth is, of course I didn't forget about Macoa after that kiss. That kiss was everything to me; it made forgetting about her impossible. Everything

I did made me remember her. From seeing a queen of hearts while playing, to seeing a girl with brown eyes made me think of her. I wanted to call her and tell her about my winnings. I knew I shouldn't have talked to her, but I couldn't help myself. I texted her asking if she was available for a phone call, but before she could answer, I proceeded to click the call button. After a couple of infinite seeming rings, she answered, "Hey!"

I was so happy to hear her voice, so soothing yet intense. She asked why I was up, and I told her about my night and how school and poker had been going. She responded, "That's amazing, Chuck. I'm really happy for you."

And even though I wasn't looking at her, I could just feel how beautiful she was. Her beauty was something else, something you didn't have to see with your eyes. It was more of a force.

After catching up for what felt like an hour, I sat content. She kept talking as I realized that the simple act of talking to somebody I felt for was real happiness, not the money I was making earlier. I realized that although my grades were impeccable, and I was making more money than the average college graduate, I still felt that something was missing. All the riches in the world were meaningless to me if there was nobody to share them with. So I decided that, despite the distance, I was going to ask Macoa to be mine. I obviously wasn't thinking anything through, but I had just had a crazy night, and I was on a poker high, and my thoughts ran too quickly to analyze them at that point of the night. It just felt right at the time.

Eventually my mind returned to the conversation, and before I could catch them, the words ran out of my mouth. "Macoa, listen, I know you're halfway around the world, but everything about you seems right to me. After that kiss, I couldn't forget about you, and maybe I'm not meant to. I've always thought about you like this, and I owe it to myself to try. With the money I'm making now, we can see each other often until I finish school, and then we'll figure the rest out. We can make it work. I will even try to take a semester in France. And I'm not kidding this time. I'm different now; I'm serious. I'm going to be a big success soon, and I want you to be alongside me," I said almost forgetting that she still had a boyfriend.

There was a pause that was at least ten seconds long.

That pause was frightening, but one can imagine for those small seconds, that finite amount of time, maybe she was mine. Maybe in those ten seconds she considered what I was saying, and in those ten seconds I was under the illusion that she was.

But those ten seconds are just that—finite. She finally broke the silence; I heard her take a deep breath before she actually spoke. "God, Chuck, that kiss meant a lot to me too. And of course I think of you too. But c'mon, you're really nice and all, but…"

And you know what, my good friend? If I could go back in time and relive that night, there's no way in hell I would continue the path I was on. Nope. I would drive home to my family, and I would talk to my mom and dad, telling them how alone I really felt that night. I would just sit there after my parents had gone to sleep, and my dog would stay up with me, never letting me stay up alone because maybe he understood that I just needed someone. Or maybe I would go to my friend Charlie's house because even though he never knew what to say, he was always the first person who tried. Maybe I would pick up my friend Sandro, and we would get a late-night snack wherever was open, and he would just listen to what I had to say.

But none of these things are the thing I'd do first because none of these things would be enough. If I could do it all over again, I would run as fast as I could and run to you and tell you to save me, to not let me go. I would tell you to stop me here, and to not let me continue making bad decisions. And I could only tell you, and only you could understand because in however many months or years you would read my story, you would be the only person who could understand. I needed you that night because the next year of my life was the darkest I'd ever felt, and I almost didn't make it out.

FOURTEEN

WHO AM I BECOMING?

Someone once said to keep doing the same thing and expecting a different result was the definition of insanity. So don't ask me why I've become the way I am. Don't ask why I'm "sexist" or "rude" now. When I was genuinely caring and nice, things simply didn't go my way. I sat around for years seeing girls' knees shake for guys who would speak poorly of them to their friends just hours after sleeping with them. There comes a point when you have to stop chasing and start being chased. Not because I'm evil or because I'm not a good person, but because I want better. All I am is a response to the pushes and pulls of the universe, and if I want to get things in life, sometimes they'll come at a cost.

Sorry, Dad.

I used to be different than the rest of the guys, but I had no success with that. So now, I'm the same.

♥

The second week of November, I had a big exam in my finance class that my college friend Brent and I studied for at the library an hour before. Brent was also from South Florida like me and also a poker player—a really bad one, but don't tell him I said that. He is my height, has blue eyes and dark brown hair; always in a good mood. He was a naturally chill guy, and always wanted to be around the "action," whatever that meant. We agreed that if we both aced the exam we would take a trip to the Hard Rock in Tampa for the weekend, as there was a big tournament going on.

There we were in the testing center, taking the exam an hour later, hoping everything went well. When I finished my exam, I waited for Brent outside until he was finished with his. A few minutes later, he walked out with a pretty big smile signaling that he felt he did well.

Thursday at 9:00 p.m., we received the notification that the exam grades were up. I checked mine first. Ninety-three. I handed my laptop to Brent so that he could check his. Eighty-seven. By the following morning, we were driving up to Tampa. I know Brent didn't get his A, but if you average the two scores, we collectively did, and that was almost the same thing.

We arrived at the hotel by 2:00 p.m. and checked in after getting a bite to eat. The tournament didn't start until five, so after resting a bit in the room and checking out the pool, we played blackjack for a bit until the tournament started. Blackjack turned out to be a bad decision as my wallet took a hit.

Walking into the poker room, we were ready to do some work. The buy-in was $250, and there was fifty grand guaranteed. We shook hands, and each proceeded to our designated tables/seats. The tournament lasted the whole weekend, so I'm not going to get into any specifics of the hands played. All you need to know is that the tournament was exhausting, extensive, and slow. It was long, and a lot of good players were there, attracting people nationwide. Playing poker naturally gets a nervous response from the body, but playing for long without an extended break starts to mess with one's nerves, and mine were getting to me after just four hours, just before the dinner break. And this was only the first day.

At the dinner break, Brent and I sped to the food court and chose the first thing we saw to eat. We only had thirty minutes until we had to get back. I told Brent about my nerves while we were eating, knowing he never showed any signs of anxiety when gambling and often losing loads of money.

"I'm not sure. I think it's the fact that I've never played this long before. I'm just starting to feel anxious."

"What do you usually do when you feel anxious?"

"I don't know. I've never felt like this. What do you do?"

He instantly smirked as if he had the cure to cancer. He motioned me to come closer to him and lowered his voice. "If you're feeling stressed out, you got two prescriptions: sex or masturbation. Both equally effective."

I thought about both of them. But I didn't have the time or luck to do either in the five minutes we had left.

"Great. Thanks."

Right before we walked back into the poker room, Brent placed his hand on my chest and reached into his pocket. He pulled out a Ziploc bag the size of a quarter with a couple of pills in it, looked at me with a grin, and said, "Here's my third prescription."

I stared at the bag for about five seconds and then looked back up at him. I had never done drugs before and didn't know what to do. I looked back down at the bag.

"What is this?"

"If you ask questions, you'll get even more anxious. Just trust me, and take the damn pill."

I did urgently need something to calm my nerves if we were going to do this the whole weekend. I gave myself a *you can do it* speech in my head as I threw a pill in my mouth, drank some water and continued to my table to keep playing cards.

FIFTEEN

I THINK I LIKE WHO I AM BECOMING

That particular tournament didn't end up too successfully for me, as I grew paranoid from my thoughts after taking the pill. I thought the pill made me too relaxed, so I would try to play more aggressively; later I would think I was playing over aggressively and would loosen my play as a result. I had a good lead up until the end of Saturday and then was eliminated early on Sunday after my chip stack was on the end of a long roller-coaster ride.

♥

When I reflected on the tournament on the ride back, I started to notice that my emotions were taking a toll on me. They were too real and intense; they distracted me more than I liked. When I was playing poker, I felt anxious and couldn't calm myself enough to focus like I wanted to, and when I went home at night, I felt the absence of the rush making me feel empty. There would also be times that normal life would be too boring for me. It's funny how playing high-stakes poker is incredibly real and makes me feel alive—I can feel cold blood running through my veins and am conscious of my heart beating as I make a risky bluff. Interestingly, when I do other things that aren't so emotionally invigorating, I get bored. Real life wasn't good enough for me anymore, I much rather preferred to live my gambler's fantasy.

But the reality was that I wasn't the One Knight Stand yet; making the switch from Charles Marquez was becoming easier and instinctual, but I still wasn't there. I acted like the big bad wolf at the table at times, but it was still an act. I was faking it until I made it. The person I pretended to be wasn't completely me because, in reality, I wasn't so brave, confident, and ruthless.

I thought about this as I drove to a downtown game to play 5-10 on Monday night. By this point, since I was pretty much playing bigger games every other week, every time I had a big win or loss, it was my largest to date. Meaning, every night I won large at the next big game, it was the most I had won; and when I would lose, it would be the most I had lost up to that point because I was buying into bigger games.

Most of the guys playing there were in their thirties who worked in finance, naturally arrogant and cocky. They all saw me as the sucker and were ready to extract my money, the type of guys who call all their losses unlucky and my wins luck.

I knew I was better than them in every sense of the game, but I still had the voice in the back of my head that filled me with doubts. It would tell me that maybe I really was getting lucky, maybe I wasn't ready to play with the big dogs. It made me question if I could really handle the stress of this lifestyle.

But eventually I tried to listen to the voice rather than ignore it. And it took me some time to realize it, but that voice that we all hear, you know what it was? The one that would tell me to not call, to not bet, to not go for it, to not even show up to the games—it wasn't my conscious—it was fear. Fear that I might actually be as good as my dreams. Fear that I actually could be great. Fear that maybe this lifestyle wasn't just a dream anymore.

This became especially true when I had aces preflop, or I had the nuts on the flop or turn. It was when I had the best hands that my heart would beat the hardest, and I would get the most anxious. When I knew I was about to make a hefty bet where I could make the most money, my insides would start to panic. I never understood this, but I just simply would have more anxiety when I had good cards and was betting than when I had a mediocre hand and was chasing.

I finally arrived at the game, picked up pocket queens preflop, and raised to fifty dollars, my heart rate beginning to speed up. On the flop came a queen, my heart rate again accelerating at a faster pace as I bet four hundred. On the turn there was both a flush and a straight draw, so I bet twelve hundred to both elude somebody who thought I was bluffing and in an attempt to end the hand there, as I didn't want to get into trouble on the river. Unfortunately, I had two callers. And of course, on the river both the straight and flush were completed.

One of the players bet only a thousand, and I was in too deep to fold. Knowing he probably made a straight or flush, I called with my trips. Naturally, he turned over a straight flush with a grin the size of my d—

I lost $3,000 that night. The most money I had ever lost in one day in my life. Before that, I was losing a couple of hundred dollars on a bad day. Now, I was down four figures in just one night.

Car rides home were always emotional. Sometimes I cried because I lost more money than most people in the world make in a month. Sometimes I laughed and called Brent to make table reservations. Sometimes I was frustrated because of a stupid play I did. And sometimes I drove in silence. The worst – silence. Thinking what I could have done with the money I lost. Thinking about the pure evilness and almost inhumanity of gambling. Forcibly closing my eyes and praying I could reverse time and not make the decisions that led to the silent drives. Promising myself and God if I would never gamble again if I could somehow have the money back. The car rides home are what separate poker with other professions or games. Poker follows you home. On the drive home, all I could think about was the money, not even putting on music, driving in silence, thinking of the cash I had lost so carelessly. Three thousand dollars? That was a lot of cash.

Guilt ran up my back like a snake as I thought of all I could do with that money. I could've fed a lot of hungry people with that. I could've helped my mom buy a nicer car with that money. I could have relieved a lot of my father's stress with that money. Had greed gotten to me to the point where I could afford to lose that kind of money playing poker yet couldn't afford to help my own family with it? Who was I becoming? What was I doing? What had all this done to me? Was it worth it?

All these questions were running through my head when I was lying in bed. The stress was so real. So real and intense. I felt trapped in my room at that point, so alone and hopeless. The walls seemed to get closer and closer the more I thought about what had happened. I reached over my bed to grab my phone to call my mom and tell her how I felt, as I would normally do when I felt stressed or alone. But I realized that she still didn't know of this part of my life, and this wasn't the way to tell her. So I put my phone down and realized I didn't have anybody to call or talk to. I launched my phone at the wall and broke down. I couldn't handle the pain anymore, and before I knew it my face was wet with tears that ran effortlessly down my face.

Not having anybody to share my pain with meant I had to start dealing with my problems and emptiness another way. I called Brent that night and asked him if he had another pill for me. I had to start hiding my emotions if I wanted to continue; rather, I had to practice numbing my emotions and not feel.

SIXTEEN

MO MONEY, MO PROBLEMS

I lost a lot of money that night, but I was still running hot. My college fund was at $16,000, and I needed to keep going. But like I've told you, I was growing anxious, as I was playing bigger games. Meaning, there was more money on the line, and messing up meant something worse each time. And the more my anxiety grew, the more I had to pretend like I was doing just fine. I resorted to vices to alleviate the anxiety that gambling thousands of dollars gave me. The more and more I played, the more I practiced wearing the mask of the One Knight Stand. And the more I wore the mask, the harder it was for me to take it off when I wasn't playing.

♥

My family came to visit me before finals. It was a nice refresher since it was the first time I had seen them in a couple of months. But when we sat down to go to dinner the first night, I remember just sitting there in silence, looking around the room. I tried not to look at my parents as much as I could, their eyes being my weakness. My parents are in their late forties. My mother a sweet, short Italian mom. My dad physically an older version of myself. My brother was there too, although I preferred if they had brought Bruce instead. When my parents would look at me I would just stare back. I was trying to avoid questions they could possibly ask me—I just didn't want to have to lie if they asked me what was new, or why I hadn't been calling them as much. I knew they could see something in my eyes, but they would've never imagined what it was.

They asked me why I was so quiet, but I didn't know what to say.

"I guess I'm just tired."

My mom told me she thought I was changing. She didn't know why or how, but she noticed arrogance and stubbornness in me.

"Do you have a girlfriend now or something?"

Seeing them came with mixed feelings, but it was soon the start of December, and finals were on my agenda. Exams came and went; I can't remember much about school to be honest. After the first week of exams, I found myself near Downtown with some girls and Brent getting a bite to eat before we took them back home to, uh, to watch a movie with! On our drive home, we passed one of the Premium Outlets that are popular shopping malls in the Orlando area. I remembered how I liked going to malls when I was a kid but stopped because of the time and money wasted there; however, most times I wouldn't really buy anything.

But I realized I now had some purchasing power.

I started to think. I realized that although very unlikely, I could've lost all the money at any moment. Sure, I had a lot of money but I was still heavily gambling. And so, before anything happened, I was going to use some of it. If I was going to adopt this lifestyle, I wanted to adopt all of it, the look included. The following day I drove to a nice mall, where I planned on making some purchases, including shirts, pants, shoes, and a nice watch.

I was in a jewelry store looking at different watches when I put one on and looked in the mirror. When I focused in on my face, I noticed I looked different. My hair was longer, I stood up taller, and I liked the person who was staring back at me. I made the purchase and continued to walk to another store. I felt powerful leaving each store. I was better now, I was better than the people working around the mall, I was better than the valet guys, I was better than everybody around me, I thought. I was twenty at the time and was making more a month than most college-educated corporate professionals.

I liked shopping at Prada and Versace; I liked the way people treated me in there when I shopped, and I liked the way people would look at me when I walked around with those bags.

But why stop there? My income was only growing every month, and I was going to enjoy the life while I could. My adrenaline was running high when I shopped, and I wanted to keep the rush going. I pondered as I later ate lunch at the Cheesecake Factory to see what my next move would be.

And then I got it: go big or go home. Next stop—Cadillac car dealership.

As I waited for my car from the mall valet, I was approached by a homeless man who asked me if I could give him some money for food. *Why do people ask me for stuff?* "No, just go work. Stop being lazy. Just because I have more than you does not give you the right to bother me."

I annoyingly walked to my car and then drove to the dealership and looked for cars after I parked. As I was doing that, a salesman walked out and asked me if I could use any help. I don't know why I was looking;

I knew exactly what I wanted—CTS-V Sedan. His face implied doubt, as I told him I wanted one, but he continued to do his job. After some questions, he realized I was serious and started talking prices to me. I said I wanted to lease the car, as I didn't want too much of a commitment. He agreed and then proceeded to try to sell the car to me, telling me that "This car is the most comfortable sports vehicle you'll ever drive, spacious on the inside and drives better than ninety percent in the sports market."

"No need to sell, man. I think I got it."

"Okay, well in case you're still comparing, this car is also great on gas!"

What? Did this guy just tell me this V-8 car is good on gas? Some people will do anything for money.

"Joseph. Can you take an Uber to the Cadillac dealership please? I need someone to drive my old car home."

After the annoying two-hour paper signing, I drove off the lot in my new Cadillac. And believe me, it felt good being king.

SEVENTEEN

AND PEOPLE BEGAN TO NOTICE

I f you think my story is moving too quickly, it's because it did move like this for me too. Looking back at those times, I find that calendars didn't matter much anymore. My life was moving faster and faster, and it was continually harder for me to slow down. One day I was drinking coffee to stay alert, the next I was taking a pill. One night I was making fifty-dollar bets, the next I was making bets worth thousands. The only real indicators of time were my growing bank account and my hair, which was longer than what it had ever been before, now halfway down to reaching my shoulders as I embodied this new persona.

It was the last day of finals, and that Friday I went to happy hour at a local bar. I was there with my roommate, Joseph, and we noticed some cute sorority girls among the dense crowd. Joseph had a dense and mysterious beard, buff, always wore black V-necks, tattoos; the type of guy I would want people to know I'm friends with in case I ever get in a fight at a bar.

"Let's go talk to them," he said to me.

"Uh yeah, let's go."

The problem was that there, I wasn't drunk, I didn't have my nice car to show, and I didn't have chips in front of me. I couldn't wear a mask or pretend to be somebody I wasn't. I was simply another kid there, no different than any of the other hundreds of students. I still didn't believe I had it in me—the ability to just get girls or be the confident guy I was when I was playing poker. I knew that deep inside of me was a timid kid who would still doubt himself under pressure.

But I couldn't say no; I told Joseph to follow my lead as I walked in their direction to talk to them. Even if I didn't believe in myself, I still had to pretend I did. As I approached them I quickly tried to imagine what the One Knight Stand would say, not what Charles would.

I walked up to the two girls, one blonde and one brunette.

"Hey, do you mind taking a picture of me and my friend," I said, handing the brunette my phone.

While she was taking the picture, I quickly caught a glimpse of her hand. She speedily snapped the photo and handed me back my phone. "Hey, Joseph, look at her nail polish. It's the same color we were talking about earlier."

"Uh, yeah, it's almost identical," Joseph answered as he looked at my serious face.

"What are you guys talking about?" she asked.

She was hooked.

"My friend and I have been having a debate all week about this. How about you decide who's right?"

Her friend had stepped closer now and listened with hesitation as I continued, "So I have this theory that you can tell a lot about girls by the color of nail polish they use. See, you have a light blue color, so that tells me you act really confident and even sometimes bold, but in the inside, you're actually quite shy and humble. Your friend has a darker red color and that tells me she likes to be independent but also values the validation from her close friends like you. My friend, Joseph, thinks it's just a color, nothing more."

They looked at each other while I looked back at Joseph. Had it worked?

"Wow. That's actually pretty accurate. What's your names again? Can you tell us more?"

"Depends on what you want to know? I'm just hoping you girls aren't like most here, shallow and unexciting."

I was in. Six months ago I would've never talked to a girl like this, without caring for the consequences. In fact, I would've probably been too busy thinking of Macoa, but now I knew what I wanted. After about ten minutes of small talk with the girls, they agreed to come out with Joseph and me that night to Downtown.

I had successfully closed; I know I did. But I still couldn't decide whether all this was good fortune, luck, or really me. I didn't know if it was actually working or the odds were simply in my favor. I knew I had started to become a different person, but was my success outside of poker due to my new attitude? Or was I just telling myself that? At that point, I didn't care, though. I was starting to believe my doubts and doubt my beliefs. See, that's the problem with gambling. You don't know what to attribute to luck and what to attribute to skill.

♥

At 10:00 p.m., they knocked on our door.

"Whoa, you guys look hotter than you did earlier today," I said as I let them in.

"We clean up nicely."

"You guys are early too. Seems like you're excited to get here."

We proceeded to pregaming, and when the booze kicked in after playing some drinking games, we were ready to head out. Usually I would've ordered an Uber, but this was my first weekend with the Cadi, and there was no way in hell I wasn't going to drive it.

We had made arrangements for a table downtown, and you already know what happens when we have a table. Once in the club, the music pumped so loud that we had to scream to even communicate with each other. The club was packed with young, depressed adults trying to get laid. But we were separated from the peasants, as the table was on the second floor, where I could oversee everybody I was superior to. After about an hour of being there, Joseph and I each danced with our respective girls on the dancefloor upstairs. If you haven't gotten it by now, my girl is always the blond. She smelled like she was covered in a $200 perfume. Just putting my nose on her neck and smelling her scent made her all that much hotter and made me want her even more. And I'm sure she wanted me too.

Looking back, like I said, I'm really not sure if it was actually that I was becoming a more attractive person, if it was that my confidence was up the roof, or my money or what. But my results were evident. Girls wanted me, and guys wanted to be around me. I guess you just show these idiots some money and a good time, and they'll make you famous. Get them all hyped up at the table, show them what they want, and they'll worship you. And worship me they did.

All those girls in the club and bars, they had different names, but they're exactly the same, every single one of them. Some just hide it better than others, but don't let them fool you. They're all attracted to the same things: power, status, and surface. Nothing more. And you're probably thinking I'm saying this only because I'm insecure, I have been hurt in the past, and that maybe I'm the one with no surface. And you know what? Maybe that's true too. But the cards were going my way, and I was cashing in. Everything I touched was turning into gold.

♥

Being broke during college? That was for chumps. I was flying high, and there was no way I was turning back.

Sometimes, I think about that era compared to where I am now and I laugh. My life was spinning out of control. Yeah, but I was driving a Cadillac, I was eating at nice restaurants, I was partying like a degenerate, and I was getting straight As in school. My life was finally a movie.

Fast forward to the next morning when I woke up next to a beautiful blond girl. My life was perfect, right?

But as perfect as my life was, I couldn't help but keep thinking that this could all be gone in a flip of a coin. This lifestyle was given to me in a matter of a few months, and it could've easily vanished as it came. So, before the girl woke up, I decided I needed one big contingency plan. I needed a plan to make an escape in case it all went sour. While she was still sleeping, I opened my laptop and searched flights to different places in the world. I looked at flights to Europe, China, and South America. I imagined myself one day leaving everything behind and escaping all my troubles. Maybe I would leave if I lost everything, but maybe I would also leave once I had enough of this life.

A bit dramatic, but I drove to the bank and withdrew $2,500, which I determined would be enough money to buy a plane ticket to pretty much anywhere in the world and have enough funds to eat and sleep for about a month until I figured something out. I put it all in a new account, which I titled "Plan Z." I put the password to access the account in a book underneath my bed. My plan was to use the money to buy a plane ticket to wherever, (probably somewhere to Asia) for whatever reason if I needed to. I knew that it would probably never come to that, but I needed an escape in case I lost everything.

As I stepped back into my room, the girl was just waking up. She squinted. "Hey, you."

"Hi. Did you have fun last night?"

"It might have been the best night of my life."

"I'm glad. There's some food outside if you're hungry."

"Thank you. I want to lie in bed for a bit longer if you don't mind."

"Go ahead."

"You know, I had never been VIP to a club like that. I felt like I was famous or something. And coming back here was even better."

"Want to do it again?"

EIGHTEEN

WINTER BREAK

I know for some of you this part is a bit boring, shallow and too easy right now. But don't worry, it gets much better and even more cliché when I die internally and lose all sense of self. So sit back and keep reading.

Or don't, you already bought the book, so my job here is done. Actually, keep reading—or at least pretend to, it feeds my ego. But it also kind of makes me dislike myself for some demented reason.

It's weird.

♥

I was running out of spending money again after going out every weekend, and I was starting to lack discipline when it came to keeping my budget. I was only supposed to be spending a certain amount of what I made, but I kept making exceptions. I needed to get back on the grind, but I still wanted to enjoy the luxuries of my lifestyle. In fact, I wanted more. I wouldn't stop until I was playing with the best players, partying with the coolest people, and sleeping with the hottest girls.

So now that I was on winter break, I would use this time to straighten out my finances and work bigger games at the Hard Rock again.

My obsession with poker began the same way other people experience obsessions. Nobody cared much toward the beginning, you know? Nobody really thinks you can do anything great. Not even your closest friends want you to succeed because nobody wants you to do better than them. Sometimes not even your family wants you to do too well because they're afraid you won't call them back. But the money was rolling in, and as I improved my lifestyle, people began to notice. Like I've always said, or at least am saying now, I really know this money isn't anything important, but it builds my self-esteem. I feel as if I am unstoppable, I think I am a king, a god. Money started to be the only reason I kept doing this and began to be the only thing I cared about. The money made me dominant, it made me unstoppable. I didn't actually care about what I could do with it, but knowing I had the possibilities to choose made me feel powerful. I was living in a world where everything was for sale, and for the first time in my life, I had the money to start buying what I wanted.

But deep down it isn't about the actual substance, it can happen with anything. Addiction isn't about what you're addicted to, *it's about addiction.* The more focused or engulfed you are with what you are doing, the less you go to your friends' events, the less you call people, the less you have time to use social media, and the less you notice other people. Not because you're a bad person, but only because you're busy working or doing whatever it is you're doing. The problem is you also forget to call the people who were actually rooting for you. Not having time doesn't mean not having time for only the least valuable or important things; not having time means you don't have any time, for anything. I was stuck in a sequence. The more successful I became, the more I cared about what I was doing, and the less I called my friends. Then, when I wasn't playing poker, I had nothing to do anymore because I had nobody to hang out with, so that made me feel isolated.

So what did I do? Just went back to poker—a vicious cycle had begun.

It's not that I stopped caring about my friends, it's that I didn't have friends anymore. Nobody was good enough for me in my eyes, and people began to bore me. I only hung out with those whose lifestyle kept up with mine. I didn't want to hear about ordinary problems anymore. You're stressed because of an accounting exam tomorrow? Give me a break. Your boyfriend isn't answering quickly enough? I don't care.

I ended the semester with all As and one A–. The A– pissed me off but I was happy that I was successfully, or so I thought, living two very distinguished lives at once. During the day I was a straight-A student with a bright future, but at night I was becoming the bull of the underground poker scene in Orlando. The fact that I could do both effectively made my ego grow out of proportion; it was during those times that I really did start to worship myself.

♥

I had returned home the first week of December, which was the same time most college kids were getting home for their break. Like I mentioned, I was planning to use the break to focus on poker and work my way up to bigger games.

One morning after a late night at the casino, I received a phone call from one of my high-school friends.

"Hello?"

"Chuck! What are you doing today?" asked Anna.

"Uh…" I looked at my watch. "I just woke up."

"It's one p.m."

"Thank you for letting me know. What's up?"

"Let's get some lunch; I want to catch up. I haven't seen you in months."

"Yeah, okay. Come over. Can you pick something up for us?"

She arrived at my house around two with Asian food, and we talked about how school was and how everybody from our friend group was doing. But she then began to talk about the normal problems in her life. I felt uncomfortable. I tried to zone out but couldn't pretend to care. I didn't want to know about petty problems; I only wanted to talk about what was important. And I know this is random, but only now when I think back at it, I realize that maybe I wasn't the normal one.

"Okay, stop right there. I don't care about sorority stuff. Tell me about something else."

Later in the evening, she said one of our old inside jokes that used to always make me smile, but now it just wasn't that funny to me. I just sat there looking at her, waiting for her to say something else. After some seconds of silence, I finally spoke. "You sound stupid saying the same things you said a couple of years ago. You have to grow up."

She looked back at me for what seemed to be the longest five seconds of her life. "Why don't you smile anymore? What's wrong with you?"

"Nothing. I just don't care for being stupid anymore. You can't just go on with your life talking about unimportant things."

She looked puzzled, fake laughed lightly, and when she noticed I wasn't kidding, her face grew red.

"Are you okay? You seemed depressed, Chuck?"

Was I depressed? Why was she asking me that? Did she somehow know of my new life? Did she see the car outside? Or did I actually seem different, and she genuinely cared?

Who was Chuck, though? I wasn't Chuck Marquez anymore; that was a character of the past. I was now the One Knight Stand.

NINETEEN

RECOGNITION

Since I was a kid, all I wanted to be was an insider. I simply wanted to be part of the inner circle. I wanted to be part of the best, whoever they were. I didn't care of what. I just wanted to be the best. I wanted to be respected. I wanted people to pay attention to me. I wanted to be somebody. I never received that as a kid, but now I was, and I was going to hang on for as a long as I could.

♥

On Christmas Eve, as I was dozing off into sleep in bed, I received a message. The text was from Macoa, who was wishing me a Merry Christmas a bit early, as she was in France where it was already Christmas day. I really didn't want to respond, as I was a bit too tired to start a conversation at that hour, but I thanked her for the message and wished her the same.

But she continued, *Guess what? I have some news!*

I give up, tell me.

I broke up with my boyfriend last week.

I know I don't introduce things enough or just jump into different parts of the story too abruptly. But this really is how I remember it. I was living my normal day-to-day life, trying to play bigger games every day, and all of a sudden this girl said that, on Christmas Eve right before I was going to fall asleep.

Was I dreaming? I had waited my whole life for this girl to be single. Why was she texting me this now? She should've told me this months ago. I really couldn't believe what I was reading; she had been with her boyfriend for almost four years, and now she was single. *The girl of my dreams is single.* I looked at the message for a minute or two, not knowing what to say. What could I possibly have said? There was nothing *to* say. It's funny when you envision a moment for so long and then it actually happens.

I was drawing a blank.

And then, another message before I could respond. *By the way, I'm going to be in Miami for spring break!*

Was there still a part of me that wanted to be with her? Would it be too late to turn around and go back to being Charles? Was this a sign that I needed to go back to my past life?

I continued to stare at the message without knowing how to answer. But then, I thought of something. *Macoa, send me a picture of that card I gave you during summer right now*, I typed. Send.

Only seconds passed. *I still have that card! I just don't know where it is; I'd have to look for it!*

I looked at the message one last time, smiled, put my phone down, and went to sleep.

Let me tell you one of my favorite stories. It's from the movie *Cinema Paradiso*, a famous Italian movie for all you uncultured kids out there. I know we're getting sidetracked, but this has a purpose, trust me.

Once upon a time, a king gave a feast. And there came the most beautiful princesses of the realm. Now, a soldier, who was standing guard, saw the king's daughter go by. She was the most beautiful one, and he immediately fell in love with her. But what could a poor soldier do when it came to the daughter of the king? Well, finally, one day, he managed to meet her, and he told her that he could no longer live without her. The princess was so impressed by his strong feelings that she said to the soldier, "If you can wait a hundred days and a hundred nights under my balcony, then at the end of it, I shall be yours." Damn! The soldier immediately went there and waited one day. And two days. And ten. And then twenty. And every evening, the princess looked out of her window, but he never moved. During rain, during wind, during snow, he was always there. The birds shat on his head, and the bees stung him, but he didn't budge. After ninety nights, he had become all dried up, all white, and the tears streamed from his eyes. He couldn't hold them back. He no longer had the strength to sleep. All that time, the princess watched him. And on the ninety-ninth night, the soldier stood up, took his chair, and went away.

I watched this in my freshman year of high school in my Italian class and actually spent my high-school days not only reading this story, but also showing it to other people, trying to decipher the real meaning of it. But regardless of whom I showed it to, I never found an answer I liked. The last day of my senior year, I walked to my Italian teacher's room and retold her the story, asking her for some reassuring meaning.

"I don't get it. Why did he leave?"

She looked at me, paused, and finally gave me the answer I had been waiting for, for four years. "Chuck, he waited for her all this time, but *she* never waited for him. He had to let his fantasies go and start actually living."

I was done chasing. That's why I didn't answer her text. That's the one thing I hated about Macoa since the day I met her—her hamartia. The thing about Macoa was that you could never feel as if she were yours. You could be holding her hand, but with her, you could never be comfortable, because you just didn't know what was on her mind. Does that make any sense? Point is, with her, one day you were the most important thing in the universe, the next, she didn't care about you. Things were always on her terms and her timing. But like I said, this was my time now.

♥

Other than the Macoa incident, my winter break was spent how I imagined it—playing at the Hard Rock most of the time. In the last week of the break, I went in to play on a Monday around 3:00 p.m. When I was on my way to the casino, I received a call from Alexander, who told me he was having a barbeque for his birthday. Yes, the same Alexander who is inside right now.

"I can't go. I'm on my way to the Hard Rock."

He and the rest of my friends grew mad at me because I was "choosing to feed my addiction rather than to be with them."

But they didn't understand that behind this addiction and glamour, I was focused on something bigger. I had a cause—I was actually working.

"Gambling isn't real work," they argued.

But it was work. I was actually working hard, suffering, and making money; the only difference was that I didn't have to punch in or out. Sometimes I actually didn't want to be there, but I needed to keep playing to make it to my goal of a hundred grand.

The only people at the casinos during the week were those who played for a living and those who had nowhere else to be. The people there were either professionals in the big leagues or lowlifes; the Hard Rock catered to both Monday through Thursday. I still question which type I was.

I made my way to a 2-5 table, and as I sat down, I saw one guy staring at me but not actually saying anything. He was one of the people whom I've seen a couple of times and seemed like a regular at the Hard Rock, but I had no idea who he was. I was positioned right in front of him, and I could tell he was still looking at me throughout the hands I played. He had tattoos all over him, a built look, was wearing a black T-shirt, and a dense and mysterious beard that hid his face.

Why was he staring at me?

Finally, later in the day a big hand was dealt where I played against him. I had two pair on the flop, but there was a straight draw on the board. So, to keep it safe, I pushed all in. He thought a moment and then finally looked at me, grinned, and said, "You've taken so much money from me this past month."

Now I understood. He had been looking at me because he had played against me before and wanted to look out. After about two minutes, I could hear him whisper to his friend, "This kid is sick."

His friend turned to me and then back to him and said, "I know, I've played with him before."

The One Knight Stand was building a reputation, and I loved it.

That Saturday night, I drove back to Orlando. It was now the end of December, and so far I had thirty-six thousand in my college fund. I had one semester left to collect $64,000 if I wanted to go to a big school. I could do it.

TWENTY

CUTTING A DEAL

When I was back in Orlando, I was starting a new semester. If all went well, it would be my last semester at UCF, as I planned to transfer by next fall. I needed to set a plan on what my future in terms of my education would look like. So I sat down one day in the library and looked up the best schools in the nation for finance and mathematics. I made a list of the most respected universities, which was about a hundred long. One of those names would hopefully be my home soon. I proceeded to narrow down the list by marking off the schools that didn't have the program I was looking for. I then went down the list again and scratched off names for any reason, whether it was in a location I didn't like or it wasn't a good enough school. For the first time in my life, money didn't affect a big decision.

I eventually reduced my list down to about fifteen schools, which included names like MIT, UNC, and UCLA and realized I would soon have to apply to all of them. I felt like a high-school senior again. It was an interesting feeling not knowing where I would be in a handful of months.

♥

Being back in Orlando also meant I had to go back to work, back to the big underground games. On the second Saturday I was there, I received an invitation to play a big game downtown by someone who also played at the other games. See, if you invite someone to a big game, the host of the game usually pays you for the referral, and this cycle benefits everybody behind the curtains. Minimum buy-in that night was $2,000. I made the drive out at eight thirty, as the action was starting by nine.

When I arrived at the apartment complex, I was instructed to go to the last floor by my friend. I know "my friend" doesn't say much, but this is about me, not about anybody else. When I got to the final floor, there was a man dressed like a formal security guard, tall, big, and bald. As I walked toward him, he asked me what I was doing there. I hesitated, but I didn't know what else to say, so I just told him I was there to play poker, and he asked me for my name and then smuggled himself inside as he told me to wait for a second. He then came back out, opened the door for me, and welcomed me in. I stepped inside and was greeted by the guy who ran the game, introducing himself as Dillon. He was a little shorter than me. Tall guy; curly hair. Was wearing a gray Spider-Man t-shirt. Tons of character. He asked me what I would be drinking and eating that night. See, these games were so big, that as a courtesy, the hosts would order whatever food the players wanted, and there was all the alcohol one could imagine.

The game started off like most, slow at first, people playing tight, people then slowly loosening up, and by two hours in, most people had gone all in at least once. As you may have noticed by now, I usually only talk to you about the huge hands I play, but the reality is that, in poker, the most important hands are the ones that you don't see. The difference maker for players is the ability to stay quiet. It's important to let go of the hands that aren't worth the risk. That's the hardest part of the game to master. It's not winning the most and biggest pots; many can do that. It's all about lessening the pots you lose and eliminating the mistakes. Anybody can make a lot of money; that impresses no one. Being able to preserve wealth is what differentiates someone from the rest. The game isn't all glamour all the time. I can easily be seated for an hour and only participate in one three-minute hand.

Later in the night, when I was sure that I was getting cold cards, I was dealt my favorite hand: ace, nine, both clubs. I raised to a hundred dollars and got five callers, a lot of loose players there. On the flop came king, king, ten, two clubs. There was a bet of $150, and I wanted to end the hand right there, not get myself into any more trouble by only calling, so I semi-bluffed by raising to $400. There was one call after me, and the original raiser also called. On the turn came a jack, unfortunately not a club. But I now had two draws—a straight draw and a flush draw. These are my favorite type of situations where I can semi-bluff and do some real damage. See, I didn't have a good hand yet, but if I bluffed and someone called me, I could make my hand on the river, and if everybody folded, I could still pick up a nice pot with no real hand. There was a check behind me, and I bet $600. Only one caller now; damn, I was getting myself into trouble. My heart beat rapidly as I forced my teeth together, biting down on nothing but themselves. I tried to keep a straight face and not show any of my nerves. On the river, five of clubs. Thank God.

All in. He called. I won.

When I cashed in my chips sometime after midnight, the host of the game pulled me aside for a quick chat. "Hey man, I've heard a lot about you, and tonight I saw what all the fuss is about. You clearly have it. You have a minute to talk?"

That was a bit weird. I had just met this guy. Did he want a picture with me or something? I didn't know if I was overly confident then, or something else, but I didn't see a reason for him to want to talk to me. I should've feared the other possibility—I honestly did think I was a god. I was superior to everybody else. All of a sudden people were interested in me, and I thought they were blessed if they had a chance to talk to me.

"Yeah, sure."

He led me to his kitchen as he kept talking. *Is this guy about to seduce me? Why do we need to talk in private? Is he mad that I made four grand against his friends on my first night at his game?* I have to admit, though, his penthouse was beautiful, and I kept looking around as I followed him into the kitchen.

When we finally reached the kitchen, he started talking. "How did you like tonight's game?"

"It was good, man. I had fun. Thank you for letting me play," I said, still not understanding why he had to take me to his kitchen to ask me this.

"I'm sure you had fun. Look how much you made!" he said, before awkwardly laughing. "Anyway, I have these games every Saturday, but on Fridays I have even bigger games, usually 10-20; minimum buy-in is about five thousand dollars. It's mostly guys who work right here on Wall Street. Their ego is massive, especially after a full week of closing deals, and they come right after they get paid. I know you can take them out."

Oh.

"Yeah, sure. Take down my number, and I'll try to make it."

He wasn't finished. "Listen, I still don't get what your strategy is. You seem to have some mix of statistical analysis and being able to predict other's actions."

"Well, that's what statistics is."

I just stood there, ready to leave. But he continued, "But I know you have it. Your style—you're like the next Tom Dwan. I was thinking we could work together."

"Not looking for a partner."

"Hear me out. I'll tell you when the fish come, and I'll buy you into the game when they're on tilt. You'll make a killing, and you give me half of your earnings. I'll make sure you win."

What is this guy talking about?

"How will you make sure I win?"

He said he would just get me into the games at the right time against the right people and continued to explain other factors he could control to put me in a better position.

I understood what he was talking about, but I didn't need to angle shoot. I didn't need people to help me. I was doing well on my own. But he was paying for my buy-in. I would simply show up and make money with no risk for me. Was it cheating? Not really. Was it frowned upon? Fuck, yes. And if I was caught, I could've found myself in big trouble. The guys I would play against didn't want an amateur showing up at their games and taking their money.

But I was in. My morals and ethics were out the door. All I cared about was the money. Did I ever ask myself how I would feel if I was on the other side of the table? I guess I did ask myself that sometimes, but my needs were more real and urgent. I was the absolute center of the universe. I was using this money to pay for school, so it wasn't that bad, I told myself.

And that night, I thought my life couldn't get any better. But it did.

TWENTY-ONE

BIRTHDAY SPECIAL

All I had to do now was wait for Dillon to give me a heads-up for the night; I would go make a killing at his game. But until then, I was going to keep doing my thing. I couldn't rely on him or anybody else. My college fund was up to $44,000, meaning I still had a long way to go to make it.

It was now the second week of February, and do you know what that meant? My birthday was on the Friday coming up.

My birthday is on February 13, but I wasn't going to really celebrate until the end of the month when I was back in Mexton. But toward the middle of February, there was a big tournament at the Hard Rock in Tampa, and I was going to play as a birthday present to myself. The buy-in was only $500, and there was a $100,000 guarantee—I just wanted to have fun and play a weekend-long tournament and enjoy turning twenty-one.

When my birthday arrived, I lived it like any other day because I knew the real celebration would be a couple of weeks later. On the second to last weekend of February, I would play the tournament on Thursday, and if I qualified to day two, I would finish the tournament on Saturday. On Saturday night, I would drive back to Orlando and go downtown and arrange for a table.

So when that week came, I made sure I finished all my schoolwork early so that I could enjoy the weekend and be distraction free. Thursday morning, I found myself driving to Tampa from Orlando. Looking back now, I laugh when I think about how I was on my way to my birthday celebration, but I was all alone. I arrived at the casino at around 1:00 p.m., but the start of the tournament wasn't until three. After I checked in, and set my things in my room, I headed downstairs to get some food to later walk around the casino floor and made my way to the event room for the tournament.

♥

As 3:00 p.m. got closer, I started to focus on what was to come; I didn't think I could necessarily make a lot of money, but there was still a hundred-thousand guarantee. I was trying to not get too anxious or let my nerves affect me too much—I was playing for fun this time and just wanted to enjoy my birthday present to myself. The time arrived, and at three I was sitting down at my table with my earphones on, ready to start the tournament. That tournament was like most others that had hundreds of thousands guaranteed—more than half of the people playing did it for a living. No messing around.

Everybody began with ten thousand in chips. My first hand: four, six off suit, I'm the big blind. Only four players to the flop: six, six, six. I looked around; was this a joke? I flopped quads the first hand of the tournament.

This is going to be a good weekend, I thought to myself. I checked, so did everybody else. On the river, I checked again, trying to get someone else to bet, but nobody did. On the turn, someone bet four hundred, I raised to a thousand; they folded. I flopped quads and only made about six hundred chips in that hand. Sigh.

I continued to run hot the rest of the day, but I was also making bad calls and playing hands I shouldn't have. So I would hit my trips, straight or flush, get a healthy-sized chip stack, but then lose half of it in the next couple of hands. I was up and down all day. Nothing too interesting to be honest, but halfway around the tournament I folded seven, jack, which is the hand I hate the most, and on the flop came seven, seven, seven. Can you believe that? But it gets sicker. Toward the end of the day, I had pocket fives and called a small raise preflop. On the flop came: five, five, six. Okay now what are the odds of *that*? Three flopped quads in one day. This time, I did manage to increase my chip stack by around 40 percent.

Again, after this, my chip stack decreased, then increased, and then decreased again. I couldn't get a solid rhythm the whole day, which resulted in me being on tilt by the end of the day, desperate to maintain a stack I could be comfortable with. One of the last hands, I was "under the gun" (which means I was first to act before the flop). I was dealt my favorite hand—ace, nine. I called the big blind. There were a couple of folds and then the button raised to twelve thousand, the big blind called. I paused, looked around, looked at my cards one more time, and pushed all in to around seventy-one thousand. Both of them folded.

About thirty minutes later, I had officially made it to day two, meaning now I just had to wait until Saturday to play. My chip stack was a bit higher than average at around a hundred and twenty thousand chips. The reason I didn't play on Friday is because Friday is another type of day one. These tournaments are structured so that half of the people play their first day on Thursday, and the other half play their first day on Friday, and then whoever makes it to day two from both days play on Saturday.

♥

Friday I didn't do much, just tried to relax. I was staying in a resort, so I took advantage by relaxing at the pool and spa. The day went by pretty fast as I was just killing time, but in my mind I kept thinking about Saturday. I had made it to day two. I was almost in the money. Although still a bit far, there was a tangible possibility of hitting the first-place payout of a hundred grand.

Friday came and went, and when I woke up Saturday, I felt like a kid waking up on Hanukah. You thought I was going to say Christmas, huh? Bigot.

I made my way to the tournament room again and was assigned my new table. I took out my earphones, gum, put my hoodie on, and found my way into my zone for what I intended to be a long day.

Right off the bat, I noticed one guy at my table who always had to commentate on others' gameplay and pretty much anything. He was in his forties but was acting as if this was his first time playing, in terms of him being obnoxious and celebrating his wins and blaming his losses on the dealer. I knew I wanted to bust him, as he was the most annoying person in a room of hundreds.

Like always, I just had to keep doing my thing, sit tight and wait for the right moment. And like always, that moment came. Next thing I knew I had jack, queen of hearts, and raised to a bit more than double the blind. When the action got to the annoying old guy, he reraised me, *no surprise there*. I called—four players to the flop. The flop came: jack, three, queen with the jack, and the three being clubs. I checked, knowing he would bet and that he did, someone called, and then I raised, and he called. It was heads up, and the whole table was not only anxiously watching, but I could tell they were also rooting for me, as they were just annoyed with this guy as I was. On the turn comes another jack, I bet this time, now *he* raised me. What the—What did he have? I call, confused.

On the river, came the nine of clubs. Still confused as to what he could possibly have, I checked, and he bet half the size of the pot. I took a while to think, just shuffling my chips, slowing down my train of thought, thinking, as this was worth more than a two-fifths of my remaining stack.

What could he have? He raised preflop. Maybe a pocket pair? Queens? If he did have queens, then he would beat me with a better full house. Did he have ace, jack? Ace, queen? Or did he make the straight flush? Or just a straight? Just a flush? I took my time to think, knowing if I made this call and lost, I wouldn't be short stacked yet, but I would take a huge blow.

I thought of when I first started watching poker on TV and what Antonio Esfandiari once said regarding bluffs: "Does the story make sense?" I had to figure out what this guy had. Why did he just call on flop and then raise on me on turn. Did he also make his full house on the turn? I doubted it, he probably thought his two-pair was good. I had to put him on a hand though.

"How much is it?" I asked the dealer.

It didn't feel right. I exhaled deeply, took one last look at my cards and was about to push them forward for a fold but right before I'm about to act, he started talking.

"I have the nuts; no shame in folding, kid."

Kid. I love when old losers call me that. I looked up at him and everybody else. Everybody was obviously annoyed. I couldn't fold anymore. *What does he have.* I studied him again and ran through the hand a couple of times. After some analyzing, I finally decided to put him on ace, queen of clubs, making a huge pair on the flop, two pair on the turn, which he probably thought was good, and now making a flush. *Got it, he definitely has an ace-high flush.* He started talking again right before I pulled the trigger.

"We can talk. We're heads up, kid. Don't be shy."

People around the table start whispering to each other. He continued, "I have the best hand at the moment. Otherwise you would've called by now, right?"

"Yep. That's right. I don't call. I double your bet."

More whispers around the table.

He looked at me with a smirk and announced he was all in.

Crap. I didn't see that coming.

I had to think a bit more, but he continued his banter. "C'mon everybody's watching you. At least crack a smile."

I was already too invested in the hand. I had to call. I thought it might be my last hand so I looked at my cards again, pushed my chips in and stood up. I waited to see my destiny. What did he turn over? Ace, queen. *I'm really good at this game.*

See ya later, old guy. Welcome to the new age of poker, I thought to myself as I collected all his chips with a smirk on my face. I doubled up that hand. I was now in the lead of the tournament. I could smell the money at that point. Just fun? Hell no; I was in this for the money, and I was close. Now I was ultra-focused and really got into my zone. I was determined to make the money; it would be by far my biggest payout up to date if I was able to make the final table. So I put my music on louder and fully shifted into One Knight Stand mode.

♥

A couple of hours passed; there was a thirty minute break I used to get some food. Coming back from eating, I wasn't the chip leader anymore, but I was still going strong. I was only a few players getting knocked out away from making it to the money. As I was playing, I felt my phone vibrate. At first I didn't pay any attention to it; I was too focused to go check what some girl on Tinder was saying. A few minutes went by, and again I felt my phone vibrate, but I let it go. Then, my phone vibrated again, so I finally took my phone out to see that it was my mom. *She is probably just calling me to check up on me or ask me something,* I thought. I put the phone on silent and tried to focus again. It's not that you're not allowed to use your phone while in the tournament; I just would've had to get up, go outside, and take the call and miss a couple of hands—but it was my birthday celebration, and I was almost in the money. C'mon I was playing top-notch poker; I had no time to be answering phone calls.

I was excited as I kept playing; I was so close to making it. I was on fire. I was making all the right calls and bets. Right before making the money, the tournament was being played hand by hand, which means every hand in the room is played at the same time until somebody gets knocked out. And right before making the money, I took a big hit when I called an all in, so I was back to an average-sized stack. I didn't want to risk the chance of losing right before the break, so I waited until the bubble was over. Finally, after ten minutes, they announced the bubble was burst, and I had made the money. I was getting paid—the first time at a professional tournament.

Then came the midday break.

During the break I was a bit tired physically but mentally exhausted, and I knew I still had a long night ahead of me, so I decided to go to my room and take a nap as the tournament had started early in the morning and I still had a few more hours to go. I was also still going to Orlando later so I needed rest. The break was for two hours, so I rushed to my room and set my alarm to five minutes before I had to be back. When I pulled out my phone, I saw I had missed calls and texts from my mom, dad, and a couple of my friends from back home. I figured that they all were just wondering where I was, as I forgot to tell anybody that I came to Tampa for the weekend, so I sent my mom a quick text before I fell asleep saying, "I'm in Tampa. Busy right now, but I'll call you later. I'll be home for spring break, if that's what you're calling about." I was so blind at the moment that I didn't even care to see the texts were in all caps. My own mother wasn't important enough for me to even have read the few texts before falling asleep.

♥

Being that I was so close to making the final table, I was surprised that I managed to get some sleep. I woke up a few minutes before my alarm went off, took a deep breath, and walked to the bathroom before making my way back to the tournament room. I was still a bit tired, so before I walked back to the poker room I dug into my backpack and reached for a pill that would help me stay alert. As I sat down, I noticed how the room was now a lot quieter; I could feel the intensity. Everybody there knew that every elimination spot they avoided meant their payout was greater. The whole tournament had started off with around a thousand players, and there were now only a hundred left. First place payout was a hundred thousand dollars, second was sixty-five thousand, third was fifty, fourth was forty-five, and the payouts kept decreasing until hundredth place who received around a grand.

My chip stack was below average at that point, so I wanted to double up or at least get a big hand in quick so that I could be on track to make the final table. In my initial table there was a guy with a Florida State polo on; he looked like a typical fraternity guy, and I apologize for the repetition, but it was obvious he had studied finance. He just had that appearance, you know?

"You went to FSU? Give me a break."

Shit. Did I just say that out loud? Some in the table chuckled a bit, but when they saw I wasn't kidding, the table turned quiet and tense. This arrogant action led me to another one, and then another, and soon I was talking most hands when I shouldn't have been. After a few hands, I was heads up with the FSU frat star, and I knew he wanted to get me out bad so on the river. When I had a strong hand, I made a huge bet that would cost him almost half of his stack. After only about two minutes, I called the clock on him. This means I asked the dealer to call over the tournament director. This action is done when a player believes the other has abused their time to think. The whole table immediately looked at me. I looked back, waiting to see what would happen until someone spoke out. "It's only been a minute and a half, man."

I knew what I was doing. I wanted to seem as if I was under pressure because I had made a bluff. But before the tournament director could get there, FSU made the call and lost.

I went from people cheering for me to knock out that loud guy back on day one to being the one people wanted out. I was being cocky, and I liked it—and before I knew it, I was the tournament chip leader. By seven, there were only twenty-five people left, and I was surely going to make the final table.

♥

A bit more than an hour later, I was sitting at one of the last two tables, still chip leader. There was a woman in the tournament who was right next to me, short stacked (her chips, not her body). I got king, eight of hearts a few hands later, and we were heads up. The flop came nine, eight, nine, and she bet, to which I raised all in. She had a nine. That hand took a small hit on me, costing me not being chip leader anymore, but I was still healthy.

In the next couple of hands, I got aces cracked, called with a strong hand to get beaten by a straight made on the river and lost other small hands. I looked down at my chip stack and realized I was down to only four big blinds. I went from the tournament chip leader to being the smallest stack, by a big margin. If I had just not played any hands, I would've made the final table and probably made at least fourth place. But now I was about to be eliminated in seventeenth.

I've told you that I don't believe in luck, and you know I don't. But at that point, I needed something. I needed the odds to be in my favor. I only had four big blinds, but I still believed I could do it. My motto in life is "As long as I have a chip in front of me, I'm still in the game." I don't care what my position is in life; I just want to be in the race. I want a glimmer of hope that I can win it all. Deep inside, I might know that I can't possibly win this, but I need there to be the possibility, or convince myself there's one.

So I put my concentration music on, and as I'm choosing the playlist, I notice that my friends and family from Mexton are still trying to contact me. *Didn't I already tell my mom I couldn't talk?*

First hand once I'm short stacked: ace, queen, I go all in, queen on the flop, I win. Next? Eight, jack, I'm big blind; I check the option, flop: J, J, eight, that *something* I said I needed? I was getting it. I go all in; I get a caller.

I was making my way back. Next hand I was dealt was five, three of hearts, and on the flop came two hearts, so I went all in again, and again, I had a caller, on the turn came another heart, and I was back in it.

But before I could celebrate inside my head, I started hearing a voice. At first I turned around as I actually thought there was somebody talking to me. The voice was intense, aggressive, and raspy. "You have these chumps. You're much better. Look at them, they're all in their thirties or forties. They're fish, you can easily beat them."

Again, I turned around and then took my earphones off—but the voice wasn't coming from anywhere exterior, the voice was within me. And again, I heard another voice, this time a more soothing and calm one. "Just focus, be humble, and make it to the final table, but call your mom before that starts."

What was this argument happening in my head?

♥

I kept rebuilding my chip stack until, finally, I found myself at the final table where all the payouts were now at least five figures. I had done it. I kept playing tight, but my short stack eventually was eliminated sixth place, which had a $22,000 payout after what seemed to be the longest day of my life.

And I know what you're thinking now—*Is this chapter ever going to end?*

I got knocked out around 9:00 p.m., and as I soon as I did, I speed-walked to the payout station to sign some quick paperwork and get my money, which I requested to be all cash. Then, I hurried to my room, took a shower, and changed into my night outfit and hurried to my car to go back to Orlando to celebrate. The effect of the last pill was wearing off, so I looked for another one in my backpack and took it to stay alive, also drinking a Red Bull. Work hard and party harder, right?

I arrived in Orlando around eleven, and I walked directly to the club I had my table reserved at. I immediately saw that a couple of my friends were waiting outside for me with a group of girls.

"Happy birthday! Ready to celebrate?" Lance asked.

I couldn't hold it in. "Guess who made twenty thousand dollars this weekend bitches?"

"Shut the fuck up!" Brent exclaimed.

They couldn't believe it, and neither could I.

One of the promoters met us outside, took my credit card, and proceeded to put wristbands on all of us. He led us to our table. As we proceed to walk in, one of the girls they were with looked to me and grabbed my shoulder. "So what does that feel like, making all that money?"

I looked down at this girl who was talking to me as if I was a celebrity. She was blond, with hopeful eyes and an I-Used-to-Be-a-Church-Girl-but-Now-I-Want-to-Have-Fun essence to her. I had no idea who that girl was, but I knew that she would be mine that night. The night was on, I was going to celebrate hard.

TWENTY-TWO

VOICES

I found myself partying like *The Wolf of Wall Street*. I was chugging bottles of vodka as if they were beer, buying anything I could get my hands on to display my new wealth, and being as loud as I possibly could, both literally and metaphorically. I remember ordering three more bottles around midnight, and after that, my memory of the remainder of the night gets blurry. I recall thinking I was too drunk, and I should stop drinking. So I did—a bit late, but I stopped. By that point I had only one goal left in mind—the girl.

I pulled Brent over. "Who's the girl Lance is talking to? She's hot. I want to make a move," I asked, stumbling.

"That's Lance's new girl; they've been hanging out for a couple of weeks. He really likes her and wants to get serious with her, so you're going to have to choose another girl."

I want what I want, and I'm going to get what I want, I thought to myself.

"I want her," I told Brent.

"Do you ever meet a girl who isn't on your list?"

"What?"

"Are there ever any females you don't try to sleep with?"

"Oh. No. Not really."

So, even though I could barely walk in a straight line, I made my way over to the girl who was on the other side of the table. "Hey, can you help me with something over here?" I said, stealing her from Lance.

She followed me to my side where I threw myself on a different couch. "Remember how you asked me what it felt like to win that much money?"

"I remember."

"Okay, well, come with me," I say as I stand up again in an attempt to continue to isolate ourselves.

"I'm listening."

The club was deafening with music. Flashing lights brightened the dark room. I made sure we were far enough where we couldn't be heard or directly seen. As she followed me deeper into my secluded side of the table, I pulled out from my pocket $4,000, and I gave it to her. "Hold this," I said, handing her the cash. "I want you to tell me how you feel when you hold this. Realize that this is more than what most people in here have in their savings. You can buy any drink, any bottle, any table here. How does it feel?"

She looked at the money, looked around the club, and then looked at me. "I feel powerful."

And again, in the midst of the music, the drinks, and me talking to Courtney (the name of Lance's crush), I heard the voices.

"You know she wouldn't like you if you didn't have money. Take her home, and do what you have to do," said the first one.

But the second one quickly followed. "That's not true; be a gentleman.

Put the money away. She likes you because of you. You don't have to do this."

And I began thinking to myself, being the mediator. *What should I do?*

The lighter voice continued, "Okay, nothing bad has happened. If you try to get with Lance's girl or try to get home, things can go wrong. You should just sober up and call an Uber."

But the voices always came in pairs. "Go home? You made five figures today. You deserve whatever you want. You can't go home yet; you're alone in this world. You might as well stay here and do what you want!"

He had a point, whoever or whatever it was that was talking to me. As I was paying attention to these voices, zoning out for a minute, Courtney tugged me. "Hey, are you okay?" And when my attention returned to her, I gave the girl standing right in front of me, a firm look, grabbing her leg decisively. "How would you feel about coming home with me and being completely mine?" Those thirteen words. Just so.

Next thing I knew I was in my car; sitting next to me was Courtney and my twenty grand. And for the last time that night, I heard the voices again. The soft and collected one started that time. "You can't drive right now; you're way too drunk. You'll ruin your life."

The other voice was always there and was always louder. "You're a god. You can do this; you can do anything. Start the car and make your way home. You have some business with this girl to take care of."

I followed the orders of the louder voice. I was able to make my way out of the parking lot. My memory from this point is only being conscious moments at a time, finding myself transporting from one place to another, not knowing how I made it there. I was then on the highway, where I was focused on trying to drive without swerving. And next thing I know Courtney was screaming. When I opened my eyes into alertness, I found that my car was inches away from another in front of me in the highway. I instantly tried to stop, but my foot didn't find the brake, so I swerved out of the way as I pulled the emergency brake. And the next flash I remember is us in the side of the highway. I looked around as Courtney was still yelling.

"Shut up! Stop screaming."

Not a scratch on me or Courtney, not a scratch on my car. But I couldn't stay there because if a cop came, I was done.

Courtney looked at me. I looked back.

"I have to keep going."

"Are you fucking crazy? I would have never come with you if I knew you were this drunk. Let me drive. You're going to get us killed!"

But before I answered, I started the car again. I assured her and myself that I was sobering up and wouldn't let anybody else drive my car. I drove as focused and as slow as I possibly could. And ten minutes later, I was parking my car at my apartment. I turned off the engine. *I made it.* How didn't I crash? Only God knows. Courtney looked at me and said, "You're crazy. This isn't fun. This isn't what I expected."

I looked at Courtney with another dead stare. *What did she just say to me?* As I feel my blood turn cold, I start talking. "Listen, when you're with me, you're going to do things you've never done before. And some of them aren't the safest things, but you know what? That feeling of your heart beating fast, like it is right now?" I ask as I put my hand on her upper chest. "It means you're alive. And you don't have that with other guys." I continued as I raised my voice, "Look at me; I'm different. You have two thousand dollars in your pocket because of me, I'm a god. *Look at me; I'm a god!*"

We made it to my building, and as I was walking up the stairs, I stumbled a bit and collapsed for a second, but I made it up and finally found my way to my bedroom.

"We're here," I said after taking a deep breath. "Now, the real fun begins."

♥

I was woken up at around 11:00 a.m. when I heard my phone ring. And for a second I thought it had all been a dream. But as I raised my head and felt my whole body ache, I turned to the right and saw twenty grand on my nightstand right next to me. I quickly looked to my left, and there was Courtney; it wasn't a dream. A wave of anxiety hit me. *What had I done?* I couldn't remember half of it which made me more anxious.

The phone rang again and I answered. It was my mom, and I could tell she was exhausted.

"What's wrong, Ma?" I asked in a low voice, partly trying not to intensify my headache and partly trying not to wake up the girl in my bed.

"Chuck, we've been trying to get a hold of you for a whole day. What happened?"

Hearing my mom's voice instantly made me sober. "Uh, I was studying all day."

"In Tampa?"

I didn't have the heart to tell her either of the news—that I had made $20,000 or that I was coming to terms with dying on the inside.

"What happened? What's wrong?" I asked again.

"Your brother was in a car accident…"

She continued speaking while I looked around and tried to understand what was going on.

"He's in intensive care."

"Okay, I'll be there soon," I said as I hung up the phone.

I took some deep breaths after hanging up and again looked around my room trying to piece the night together. *It had been a long night*, I thought to myself. I stood up and made my way to the bathroom, leaving Courtney on the bed. Once there, I used the bathroom and continued to wash my hands. And as I was doing so, I spotted myself in the mirror. I looked up and took a deep stare at myself.

This was the moment that I consciously acknowledged that I had created something great. I had created a godly figure. Even if it was evil, this monster in front of me, I was the artist; I was the maker, and I could only admire what I had generated. I was full of shame and dying from anxiety as I looked at the mirror and it did break my heart to see all the pain I had caused, even if most of the pain was to myself. But I finally did something; I had made it. *I'm alone, but I'm here.*

And I had come too far to turn around.

TWENTY-THREE

CONSCIOUSNESS

B ut you know the worst part of being a god? What people don't think about, what nobody realizes—this all-powerful figure, this all-mighty idea, is just there. Very powerful, but very alone.

♥

I drove down to Mexton to see my brother at the hospital that same day, which was Sunday. I drove in silence, just thinking. You know when you're having a bad day or something is bothering you, but all of a sudden you think of something else that makes you happy, and it's all okay? Well, that day was interesting, as I was reflecting the whole time, and I consciously acknowledged that maybe I had taken this too far, that maybe I was becoming something I wouldn't be proud of. But I couldn't help but also think I had made twenty grand; I was on top of the world. And whenever

I would remember it, it made things okay.

I made it to Mexton by nightfall and went straight to the hospital. My brother had driven into a school bus and had been crushed under the bus; he was in a bad condition and had needed to be airlifted to the hospital. His leg was shattered, for lack of a better word, but other than scars, he was going to be okay. It would be a few weeks until he found out if he would be able to completely walk again, but I knew he would. I stepped into the ICU and asked him how he was feeling.

"I'm just happy to be alive. It will be a while until I walk again, but I'm good."

I asked him if I could have one of his pills they were giving him.

"The nurse only gives me one at a time and watches me take them."

♥

Once my brother was knocked out from the medicine, I called my friend Sandro to come over to get a bite to eat. Sandro was a friend I had from childhood. We grew up next to each other and spent the majority of our days together as kids. He has a built look, was always notably taller than me, and has great curly hair. We had made plans as kids to go to college and do everything else together but life got in the way. But we were still close and continued to hang out whenever I was in Mexton.

I picked him up, and we drove to get some dinner before coming back to my place, telling him about the night I had had the previous evening and everything that had been happening to me while we were in the car. By the time I finished the story, we were back in my house. "Yeah, bro, I'm killing it now."

He then looked me in the eye, not even grinning. "Are you okay?"

Here we go.

He continued, "Chuck, your brother almost died yesterday; we all tried to call you, and you were too busy playing poker. And all you care to talk about is your night; you treated this girl like shit. How are you laughing right now?"

Why is he being so hard on me? Little did he know I wasn't laughing because I thought it was funny; I was laughing because I didn't know what else to do. I was hiding. I had wanted to eat with him so that he could congratulate me on my success and distract me from my thought, not to make me feel like more of an asshole.

"I'm just having a good time; things are going my way for once, and I'm enjoying the ride. Where's the sin in that?"

He answered instantly, now getting louder and more intense. "Do you not get it? Your brother almost died yesterday, and you wouldn't answer your phone because you were playing poker. You're not even producing genuine, Chuck; it's all a facade.

"Chuck, you worship yourself now," he added, bringing his voice down.

"What's wrong with that? Listen, I've become a better person. I'm more confident now. I've learned to read people and act correspondingly. My lifestyle has improved—I go to the gym and eat better now. I hang out with smarter people who are actually doing something with their lives. I used to be a chump, but now I can get any girl I want, when I want. And that's not a coincidence."

He looked me dead in the eyes. "These people you hang out with, these girls you have now, do they like you and all that you've become along the way? Or do they like your money and the fact that they can have these nights with you and post it on their social media? Would they hang out with you if I took away the nice car, the money, and everything that comes

122

with it?"

That's what he didn't understand. It wasn't the money. It's what came as a result *of* the money. I became confident, and I saw myself as a god, so I treated myself accordingly, so others did the same.

I looked at him as I had an epiphany. "What about you? You also attract others because of your humor; you're the life of the party. You don't see me telling you to change."

But he had a reply for that too. "Yeah, but that's who I am; I'm being myself. I never had to change."

"Okay, well, being myself never worked for me, so now I'm trying something else, and it's working. I don't lie to anybody. I don't cheat. And I'm not even becoming something else. I'm just becoming an improved version of me."

"You're selling your soul, man. The way you talk to girls now, it's not you. You're changing! You're molding into something different. There will come a time when you can't help but run this game you play; you won't even be acting anymore, and you will actually become this cold guy who isolates himself. You need to understand these things don't bring true happiness; they're just temporary. They don't really mean anything at the end of the day. This dream of money, women, and cars we all were sold when we were kids isn't real. There's a truth, and that isn't it. Listen to me; I've been meditating a lot, and I've realized many things. You should try it. The point is, if you continue on this path, you'll come home one night with all this money, and you'll feel alone and it'll be too late to turn around.

"You're going to look back when that happens and wish you hadn't changed. You'll drive your family and friends away from you until you push them too far to get them back. You'll one day be a millionaire and then what? This game won't distract you anymore. Only then will you realize that all this is a mistake. You're going to meet a girl you actually like, and you will run on autopilot and run the same game on her as you do with all these girls. There's lover's karma out there, you know?"

I looked at him, a bit more serious now. "I did meet her, Sandro," I said as I slowed down the conversation and lowered my voice to almost a whisper. "I met her, and when I did, I didn't have this power, so she got away. She didn't notice me. But I guarantee she would like me now if she met me at this point in my life. If I met her now, she wouldn't see me as just a friend."

He brings back his tone to an aggressive one. "Please don't tell me all this is about her. Chuck, Macoa wasn't the girl of your dreams; forget about her. Stop being a fucking bitch. You chased her your whole life, and she never wanted anything, who cares? Let her go. You're better than her anyway. If she didn't want you, then screw her. But don't do all this because of one experience."

"Well, that's the thing, bro—I don't chase anymore. I've turned the tables; I choose what I want now, and I get it."

"You just don't get it. You're not conscious. This isn't what you actually want. I'm done trying to save you. Don't call me when you realize all this was a mistake."

I sat at the edge of my seat and fired back, "You can't do this to me! I'm finally making it. I don't need this shit, not now."

"That's the fucking problem. It's all about you!"

"No, I can finally do something special, and I don't need any of this bullshit. It's important to me. Go take your jealously somewhere else. I know what I'm doing is worth the sacrifice. This life allows me not to be scared anymore. Nothing can stop me. The fear of death is invisible when I'm playing."

"Wake the fuck up! This isn't anything special. It's poker. You're at a casino. That is where the lowlifes go to spend their days. You're not scared of death? Well it's because everybody there is already dead; they have nothing to live for. They're not different than people who spend their days doing drugs or at the strip club. You spend your days with a bunch of losers."

"Listen to me. I'm not one of them. I just make money off them. This is something I've been waiting to do my whole life. I've had a plan all along, and it's working. This transformation, it's working."

"No, now you listen to me. Nobody gives a fuck about your stupid transformation. You do this because you have one goal—to be relevant. But you're not; you're just not. The only people you impress are pretentious assholes and shallow girls. You're not relevant to anybody of substance; you're a nobody. We're all nobodies. Nobody cares about your Snapchats or pictures of chip stacks or money or the clubs. Nobody's thinking 'I wonder what Chuck is doing right now!' You disappeared to do this poker thing, and nobody has even noticed you are gone. You're scared of being irrelevant; well, so is everybody else. But you think you're so important and special. *You're* the one who thinks you have a God-given right. You're the one whose ego is so inflated you think people care about what you have to say. Guess what? Chuck Marquez, or the One Knight Stand, whoever the fuck you think you are doesn't exist outside of your own stupid world. You're not some hero or a character worth their own book. Get over yourself. Accept it, okay? You keep living like this, and you'll die how you are now—dead on the inside and completely alone. You only do this because you're an insecure loser who's scared of being the real him because he got his heart broken."

I didn't say anything as I felt my eyes starting to change texture. "You're right," I finally answered and looked down for a few seconds.

There was another moment of silence.

"Chuck, I uh didn't mean all of that."

I finally looked up. "Do me a favor," I replied.

"Yeah."

"Get the fuck out of my house, you poor piece of shit."

What exactly was he trying to save me from? I was having more fun than I ever had in my life. Maybe he was the one who needed to be saved. He was a friend who I dreamed with as a kid of becoming rich and famous, and now he was telling me there's a bigger truth?

Honestly, was it immoral to become rich and confident? Are you kidding me? I didn't think so.

You ever notice how it's the poor and ugly always mocking the rich?

TWENTY-FOUR

COLLUSION

What Sandro didn't understand, what even I didn't understand, was that I didn't need to be saved. I needed to be accompanied. But I was officially alone now; everybody had left me. Even those who were supporting me when I began to change were now saying I had changed too much. I couldn't look to anybody who still accepted me.

But you know who is with me? You are. I've been telling you my story this whole time, and you've managed to stay right here with me. How are you doing it? I've been telling you all these immoral things I've done and showed you who I've become and how I treated people. But you're on my side, aren't you? You're still here because you're on my side, right? I know you're on my team because you're still listening to my story, and I know something inside of you is cheering for me; you want me to win. But why? Why do you want me to win?

Listen, my friend, it's only us now, just you and me. I'm here with you right now as you hear my story; I'm not just an abstract idea or some character in a book. I'm present, now. This relationship we have, you and me, it's not notional. It's real, and tangible. We're in this together, you and I. Both in imagination and in reality. You can call it fiction all you want, but you're sitting or lying down right now, holding my book in your hands, listening to what I have to say. You're coming along for the ride, feeling what I really felt. It doesn't get more real than that.

♥

I needed to be back in Orlando on Monday morning for school, even though I didn't see the point in school anymore. I would soon come down to Mexton again, as spring break was just around the corner. My week went by how it usually did, but it was around this time that all the deadlines to submit an application for all the schools on my list were coming closer. I had already submitted an application to my number-one choice— Massachusetts Institute of Technology. But now I needed to decide which other schools I would also apply to.

I knew MIT was the school I wanted to go to as it had everything I wanted, and it was more than respected, often being called the best mathematics school in the nation. I had planned to submit a couple of other applications before the deadline of spring break in case I didn't get into MIT, but I then had an epiphany—my life wasn't meant to have backup plans; I didn't need one. I was a *gambler*, and I was going for all or nothing. So, as I stared at my other applications, I closed my laptop right then and there. What was the point in doing something just as a backup plan? What was the point in going to a school that wasn't the best or my number-one choice? It was MIT or nothing, and I would find out mid-May.

♥

Later in the week, on Thursday night, it was finally time to work with someone else. I received a call, and I didn't have the number saved, so I answered waiting to see who was on the other line.

"Chuck, it's Dillon. It's time. Are you ready?"

I had forgotten about the deal we had made, but I was ready to play at these so-called big games.

"Yeah, what's happening?"

"There's some guys here playing a pretty high-stakes game. I'm in the process of getting them loose; be here in an hour."

I was there in forty-five minutes. I marched straight to the table. Normally, people who gamble a lot of money aren't in the mood to shake your hand and say hello. But, to my surprise, all the players were oddly nice and greeted me. This time around, there seemed to be a bodyguard for the same number of people who were playing. *Who are these guys?* I wasn't sure if I wanted to find out. Dillon sat me down in between two tipsy middle-aged men who I could tell didn't care much about the money they lost.

"How much do you want to buy in for?" Dillon asked.

"Ah…" I didn't know. I thought he was buying me in, so I just looked at him confused. He then gave me a stare trying to signal me, and I quickly realized what he was doing. These people couldn't know I was his friend; they had to think I had gotten into the game the same way they did, however that was.

"Give me whatever the average stack is."

The players would laugh as they bet $5,000, and when they would lose they would just say, "Crap." It was like I was playing against drug lords who were simply trying to have some fun with small money. And I knew some of the guys there might have been involved with celebrities or just had a lot of money. How did Dillon organize these games with these people? I didn't ask, and I didn't want to find out. I was also sure that many people here were playing for the first time. One of the later hands of the night was against someone who went all in on the river with a flush and straight on the board; he flipped over a pair of sixes. Had he bluffed or was he really that bad?

Who are these people?

The first hand I was dealt: pocket rockets. Whoa, he wasn't organizing the deck for me, was he? I thought I was in a movie, and I grew paranoid. All I had to do was play normal poker. These guys didn't really know what they were doing, and they didn't care. And I didn't care either, I was going to take what I could. I just did my thing, and when it was around 2:00 a.m., people soon started to leave. I wanted to stay and make as much money as I could, but I wasn't allowed. I had to leave so that they wouldn't notice I was colluding with Dillon.

I left twelve thousand up that night. I would need to give Dillon $6,000 from my earnings, but it was still a killing. I had almost made enough money to reach my goal, and it was all before spring break. I arrived home and put my share of the twelve thousand in my shoe box, which had been an upgrade from the envelope. My fund was at seventy-one grand now.

Addiction is scary. It's terrifying because you realize that there's something inside of you that has power over your own brain. Once you realize the simple fact that something can control you, your life vision shifts. Because when something can control you, it makes you do things you don't want to do. You hate it, but you can't help and go back to it.

PART III
LONELINESS

TWENTY-FIVE

"AND WHEN I FINALLY GOT SOBER,
I FELT TEN YEARS OLDER."

Nobody wakes up and decides they want to become a bad person. Nobody even really asks for their life to change in the way mine did. A year ago, I had no idea this would happen. It was a slow, blind process. I was now at the point where even my friends didn't support me, something I never wanted. I know I said it was a series of very small and slow decisions, but my life had changed before I had time to stop and think about what I was doing. One second I was doing just fine, the next, I was in this world all alone. Listen, you have the right to think whatever you want of me, and I don't care what that is, but you need to understand that I never intended for it to get this far.

♥

Two weeks later I was back in Mexton for spring break. I was almost there; I need a bit more money. I only needed around $20,000 more at this point. I was almost done—just a few more nights and then I could relax and wait for my MIT decision.

But it was break now, and I could have used some time to reduce my pace; everybody was back in town and was using the week to relax as well. While there, I decided that I would have a big party to celebrate the huge win of the tournament and also a belated birthday. It was the perfect time to do so, as my parents were out of town for the week, and I could use the house to celebrate. To be completely honest, I was having this party as a way to loosen up and let go of some of the stress I had felt earlier. Because after all the stress I was under for so long, I just wanted to have a good time with my old friends. I wasn't playing much poker during break, so I needed a distraction. I also figured that I could use the party as a way to regain some of my friendships that were dying off.

I decided I was going for it and was soon into the planning. The theme I was having for the party was one I had wanted to have for a while—Stratton Oakmont Office Party. Don't know what that means? Look it up.

Instead of personally inviting everybody to the party, I posted a Snapchat indicating I would be having a soiree and spent the rest of the day prepping for the event. Gentlemen were instructed to come in office-like button-down shirts, and ladies would pretty much look like office sluts, for lack of a better description. I know. I'm an asshole. No way to hide it anymore. I hired a DJ I knew from some of the clubs in Miami and then proceeded to look for a snake I could rent online so that people could take pictures with it. Why did I rent a snake? Why not?

I instructed some of my old friends to show up a bit early; I knew they didn't exactly love me at that point, but they wouldn't turn down a chance to party, and it was the celebration of my birthday, so they couldn't say no. Maybe I could make amends and get them back on my side by the end of the night. At 10:00 p.m., I finished getting ready—I wore a new pair of pants I had bought for the party and a nice purple shirt. Before I walked downstairs, I looked in the mirror to the guy staring right back at me— he was five eleven, Italian, muscular, with long hair slicked back. I was ready—I would be *The Wolf* that night.

I knew it was going to be the first time seeing many of my old circle of friends in a while, and I would be stressed about my house, making sure nothing got broken. This meant I also knew I had to start drinking to take the edge off. My friends showed up soon, and we proceeded to open some of the twenty bottles I had bought for the night. My friends felt a bit distant as if they were expecting me to say some sort of apology, but a king like me apologizes to nobody. Instead I toasted to a good night and was ready to have one. I was going to keep drinking until I was done worrying about my house and could enjoy my party.

At around eleven, people started to show up; all the girls were looking good, and I was still drinking, everything going according to plan. The DJ began to play music, and the night was well on its way.

♥

It was sometime past 11:00 p.m. when more and more people shuffled in, and I was already starting to feel the effects of the rum. Next thing I knew, I was in my kitchen, leaning back against the counter, talking to a couple of people. Suddenly, Macoa walks into my kitchen. Yes, you read that right; the girl I hadn't seen since summer, the girl who lived half way around the world was at my house. I had no idea what was going on and thought maybe my eyes were lying to me, but I hadn't done any drugs, and before I could say anything, she hugged me with a smile from ear to ear. And as she hugged me, I remembered she had told me she was going to be in Mexton during the break. I still couldn't believe it; how had she known about the party? Had she seen my Snapchat post and just come? If there was one girl who would come to a party alone, it was her. But, I quickly noticed she wasn't alone. There was a girl walking directly behind her. This other girl was a slightly taller, slightly sexier, slightly goofier version of Macoa. "This is my best friend from France," Macoa said as the girl proceeded to kiss both my cheeks as I was still trying to figure out what exactly was happening.

I didn't want to seem affected by her, so I just tried to play it cool, and the rum helped with that. We caught up for a minute; I served them drinks, introduced them to some of the people, and then let them go. I was throwing a party and didn't have time for her, I told myself. And, more importantly, I couldn't pay too much attention to Macoa, as I was interested in other girls that night. I hadn't seen much of the girls who were in my house for months and was going to use this chance to really see them if you know what I mean. Do you know what I mean? And wasn't going to diverge from my plans for an unpredictable girl.

♥

As the clock struck midnight, I found myself shuffling around my house from one group of people to other groups of people, welcoming everybody, serving girls drinks, and making sure nobody went upstairs, and my house didn't erupt. Each time I walked past Macoa, she would grab my hand, and she would just look at me without say anything. It wasn't my fault she didn't know anybody there. But she followed me to my kitchen.

"Why are you being so distant?"

"I'm throwing a party; we can catch up later."

"Fine, but at least dance with me now," she commanded as she stepped closer to me and pulled me toward her.

What was going on? Didn't this girl reject me a couple of months earlier? Why did she want to dance with me now? *Why is she even here? Was she put on this earth purposefully to confuse me?*

Next thing I knew, I found myself dancing with her on the dancefloor. What was I supposed to do? Say no? She was dancing on me as if she was trying to make me fall in love with her again. She was moving her waist like only she could, as she had practiced dance her whole life. I couldn't fathom what was going on, and I had no time to analyze; I could only do. Damn, she danced like a goddess. We continued dancing for what seemed to be twenty minutes. Each song that played, our bodies moved closer and closer together.

I eventually turned her around so that she could face me. I couldn't resist the urge of wanting her. I normally wouldn't have said anything to her, but I wasn't an insecure kid anymore; I had confidence now.

And I was really drunk.

My whole life I had seen her as this angel, a princess; I had seen her as something delicate and majestic, but now that she was grinding on me, now I could see her as a woman. Maybe it was me who had changed, not her. Maybe it was the fact that I wasn't warm and romantic on the inside anymore. I had always seen her and dreamed of the possibility of just kissing her. But that didn't matter now; I saw her as a woman now, a woman whom I wanted to bring upstairs. So after turning her around, I looked straight into her brown eyes. I knew what I was doing. It was going to happen. She was single now. She came to my party uninvited. She was the one who asked me to dance. We were in my house. This was *my* party. I was the One Knight Stand now. I was going to do what I should have done years earlier.

After a couple of seconds of looking at her, I kissed her neck—something I wouldn't have done a few months earlier. But I was a kid then, and I wasn't ready; I was ready now. And then she looked at me, shocked that I had just done that. It was time. I grabbed her by the lower back and leaned in to kiss her, my heart pounding as if I had just made a bluff at the poker table.

But, to my surprise, she called the bluff—she moved her face out of the way. She looked at me with a smirk, *just* like the smirk of players who had successfully won a hand, and told me she "didn't want to hook up." *What!* *The—Fuck* that. I grabbed her again. "What are you doing? You come all the way here to my party, ask me to dance, and you're not going to let me kiss you?" It was all my evil twin and rum talking now.

And without saying anything she leaned in and touched my lips with hers. What was it about this girl and pity-kissing me?

I laughed it off and left her alone on the dancefloor. I couldn't let that bother me; I was still throwing a party, and there were still other girls to be taken care of.

Sometime later in the night, I was too drunk to focus and found myself at the DJ booth. I was feeling confident and told the DJ he could take a break and played the songs I wanted. And then, for the first time in my life, I saw and felt real pain. As I was in the DJ booth, playing my tunes, I looked directly in front of me, navigating through some people, and saw her dancing with a friend of mine. Yes, Macoa was dancing with one of my best friends. *That bitch. This can't be happening; I won't let this happen. Not at my party.* I quickly changed the song to "Smack That," one of my favorites, knowing that both of them knew it was my favorite song and maybe they would look for me. But it made it even worse. What happened next could only be described as Brutus stabbing me—I saw my best friend betray me in front of my eyes. They kissed, in my own fucking house, to my own fucking song.

I promise you I no longer had feelings for that bitch, but her kissing someone else at my own party? *No bueno.* And not only that, but one of my best friends. Maybe my friends really *did* hate me now. That shit hurt, a lot, but I wasn't going to do or say anything to them. I had too much pride for that. I was heartbroken by the situation for a minute. But my sadness soon turned into anger. Into rage. Nobody does the One Knight Stand like that. Not at his own party. Fury ran through my blood as I pulled out my phone to text Brent. "Hey, can you bring me some…"

I knew what I had to do. I marched from the DJ booth to find the real DJ. "You're back on."

Next, I walked directly to Macoa's friend who was talking to a group of people. I walked over to the group. "Hey, I need to borrow her for a minute," I said as I grabbed her hand and led her to the dance floor.

"Pardon my French, but you're coming with me."

I know, cheesy, but in the moment, it sounded cool. I was still drunk, but being drunk was on my side now.

"Ha-ha, I speak English. Where are we going?"

I didn't answer. I had only one thing in my mind right then and there. It was my life's mission to hook up with Macoa's friend that night.

We started dancing, and I knew I would die before I would let this girl not kiss me where Macoa could see. I told the DJ to put on some songs we could continue to dance to, making sure to dance with her right in front of everybody. But I wasn't interested in just dancing. When I felt she was ready, I turned her around with more determination and confidence than I had turned Macoa around just an hour earlier. I looked at her; she anticipated. I let her anticipate a bit longer and then I kissed her. She kissed back.

Bingo.

We kissed for a couple of minutes, but I knew the job wasn't over. I needed to do more. I stopped to look at her. "I don't know how it is in France, but I don't like kissing you here in front of everybody. We need some privacy."

She agreed.

"Let's go upstairs to my room."

She agreed again.

But I looked up, and Macoa wasn't anywhere to be seen. I had to wait. I led the girl to the kitchen to get a drink of water. I knew Brent was at the party by that point, so I left her in the kitchen so that I could go find what he had brought me. As I was pushing past people, I ran into my friend Charlie.

Charlie is another friend from my childhood. We met in middle school. Instantly clicked. Probably the best person I know. Skinny guy. Don't know why but I'm pretty sure in the ten plus years I've known him, I've never seen him wear shorts. Anyway, he's the only friend who never gave up on me. And it was perfect timing to run into him.

"Yo! I need your help! Find Macoa and make sure she's near, but not too near the staircase in a couple of minutes."

"What? Why? And how?"

"Just figure it out, man. Make sure she's there or at least looking in that direction in exactly two minutes!" I told him as I continued to look for Brent, whom I eventually did find.

"I got you."

Next thing I knew Brent was in front of my face.

"There you are. Do you ha—"

"Yes. Here it is. What's up? Why the urgency?"

"You're a lifesaver. I'll see you later. I have to take care of something."

I sped back to the kitchen, and she was still there. I grabbed the French girl and stalled a bit longer before I took her to my room.

Two minutes later, Macoa's friend and I made our way upstairs. I wasn't going to check if Macoa was looking, but I was hoping she was. As we found our way up the stairs, I made sure to not look back. We made it to my room. But as we got in, I saw my dog, which I had forgotten I had put in my room during the party. "Oh my God! She so cute!" she said in her French accent.

Come on girl, no time for my dog right now. "It's a he."

I grabbed her and led her to my brother's room (sorry if you're reading this, bro). I continued kissing her in the hallway upstairs; she tasted like a sweet flower. Her kisses were wet and memorable. Wet in a good way, not in a sloppy way. She continued to follow me. She was letting me do the leading. I told her to go into the room. She did. I told her to lie down. She did.

I got onto the bed to meet her, one thing leading to the next. "Take these off," I said. But before I said anything else as she was undressing, I slid my hand into my pocket to find the Ziploc bag Brent had given me. I pulled it out, and there it was—white pixie dust.

"You want some?" I asked her.

"Fuck yeah."

Who the hell was this girl? And why was she hanging out with Macoa? I made a line with the powder on her naked body and snorted it into my nose as I felt a rush of energy and a greater need to have sex run through my form. It was her turn now. She did the same. When we both were done, I took off my clothes to match her and made my way to the bed.

"Are you going to make love to me now?" she asked.

That was either the sexiest thing or the lamest thing I had ever heard. I told her to close her eyes. She did.

♥

Fast forward an hour, and we were walking down the stairs to rejoin the party as it was still going strong. This time I noticed that Macoa did see us walk down, and the look on her face said it all. What I had wanted.

Macoa ran to us. "What were you doing with her?" she asked in a shocked tone as I made my way off the final step.

"She was teaching me some French. Now excuse me, I have a party to host." I pushed past her and went to go find more alcohol.

Listen, I can keep talking, and you can keep judging me. You can come up with a thousand reasons why I'm so messed up, but what else was I supposed to do? Tell me, what should I have done? I feel and I felt like shit. And maybe I regret it but I want to know the sane response to chasing a girl for years and then seeing her do *that* in your house. And as you're listening and thinking that I am crazy, I hope you're never in my position. I really do because if you had felt my pain, I fear you might have done worse. I hope you never have to deal with what I've dealt with. You think I'm a bad person? Fine. I never said I was a good person. But you don't know all the factors behind my addiction and how I felt that night. Conscious or not, at the end of the day I'm just telling you what happened.

Truth is, I felt horrible the rest of the night. All the transforming in the world couldn't help me not feel for Macoa. I was heartbroken over what happened. As the high wore off, I looked down at my watch that marked

3:00 a.m. I had to end the party early; I couldn't pretend like I was having a good time anymore. I walked over to the DJ and told him to only play a couple of more songs and then shut it down.

Man, that feeling was horrible; it really was like a dagger into my heart when I saw them kissing. I know it's cliché but it's the only way I can describe how I felt. I was sitting down alone on the couch thinking what to do next when the music ended and people began to make their way out. Right before everybody was out, Macoa's friend came to me with shock quake written all over her face. "Why is Macoa upset? Did I do something I wasn't supposed to? I didn't know, I promise! Should I tell her nothing happened upstairs?"

She continued, but I wasn't paying much attention now. It was only then that I realized I really was only peripheral to Macoa. That's all I was to her. All my friends knew how I felt about her, but she had told her friend nothing about me, because I was nothing to her. The dagger had gone too deep. I had had enough.

"I have no idea what you're talking about. But, listen, I want you to tell Macoa exactly what I did to you upstairs in detail. Vivid detail. Make sure she knows precisely what happened. And tomorrow, I want you to come back, and we'll do it again."

Minutes later I was there alone, in my house. A few minutes earlier, half the city's kids had been in the first floor of my house with music blasting. But now it was just me, in silence. I couldn't help but think it was just like playing poker. One second my heart was racing and I was full of adrenaline, the next I was home, alone. But I was exhausted; it was 4:00 a.m. when everybody had made their way out, and I had finished the initial cleaning before I realized I needed to order a full-on cleaning service. So I made my way up with the last bit of energy I had and collapsed asleep on my parents' bed. Just me and my dog.

♥

I woke up dehydrated. Well, that's an understatement. My throat was so dry that it hurt. My tongue was sticking to my mouth. I squinted as I looked at my phone—noon. My head hurt, and I was dying of thirst. I needed to make my way downstairs to get some water. When I first stepped out of my bed, I stumbled and realized I was still a bit drunk. I squinted my eyes harder and stopped walking for a second to hold my head, which felt heavy. At first I chuckled to myself, as I was midway down the stairs, when I thought about the French girl and when I was in the DJ booth playing songs.

But then, I finally got to my first floor. I stopped there and looked out before continuing. There it was—my house. Completely empty and destroyed. Just a few hours before there were about a hundred kids there. Now, my home that is normally filled with furniture, was filled with cups, bottles, and everything that a party leaves behind. And then it hit me— what really happened the night before. I couldn't help but think of what had happened with Macoa and her friend. I felt a cold rush of anxiety again. Had I made the right choice? I had gone too far. My smile was quickly washed away from my face. I looked at my house, and it was vacant. It looked so vast yet so unoccupied. I realized I had nothing. I hated that feeling. I felt scared.

I immediately sobered. And I had never felt so alone in my life.

TWENTY-SIX

FOOL

I know I say and do a lot of messed-up shit when I'm drunk. But I sleep like a baby because I don't have to face the consequences until the morning. It's only in the morning where I felt like shit; only in the morning does my anxiety, shame, and guilt set in.

There was nothing for me to do when I reached the first floor. I just had to keep swallowing my emotions and continue to move toward my goal that was so close now. Maybe it was brave of me, that despite how I felt on the inside I was working toward something bigger. Maybe I was being a coward and didn't face my reality. But it's easy to look back now and draw conclusions. In those times, my life was moving too fast for me to question what I was doing. Things were just moving too fast.

♥

The next day I was at the Hard Rock, playing one of the biggest games they had—25-50 deep stack, minimum buy-in—$10,000.

Have you ever broken a bone? Or had any major physical pain? If not, imagine the sensation of it happening. Because, when somebody does, all they can think about when it happens is the pain, in that moment. The agony rushes to your brain, and your thoughts are clogged with acknowledging and attempting to react to the pain. Now, have you ever scored a goal or touchdown in a big game? Or been at a concert that makes you feel something you don't usually feel? Similarly, all your brain can process is the euphoria in that moment. All of a sudden, in these instances, you forget about your girlfriend, you forget about school, you forget about the book you're reading; you forget everything else in your life because all your brain wants to do is process what's happening in that moment and try to react to it.

When I play poker and have thousands of dollars on the table, I can't help but only think about what's going on. The chips and my cards are the only thing in the world that matter in those hours. It's the reason I do it—to forget about everything outside of the table. I am forced to concentrate and only process the table's action. I choose not to deal with pain. Instead, I choose to live the fantasy of being a professional poker player.

Many people imagine having a lot of money takes away all the stress in one's life. I found it to be the opposite; all this was incredibly stressful. The more money I had, the more I could lose and the less I liked stepping into a poker room. The more money being wagered, the more anxiety I had. But it was different now—even though I hated playing for so much money, poker rooms were my home by this point. Having so much in life can be a burden, but the more pain I felt those days outside the poker room, the more I fought to silence it and focus on poker. I was addicted to the cycle of stress by now, it was the only thing I had, and I had learned to love it.

As a consequence of wagering so much money, my game was changing. I couldn't afford to lose the money I was playing with now, as the buy-ins to these games were more than 10 percent of my entire bankroll. See, the thing is that when I was playing for a hundred dollars, I was playing against adults who could afford losing a hundred dollars. And when I moved up to bigger games, I was playing against bookies and nerds who could afford losing a thousand dollars. I was always playing against people who could afford to lose. But I never could. This whole time, I was buying into games where I simply didn't have the ability to take a loss or have a bad run. I play with my heart because I don't have the luxury of not doing so.

♥

I was up two thousand at the Hard Rock when, I heard a whisper behind me. "You should leave. These games are too big. You're playing against millionaires now. They don't care about ten thousand dollars. They'll destroy you."

The voice was back, and the next one followed. "Exactly. They don't care about losing ten grand. You can beat them out of their money easily."

I never knew which one to trust when it came to the voices, but the evil one was always more attractive. The nicer one was a bit too boring. "Stop this before it's too late. The money you have is enough. You can pay your way through most of college. You can start a business. It's enough, you've done enough. If you keep going it will only get worse. What else do you need to lose?"

Maybe it was enough, but I needed more.

I eventually was dealt pocket kings. I raised to seven hundred after three folds, and everyone else also folded except for one guy who was in position and had the most chips in the table—he took a while to think but eventually raised me to two thousand. I suspected he thought I had nothing and was just abusing his position and stack size. *Fuck that.* Nobody was going to push me around just because they had more money. I reraised to thirty-six hundred. Then, he finally four bets me to six grand. Did he actually have something? I had two options now: call and hope an ace doesn't come on the flop, or shove. I don't like to go all in before the flop, but I needed to send the message that I wasn't scared. So I announced it: "I'm all in."

And then, he called. We flipped over our cards, and he shows ace, queen of hearts. I had him. All I needed to do was avoid an ace. The flop was about to come.

And then it hit me, as if I was sleeping before. I had gone all in. This was it. All my chips were in the in the middle of the table. And here's the scary part about that—it doesn't matter if you're a 99 percent favorite to win a hand in poker, once the chips are in the center of the table, they are no longer yours. Ninety-nine is always a great number, until that 1 percent hits.

The next five cards were worth almost $25,000. My heart raced faster than it had ever before at a table when I realized that. In thirty seconds I would be either thirty grand richer or poorer. All I could do was stare at the table, and all I could think was *Don't you dare put out an ace!*

The dealer dealt the flop: ten, three, ace. I immediately felt as if Mike Tyson had punched me in my stomach. I couldn't believe it, but that's the problem with playing this game—the best don't always win.

And I wasn't one to ask God for favors. But right then and there I couldn't help but look toward the ceiling and cry out to God and to the universe in my head; I just needed this one favor. *Come on, one time! Give me a king!*

The next card comes: queen. *You got to be kidding me.* But then I realized I had more outs. I needed a king or a jack now. I didn't want the last card to come, because I didn't want to accept the fact that I was about to lose this pot. I just wanted to disappear. I didn't want people to look at me the way they look at someone when they've lost a huge pot.

The river: jack of hearts.

And if you would've looked at me in that moment, you wouldn't have thought I had won $30,000 because I was in shock. I was in shock from the ups and downs that I had lived. I had won the biggest pot of my life, but I wasn't smiling. I was starting to hate this game; even though I had won that particular hand, I didn't like what this game put me through to win anymore. It was giving me too much anxiety that could only be cured by playing more.

In two hours, I returned home and fell into bed, staring at the ceiling. My heart had pounded so much throughout the day; I could still feel it when I arrived home. One of the worst parts about poker was that the anxiety lasted for hours after I played; I felt like throwing up as a result of my heart beating into my chest hours after the action had unfolded.

As I lay on my bed and was completely still, I had a chance to reflect on the last couple of months. How it had all just started the previous summer and where I was now. How I had won that initial tournament and decided to follow this crazy dream. I never actually had time to think about everything that had happened—how I had won sixth place in that small tournament in Tampa and the night that followed it. How I was now so close to having six figures in cash. I was proud of myself. I had done something respectable; this wasn't easy—not just anybody could do it, but I had done it. All alone. But despite how proud I could be, I knew I couldn't go on with this lifestyle much longer.

The lucky are born rich. The lucky are born good looking. The lucky are born charming. I wasn't. I wasn't born with fortune; I had to go out and find a way to get it, *unluckily*. Not unluckily because it was hard to go and get it, although it was. Rather, it was because of what I had to become to attain what I wanted. I needed to change to get money and women.

Yes, I had money and girls now, but I had to change to get it; that's the whole point. I had to become something I wasn't. Maybe the reason I don't believe in luck is because I never thought I was lucky. It was while thinking about this that I came into the realization that I was a fool. Do you ever feel that way? About the things we have to compromise to be who we are? Maybe it's not worth it?

I was a fool, because I became something else. I was dead inside. Talking to girls the way I did, taking money from people the way I did, I had to be dead; I wouldn't be able to do these things if I were alive. Chuck wouldn't have done those things. Chuck couldn't live this type of life. I had to turn off my emotions to do the things I did. I wish I had been naïve, rich, and happy when I was born. But I wasn't. I was ambitious and smart, too smart. I knew what it took to be rich—what I wanted my whole life. But I hated what I needed to become to get it.

TWENTY-SEVEN

NOTHING TO HIDE

W e're almost there, just one more week to where I am now, and why tonight can be life changing. Almost done catching you up—hang tight.

It was now early April, I was back in school, and my fund was up to $89,000—only eleven thousand more, and I was there. It would soon all be over, MIT decisions were only a month away, and I would be able to start my new life once I was admitted. And if I didn't get in? I had no idea what I would do.

✦

I wanted all the stress to be over soon, and I knew I needed one more big win and I would be done. So the following Thursday, while I was still back in Mexton, I bought into a $5,000 cash game. This game was the first underground game I had played in Miami which is a short drive from Mexton. I was told about it by my connects in Orlando. This game wouldn't be as stressful as the $10,000 game I had just played, and I knew if I played well, there was a possibility I would reach my $100,000 target and finally be done.

As soon as I sat down for the game, I noticed there was a kid there that I used to see playing at the smaller games when I had first started here in Orlando. Each time I played these big games, it was common knowledge that the kids were the aggressive ones, and as a result each time I played with another young kid at my table, we would clash heads. He kept looking at me, and I'm sure he knew about my poker success as most people in the community talk. He was wearing a brown sweater. When I sat down he asked me what school I went to.

"I'm transferring to MIT."

He chuckled.

"Why? Where do you go?"

"I graduated from Harvard last May," he replied with a stupid smirk on his face.

I would make sure he would go broke.

Right before the game started, another kid from the cash games from when I first began to play sat down. He had black hair but was wearing a hat this time. He was positioned right next to me. Was every kid a professional poker player now? We started to play, and I won the first hand, off to a good start. Right off the bat, the Harvard kid lost about half of his stack. I was happy he was losing, but I wanted to be the one who would take his chips. As the game proceeded, it was obvious that the other kid next to me was going to be overly aggressive the whole night. He was a good player most of the time, but his aggressiveness would come back to hurt him, I told myself.

Next hand, the aggressive kid raised five times the big blind. I looked at my cards and I had pocket tens, so I then raised it to thirteen times. After some folds, action got to the Harvard kid who called and then everyone else folded except the original raiser. The flop came: three, six, eight. The original raiser checked, I made a small bet, and the Harvard Kid went all in, I called. I knew all he had was ace high, probably with a queen or king. I turned over my pair of tens. He turned over ace, king. My reading skills were there. I was about to knock him out of the game. The turn: king.

Now I was short stacked. But all I could think was that I needed to get back up to knock out the kid from Harvard who had pissed me off by simply laughing when I told him I was going to MIT. The next decent hand I got, the Harvard Kid raised, and when most people folded, I checked my cards and had pocket eights; now I went all in. Harvard kid called. Again, he had ace, king. The flop: ace, king, three. *You got to be kidding me. Fuck.* I didn't even wait to see the turn or the river. I was on tilt now; I made my way to the game host to buy in again for another five thousand. It wasn't going to end like that.

I bought back in, now only thinking that I wanted to take the Harvard kid's money. He had all my chips and started acting like the big-stack bully. I wasn't going to take it. Once I was dealt a good hand, I was going to make sure I was paid off. After a couple of minutes, he raised again, and I looked at my cards when the action got to me and saw pocket fours, so instead of doing anything stupid, I just called and hoped to see a four on the flop. Four players to the flop: eight, four, five, all spades. I knew no one probably hit their flush on the flop, but someone had to have at least one spade. After the aggressive guy checked to me, I made a hefty bet, trying to protect my trips, hoping the action would end there and prevent anyone from hitting their flush. The Harvard kid asked me how much I had left. I tell him I have around eight thousand behind me and he then puts me all in. *Give me a break.* I called. He showed an eight of diamonds and a nine of spades. The turn: another spade.

I hated the fact that I was losing even though I was outplaying everyone. Again, this was not over. So I stood up and walked to the end of the room where the host was and bought in again. When I sat down for the last time, I was only looking at the Harvard douche. After an hour went by, I was up a grand even factoring the times I had bought in again, meaning I was able to break even despite buying in three times. But I wasn't leaving; my enemy and I were at the same stack size, but now all that mattered to me was taking his chips. I had something to prove, as I declared war on him in my head. It was time for real poker; I was going to make him pay. I then got my favorite hand: ace, nine, so I raised to four times the blind. Only Harvard called. Of course. The flop came: jack, queen, five. I bet 25 percent of my stack. Harvard stared at me for a minute.

I stared back and opened my mouth. "Bro, stop looking at me. You can't read me; I have no tells. I don't need to wear glasses like you or any of these other people. You won't find anything when you look in my eyes."

He chuckled just like he did in the beginning of the night.

"What do you have?" he asked.

"I have ace high. You want to gamble? Let's gamble."

Why did I just tell him what I had? Well, sometimes in life all you have to do is be honest, and people will laugh.

"I don't believe you."

"You want to see one? I'll show you one card, all you got to do is ask."

"Show me a card."

I showed him the ace. He called. *That didn't work.* The turn: a nine. I knew he probably had a jack or a queen, but I had to win this hand. I bet 50 percent of my remaining stack. He thought about it for a minute, but he called. The river didn't change anything; I went all in. He took two minutes to call, but he did eventually.

God, I hate this feeling, coming home to nothing. I can't sleep for how alone I feel.

TWENTY-EIGHT

DEATH

I lost nine thousand that night. I grew to accept that the worst pain I would feel would be losing the money I had worked so hard to make. Rock bottom to me was after having a bad run. I didn't care if I made $90,000 in a year only being a twenty-year-old. I didn't care that I was surrounded by cute girls when I went out. I didn't care that I was healthy and drove a nice car. Losing nine thousand was terrible for me. I hated the feeling like nothing else. And these bad runs would generally last at least a week. Yet I would still go back. It wasn't just addiction; it was being mad. Why would I go back knowing there's a possibility that I could hit rock bottom? If I knew that I could experience the worst pain by playing poker, was it logical to even play? I consciously walked into poker rooms knowing that I might leave severely depressed. I was going crazy and losing my logic. And the worst part was that even when I lost a lot of money, I knew I would be back. It was scary knowing that there was nothing I could do; acknowledging the fact that this stupid game had all the power over me was frightening. Even in the worst times, I still knew I was hooked. Poker would spit in my face, and I still told her I loved her.

Thinking about it, I knew what it felt like to be losing; I knew what this terrible feeling could do to me. And like I told you in the beginning of the story, for someone to win, someone else has to lose. So for me to be happy, it would mean I would have to hurt someone else. I would have to make others feel the pain I hated. Was this moral? Was it moral to make money and prosper at the expense of others?

✦

The following night I was in the Hard Rock looking for the sucker. But you were with me last night. Remember? I know we took a while catching you up, but you were with me. We found the sucker, took her money, went out to celebrate in Miami, and then took that blond girl back to Alexander's apartment? Well, where do you think we are now? Still here. The girl is still in the room, and Alexander is still inside.

That was last night; go read the first two chapters again if you forgot about it. But I've caught you up now. So that was my story. Did you like it? I hope you did. Now we're in real time. I don't know what's going to happen, but you're welcome to come along for the ride.

As I make my way back inside toward the room to wake up the girl, I see Alexander at the door. "I'm not going to let you do this. You can't play anymore."

"I don't need your permission. I know what I'm doing."

He grabs me and stares at me until I finally make eye contact with him. "You don't need to do this. You already have ninety thousand. Why would you risk half of that just to make a bit more? Stop this. Let's go get dinner. Let's be normal for one night." His eyes are pleading at me stronger than his words.

"I'm sorry. I have to finish what I started. I'm going to wake up the girl, take a shower, and get ready for tonight."

I just want to get all this over with and finally hit my mark of a hundred thousand. Maybe once I make it, I can finally be at peace and let go of this depression. I know that I will eventually lose my sanity, if I haven't already, but I need to hit the six figures; this goal is the only thing I have keeping me going. That'll be enough to pay for MIT and then I can stop.

✦

Okay. I'm back in Orlando now. I said my goodbyes to Alexander, packed my stuff and drove up here. There's only one thing to do now—keep playing. If I win tonight, I can hit my mark; it can be done tonight. It's 11:00 p.m., and I'm on my way to Downtown for a big game.

As I get escorted in and look around, I think that hopefully this will be the last time; I look around at the room that I have spent hours and hours in this past year. The dealer asks me how much I want to buy in for.

"Give me a dime."

It's time. This has to end. All I have to do is win and then it will be over. I'm not too anxious because I just won $15,000 last night, but I'm still aware that tonight could be the biggest night of my life.

The roller coaster of winning one day and losing the next is making me numb. I sit down and look around. But I don't actually see; I just look.

It has been half an hour, and I'm sitting here, no sucker. Why are we all here? What's the point of all this? The thing about gambling is that it's not about the reality; I mean, people can't honestly believe they're going to make a lot money, right? Nobody actually makes a lot of money in the long run. Why do people play slot machines? Why do people play the lottery? People don't actually think it's smart to play, do they? I don't think people are actually that dumb. The math is simple—you play a hundred times, and you'll lose at least fifty-one. So why do we play? Where's the logic behind our stupidity? Are humans actually too dumb to realize this? Or do we do all this for some other reason?

I think it's all about the illusion. The illusion of what might happen when we do hit that money. We know we won't win, but until we lose, we can fantasize about the possibility of winning, and maybe that's enough.

It is past midnight now, and I have won some hands and lost others. I can't help but think how repetitive this game is. The same things happen, all the time. I am slow rolling the same hands I always do, making the same mathematical bets when I have to, and people are saying the same things when they lose against me. I am playing with the same strategy I have been playing with for a while, and it does make money, but it's boring now. This isn't fun anymore; the money means nothing to me anymore. I know I said I wanted to hit my goal and I still do. But these chips, the cash, the actual numerical value of all this doesn't faze me. I don't care about a couple of thousand dollars. What will that do for me outside of here? Whether I make money or lose money tonight, my life outside the poker room will be relatively the same. Even though I do need the rush the game gives me, it's just starting to get boring.

Sitting down at this table is boring. These people are losers. What am I doing here? I'm twenty years old; I literally have ninety grand in cash back in my apartment, and I'm sitting down with people I don't know, in an apartment I'm not familiar with, playing a stupid game that I know better than most people who have been playing it the same amount of time I've been alive. What's that point of doing this? *I already won. Why am I still here?* Tell me what's the point of this obsession with becoming successful and having money. We do all this, but at the expense of what? My journey to happiness has cost me everything, especially happiness. But the worst part is that this is the only thing I have. I do feel bored, I do feel anxious, and I do even feel a bit dead. But there's nothing and nobody for me outside of this room, and these feelings are better than feeling nothing. Don't you get it? I do hate who I am in here, but I hate the person outside of this room even more.

✦

It is 2:00 a.m. now. Up a lot. Still here. I'm getting anxious; my mind is starting to race again. I don't like the feeling in my chest and my hands right now. I bite down on my teeth.

I look down at my stack, which is the biggest it's ever been. And now I look up and analyze everybody at the table. Some of the guys here are down a couple of thousand dollars, some are down even more, and some guys are up tens of thousands of dollars. But, regardless of everybody's losses or profits, we are all losers—that is, we are all losing something by being here. Some of us are only losing money—the lucky. But some of us, most, are losing money, time, morals, or sanity, but even worse, we are losing our lives, *we are losing sense of reality*, of ourselves, of our conscious. Being here we are losing our connection to what's right. Everybody here at the table has experienced the euphoria of winning thousands of dollars where one really does feel like nothing in the world can stop them—I promise you that this feeling of collecting chips is one that transcends time. And that's why we're all here. But it is 2:00 a.m. on a Sunday, and we are all still here and we have been here before and we will be here again.

We are all losers, dying together yet very alone.

TWENTY-NINE

MADE IT

It's 5:15 a.m., and I'm on my way home; the sky looks as if it recognizes only the lonely are up at this time.

I open the door to my apartment and make my way to my room. As I step inside, I know exactly where I'm going—my shoe box. I open it and start counting the money. Ten thousand, twenty thousand, thirty, forty, fifty, sixty...seventy...eighty...ninety...and I add what I made tonight—$100,011 total.

I make my way over to the mirror, and I take a second to look at myself. I hear and almost see the voice that had been inviting me to the dark side pop up behind me—the One Knight Stand: "Look at us; we did it. We are the One Knight Stand. We made six figures playing poker in eleven months. I told you this would be fun. I told you we would make it."

The edge of my lips makes a slight smile, and I take my clothes off and finally lie down on my bed to get some sleep.

Loneliness is a feeling that simply makes you feel distant. You can be in the middle of a crowd but feel miles away from humanity. It makes you feel alienated, like nobody speaks your language and nobody can. It's questioning yourself because maybe it's not that people don't get you; maybe it's that you are the different one. It's like screaming at the top of your lungs in a glass room, realizing that nobody can hear you. It's not being able to make a connection, and it's such a terrifying feeling because you wonder when you'll start to feel connections again, if you ever will.

PART IV

ANXIETY

THIRTY

WHAT NOW?

hat was a short chapter, right? I know. I had gotten home tired, and I needed to sleep. But I'm awake now.

I wake up at around noon, and I can't help but smile. The first thing I do is jump out of bed and check my shoe box again and recount the money; I make sure it wasn't a dream. But it wasn't; it was real. I have done it. Eleven months ago, I had a goal to make this money, and it is right here in front of my eyes; it's real and tangible. I decide I don't want to go to school today. Screw my finals; I'm already making six figures. I don't need to take a test at this point of my life.

✦

It's 3:00 p.m. now. I went to get a bite to eat earlier, and I'm in my apartment now, doing nothing. I'm literally pacing back and forth around the living room trying to think of something to do. There's nothing that comes to mind; I'm just pacing around. I go to my room and look at my shoe box one more time. I count the money again. It's still there.

I sit in my living room again, and I stare at the wall. I look at my phone—no one has texted me. I stand up and go to the shoe box and look at the money. Still there. Back to the living room now. What do I do now? I'm too good to go to school. It's too early to play poker or go out drinking.

I begin thinking of why I have nothing to do. Nobody has called me in months. I have no obligations. It's just me and what's inside the shoe box in my room. I don't care about her, but I start thinking about Macoa. I think that she probably still doesn't want me. I had imagined as a kid that maybe she would want me if I looked better and was successful. I think how maybe I'm still not good enough. I think about my parents, how I left Mexton after I went to go visit my brother at the hospital, and how they must think of me now. I think of their meaning of success and how I told them I would be successful for them. But I'm not a good son; I haven't made them proud.

My breath begins to get harder and more intense. I look all over the room as if someone is watching me. My thoughts are going a mile a minute. My heart starts to speed up. My hand feels like it needs to be doing something. I need to get out of here; I need to go somewhere now. I walk down the stairs, and as soon as my feet touch the floor, I start running. I feel the need to escape. But as I'm running, I realize I can't run fast enough; I can't escape my anxiety.

I go back to my apartment and sit down. I look around again. I start pacing around even quicker. I step into room, check the shoe box. Look at the money. Count it. Still there. Put the shoe box back. Get out of my room. Find my keys. Walk downstairs again. Walk to my car. Turn it on.

On my way to Mexton.

✦

I finally get to Mexton two hours later and sit down again in my living room. My mom gives me a hug, happy that I "surprised" her. "Don't you have finals, though?"

"Yes. I have four days in between my next exam though. I figured I'd come and be with the family for the week."

Again, I sit down in the living room, and I can see my mom right in front of me, and I can see her mouth moving, but I can't hear her or make sense of anything. Time seems to be melding together.

"I'm a bit tired. I'm going to get some sleep."

Again, my hands and feet feel like they need to be doing something. I try to put on music as I close the door to my room, but I can't pick a song. I don't know what's happening to me. It's really hot in here, the walls seem to be growing closer and closer. The walls aren't moving but the room seems to be getting smaller. My heart is racing, it's getting harder to breath, and my body is getting warm even though my blood feels cold.

I can't take this. I don't know what to do. I can't focus on anything; my mind is being loud. I feel trapped in my own body, inside my own thoughts. I need to get out of here again. I race to my car, turn it on.

Don't you get it? That all this is a facade to hide and forget how alone I really am? That maybe I treat people the way I do because I'm insecure? That the stress, the adrenaline, the distraction of the money is what I do it for? That I'm addicted to the stress, that I'm addicted to the feeling I have when so much is on the line? That when I have thousands of dollars in my hand, people look at me and pay attention and that maybe that attention is just fulfilling what I don't get outside of poker rooms? That I don't come here to get away from the reality of my life? That I come here to live my preferred life? That I'm afraid of being incapable of doing anything other than living in this intermediate phase of being almost there, of forefeeling that rush of accomplishment and self-actualization? That I'm actually scaring myself to death of being a big fucking fraud, that I'm scared I'm not capable of being normal? That I'm terrified I might actually be a psychopath? That I'm trying as hard as I can to actually be something? That I'm addicted to living this fantasy that goes away when I don't have cards and chips in my hands?

THIRTY-ONE

TEMPTATION

I'm in this car driving ninety miles per hour to the casino, not because I need the money, not because I don't have anything else to do, not even because I want to have some fun. I'm going to play poker because I need to.

I sit down at a table at the Hard Rock and feel cards slide into my hand, and even though it's like taking a shot of vodka to treat a hangover, it gives me another moment of saneness. My hands and feet finally stop shaking, and my mind can be silent for at least some time. I know that my long-term health is very much in danger at this point, but I'm not looking for a lot of time. I'm just focused on being able to breathe. And this money, in the form of clay with ceramic known as casino chips, allows me to breath.

So why don't I stop? C'mon…who possibly could? Poets say love is the most powerful force of the universe. Fine, but greed is a close second. I need more. I can't stop. I won't stop until I really make it. At this point, I'll keep going until I am a millionaire. Until I'm good enough.

I start to play and sense my body slowing down and feeling better. The only thing different now is that for some reason today I just can't find the sucker. I know I have to leave this table, and I decide that it's time to go back to Orlando. Even though I was just here for a couple of hours, I need to leave Mexton if I want to play bigger games.

✦

It's Friday now, and I'm about to sit down at a table. It's a 25-50 game again, and I buy in for fifteen grand. I do that thing I always do first—look for the sucker. As the first few hands of the game are dealt, I still can't find one particular sucker. And after a few hands of me not landing any cards, I get seven, nine off suit. I raise to $300 when the action stops at me. The little blind, who is a middle-aged Asian guy, reraises me to twelve hundred. I can't tell how tall he is because he's sitting down but he somehow has a big physical presence at the table. He is wearing a white button down shirt. Wearing glasses. In a nonracist way (that's when you know something racist is coming), Asians are the hardest to play against. On the one hand, they might be mathematical geniuses who calculate every move. On the other, some of them are just crazy gamblers. Look, let's admit it; some stereotypes are true—Asians are crazy gamblers.

I take a second, but I know I'm the best here, and the universe loves me, so I reraise to nineteen hundred. He calls. The flop is: king, seven, jack. He bets a grand. *Do you know who you're playing against, old man?*

"I'm all in."

And I know what you're thinking. "Chuck, he three-bet you on the flop. There's a king and a jack on the board; this isn't the right place to bluff."

But let's not forget who's the player here. Your job is to sit and listen;

mine is to make money.

And you know how I can't find the sucker? I get it now—it's different nowadays. Everybody who plays against me is a sucker. I mean, I know I'm better than everybody here; all I have to do is play my game. There's not one particular sucker whom I need to focus on. I'm here to take everyone's chips. The middle-aged Asian guy takes two minutes to think about it and finally folds and shows his cards: ace, king.

"Thanks for sharing," I say under my breath but loud enough for some to hear as I collect the chips.

"You got aces or king, jack, don't you?" he asks.

I show my cards, and his face says it all—*you mother fucker.*

I keep doing my thing for a bit when I get a message on my phone. I look down—it's Macoa. *Here we go again. Didn't we put an end to this over spring break?*

"Hey, what's up?" says the message.

I'm not in the mood to start a conversation, but I can't help but answer, "Poker."

She replies instantly, "Ha-ha of course you are. I wanted to catch up with you. I feel like we left off on the wrong foot."

I really don't want to deal with this right now, so I put my phone in my pocket. But a couple of minutes go by, and I hear my phone vibrate a couple of times, and I know it's her. But now I'm in a hand. And again, I'm up against the same guy. I don't get much on the flop, but it's heads up, and I bluff again.

"You're not bluffing me again, are you?"

"Nope, I only bet when I know I'm going to win, so it wasn't really bluffing. But no, I'm not bluffing again; I wouldn't bluff twice."

While the sucker is thinking about calling or not, I read my phone.

Macoa has sent me a couple of question marks.

Finally, the guy folds, and again, I show my cards.

"Listen, kid, you keep bluffing like that and you're going to get yourself into a lot of trouble."

"I appreciate the advice, old man, but I made a hundred thousand dollars in less than a year playing this game. I don't need guidance from a car salesman."

He shuts up. Again, Macoa sends me another question mark. I am making about a grand an hour playing cards; Macoa is starting to really bore me.

"Why do you say that?" I finally answer.

Her texts pop up instantly. "Well, I assumed you saw me kissing your friend, but it's not what it looked like. And then I saw you with my friend."

"It was just a party," I tell her. But she kept wanting to talk, trying to explain to me how she didn't actually want to kiss my friend. I cut her off.

I finally am ready. "Listen, when I was in high school, I would've been obsessed about all of this. But now, you're just another hot girl to me. There's no substance to you, at least not anymore. What we did is okay. It's cool. No hard feelings. It was just a party. I appreciate the message, but save it. I'm trying to make some money here."

She didn't answer immediately like she had been. But eventually, after about half an hour she does. "You've become such an asshole."

I've been told. I inhale deeply.

I have to focus anyway. There's twenty-two grand sitting in front of me now. I have no time to talk to girls halfway around the world.

✦

Eventually, I lose some of the money back to the Asian guy, but I am still able to keep my stack higher than it was when I started. I get up ready to leave but hear the Asian guy behind me. "Hey, kid. You have some milk on your lip."

"Do you want to come here and take it off?" I reply.

"Hah. Don't tell your mom how much you lost to me tonight. She won't be giving you anymore allowance."

"What did you say? You're a thirty-five-year-old virgin making fun of a kid who's more than a decade younger than you. You think I'm worried about you taking a grand from me? I make more money in a week than you have in your savings account. Don't try to act cool in front of your buddies here because you made some cash."

I am still up and consider staying, but I decide I should leave before I get myself into more trouble. Now, I make my way to cash out, and I notice the same guy sees me, gets up, and follows me. I assume he's going to threaten me and ask for some money, but this is poker, and I'm the One Knight Stand. You don't get your money back. Anyway, I was close to Tony, the host of the game. And I knew his security guys too. He finally comes up to me and extends his hand. "It was nice playing with you. You got some real talent. I was only joking earlier, kid."

"I appreciate that."

He continued, "Listen, there's a private game we have on Saturdays. It's a 50-100 game, a lot of money on the table. We usually don't invite more people, but it seems like you can spice things up. Buy-in is around fifty thousand dollars. You should come."

I've heard this line before. "I appreciate it, but that's a bit much for me right now. I'll keep it in mind, though."

"What? You scared of losing more money to me? Can't back up your talk?" he asks, smirking.

"Thanks for the invite, old man," I say as I turn to walk away, but he grabs me by my arm.

"Look, some people are good there; I'm not going to lie. But most are millionaires with stupid money. They don't care about it. All you have to do is show up, do what you do here, and you'll make a killing. *Guaranteed.*"

"You just said you guys don't usually tell people about it. Why are you telling me?"

"It's not easy to find players to buy into these types of games, but when we do, the host gives us a cut for bringing in new players. They'll see that you're young and want to take your money. And I also want to give you a chance to get some of your cash back," he answered with a sleazy smile.

The great thing about poker is everyone thinking they're talented; everyone can lose and still think they're the best. Makes my job a lot easier.

I look at the dumb expression on his face and give him my number. I can't believe how stupid these people are. These people with all this money, they're vapid; they're primates. Seems like the actual smart people are broke, and the loud idiots are the ones with all the money. But that's for another book; my job is to make money off these idiots. "I'll see you Saturday."

THIRTY-TWO

SUCKER

Driving to his apartment, I am ready to take some money from some millionaires. I love the fact that I'm a college kid taking money from older rich people. There is a thunderstorm outside, so I park at the curb to wait a couple of minutes to see if the rain goes down. I wait for ten minutes, but the rain is only getting stronger. Some of George's (the old Asian guy) employees come outside with umbrellas and escort me inside, and we make our way up to the apartment. George is waiting at the door and welcomes me in.

"What are you drinking?"

"Water is good for me," I respond.

When I get inside, there is a full table ready for me to sit down, as if they had been waiting for me to start.

Everybody has around $70,000 in front of them when I walk in.

"How much do you want, kid?"

Stop fucking calling me that.

"Give me a hundred, old sport."

I know, risky. But look at these guys—they're idiots. It's not a risk, at least not for me. It's a big bet, but if all goes well tonight, I will be up to $200,000.

I sit down and look around. Mostly older white men as I expected. There is one guy who seems to be Latin. And there is one woman who is wearing more jewelry than I even own. We start to play.

An hour has gone by, and I am only at a hundred and seven thousand. Nothing too interesting has happened.

"You sure you don't want anything to drink?" George asks me.

This game is getting boring; maybe I should actually drink something. "Do you have Bacardi? Limón?"

He did. Maybe this will make the game more interesting. If it doesn't, I'll just head downtown later.

Another hour later, I start to feel the rum kicking in, but I am still only at a hundred and twelve. I can't figure out why the game is so slow; it's like nobody wants to actually play. As I'm thinking this, there's a knock on the door, and George looks at the camera display on the TV. It's three girls.

"Let 'em in," he tells one of the guys in suits.

They make their way in, and like always, they're wearing basically a bikini under their jackets. They look Russian.

George asks, "Anybody want a massage? It's on the house."

It's 11:00 p.m. on a Saturday; there's around a hundred and fifteen thousand in chips in front of me, I am pretty drunk, and there is a Russian model massaging me. My life is pretty good, and it is about to get even better, as it's time to take these losers' money. Dealer shuffles. I get two black aces. I raise to two thousand and get a couple of callers. The flop comes five, six, eight, rainbow. I check, making them think I don't have anything. George bets five grand. Did I mention he bought into his own game? Yeah, I know. Weird. Everybody folds and then I call, making sure I take my time. Turn comes, a ten. I check again, knowing I'm still ahead. George bets nine grand. I call. The river: ace. Brilliant. George checks, and I bet $11,000 trying to get a call. He raises to twenty-five. I think about it but call before taking another sip of my drink. He turns over a straight. *Shit.*

Fucking shit, my heart slows down. George looks at me straight in the eyes. "See, kid, eventually your luck runs out."

This guy doesn't know what he's getting himself into. Some hands go by, and I'm down to about $70,000. Should I stop playing? Am I drunk? My chip stack is disappearing pretty quickly; maybe I shouldn't be drinking. Crap. This can't be happening. I need to get this money back.

What did I just do? What's going on here? Why am I not winning anymore? I feel weird.

Finally, I get aces again. They're black, like last time. And I start to plot my hand in my head. This time, I just check under the gun. George raises to three thousand, and there's two callers, and I call too. Flop comes ace, five, five. I check again. *Okay, this is it—I have to play this hand right. This is fucking it.* George bets five thousand. Everybody folds; now it's on me. I take my sweet time, eluding him, trapping him, ready to make him one of mine. I raise to eleven thousand, and he snap goes all in. And I can't help but feel bad for this guy. Here he is, a rich middle-aged man. He thinks he's on the top of the world because he makes more money than a whole neighborhood. And here I am, in his penthouse apartment, drinking his rum, getting a massage from his girls, who will probably give me a blowjob after this, about to take his money, again.

We did it, friend. We did it. I win. Nobody can look down on me anymore.

There's only one hand that can beat me and there's no way he has it.

"Call," I said, more than eager to collect the chips.

I wait to see his cards. Two hundred thousand dollars on the line.

He flips over his cards: pocket fives. *No. No. No. That can't be right.*

I look around and realize everyone is looking at me. His security is right next to the table. I realize I have nothing else to do. And in one second the beam on my face is wiped off. My blood turns ice cold; I almost choke a bit. My left hand starts to twitch.

This last year I have worn a mask of the One Knight Stand where nothing can hurt me, but in this moment I feel so vulnerable and naked. The universe brings me back to reality, to being Charles. My mask is nowhere to be seen. Everything I have worked for throughout the last year is right here in front of me.

God, put the last ace out there, and I will never gamble again.

The turn comes: deuce. My eyes close slowly. I need the last ace, or I lose everything. I take a deep breath. *This can't be fucking happening.* I think about of saying something. I want to stop the dealer. I want to go back in time. I want my chips back. But the dealer hits the table with his fist twice signaling he will put out the last card.

I have about a 3 percent chance of the last ace coming now. I know it's not much, but I need it. I start to sink in my seat. If an ace doesn't hit, that's it. I lose it all. *How did all this happen? Come on! One Time! Come on!*

The river: jack of spades.

I close my eyes again and realize how my world is turned upside down. The dealer then pushes the chips away from me, and I see the past year of my life disappear.

I can't even speak. I want to scream, or to cry. But I can't do it here. George talks. "Tough beat, kid. You want to buy in again?"

But I have no more money. I do not have more not only here, in cash, but also anywhere. I am done.

"Nah, I'm done for the night. Maybe I'll be back next week."

I make my way to my car and start to think to myself, *Now what?* I step into my Cadillac, sit down, and lock the door. I try to process what has just happened but can't seem to think straight. *I'm I drunk? Should I go in and ask him to stake me?* I scream at the top of my lungs and laugh.

Eventually I stop laughing. And all I do—cry and scream for minutes. Charles Marquez—the kid whose parents were so proud because he was a Dean's List student and who they thought was working on the side to be able to pay for a car. The kid who was always smiling at parties and who always had something funny to say, the kid who could make the pretty girls laugh. The skinny kid who grew up trying to figure out what was wrong with him. Charles Marquez, not the One Knight Stand, is right here, alone and scared, crying. It's over.

And then, I look up and see all the guys and the Russian girls leaving the apartment complex. They are all walking together and laughing going to their cars. Why are they leaving so soon? Did they all bust? Why is the game over? It hits me—they aren't leaving because they have no money left, they are done for the night. For the first time in my poker career, I realized that *I was the sucker.* I was being hustled this whole time—not by one particular person or group of people, but by the whole system. The whole organism of poker was hustling me. It told me that I was special, that I had *it.* It sucked me in, made me think I was different. And every time I got comfortable, it reminded me who it truly thought I was.

THIRTY-THREE

LOVE

I love you.

You were the best part of me. I remember the first time I met you, how you made me feel. It was something I'd never felt before, at least not to that extent, and it felt right. Being with you felt right. I knew this wouldn't be the average relationship—it couldn't be. I wanted to spend whole days with you; I wanted all my friends to meet you. And they did, and they liked you too. How could they not? They are human like me. But when they just enjoyed you, I became obsessed. I fell in love, I really did. How could I not? It wasn't coincidence I met you; it was like you fulfilled something I had been missing my whole life. Sooner or later I would've run into you; you just happened to come at the right time. And ever since that day, all I can think about is you.

I was vulnerable when I first met you, and you gave me an outlet. Being with you let me breathe again. But the problem with finding an outlet when dealing with other mental issues is one imagines this outlet is saving them. They become addicted to the saving. And the problem with love is drawing self-worth from the thing that is saving us. And I am no different. I fell for you quicker than water dissolves into the sand at the beach. It's the evil form of love, though. I stopped taking and only gave. I wanted to give you everything. I wanted to immerse myself in you. I wanted to become a better person outside of our relationship for you. But being in love this way isn't ideal because I was never at peace with this love; I was always in the pursuit of being better so that I could finally please you.

And then my friends didn't want to be with you; they even told me I was spending too much time with you. And then you didn't let me be with my friends; you didn't let me do anything. So it was only you and me. I said *okay*. As long as I got to be with you, I would've left everything, and eventually I did. I loved you, but I realized I would never have you—not anytime soon.

I'll never have your love because I'll always chase to be better. I'll chase the rest of my time with you, trying to be good enough, and you'll never love me back. The more I want you, the more I love you, and the more I try to be better, the more you control me, and the less you love me.

You are the worst part of me. You drove me away from my family, from my friends. I stopped watching soccer; I stopped doing things for me—I stopped caring about school and my future. Because at one point, you *were* my future. Do you not understand all the sacrifices that I made? Everything I have compromised for you, you fucking bitch? All I cared about was getting back to you. And every time I thought I finally understood you, you let me down. Every time I thought I could finally be comfortable and do things the way *you* taught me, I was made a fool. You made me into something evil, you made me treat others and myself poorly, and glorify and worship you. I did things I didn't even know I was capable of doing.

Why didn't I leave you? How could I? You were glamorous; you were *the* show. I could show you off everywhere I went. I couldn't return to my regular life anymore; going back to the old me would be too late. I had turned down reality, for you.

The problem is that I learned that you would only love me until I was a better version of myself. You would only love me when I stopped chasing you, but this would only make me chase you more. You could only love me to the degree to which I loved myself.

Your love was the type of love I needed to earn. I had to become somebody special to have it. But the funny part is I was better only when I was with you; you *were* the special part of me. You brought out the worst in me. And once I earned this love; I didn't need it, or even want it.

I hate you, poker.

THIRTY-FOUR

DONE

When I arrive home, I make my way to my shoe box one last time. I get the little cash I have in my wallet out, and I look around the room for any other money to put it all together and count what I have left. One, two, three, four, five, six, seven, eight, nine, a thousand. A thousand and one, a thousand and two, a thousand and three, a thousand four, a thousand five, a thousand six, a thousand seven, thousand eight, thousand nine. Two thousand, two and one, two two, two three, two thousand and four hundred dollars. Twenty-four hundred.

And people say the first heartbreak is the deepest, and the rest won't hurt as bad. But that's just a fallacy; it's all relative. Macoa tore my heart, I have lost money before, and I have felt alone before; but none of that can prevent this pain in the slightest way right now. I feel shredded, man. What the hell did I do? I'm an idiot. Why would I bet so much money in one game?

I take a moment to myself and scream. Again, thinking that maybe if

I cry and scream loud enough, I can make my money come back. I want this to be all a dream. I want to wake up tomorrow morning and still have a hundred thousand dollars in my shoe box; I want to wake up tomorrow and not know what poker is. I want to wake up tomorrow and it be May from last year and lose that first tournament I ever played and continue my life like a normal college kid. I just once want to wake up and feel normal, feel happy. I don't want to go to sleep—I'm too scared to wake up tomorrow morning. I stand up and leave my room.

I open the screen to the balcony and step outside. As I feel the cold reenter my body, I make my way onto the balcony and look down at the few cars passing by. I think about how this life gave me it all just to take it away. I think about how I am in a world of seven billion people but feel isolated. I think about my anxiety; I think about Macoa and that night of my party. I think about how I haven't really talked to my mother in weeks. I look down at the street again. I step further onto the railing of the balcony and think about how much of an idiot I am. How I don't deserve or want to be on this earth. I look down from the edge.

But I take a step back.

What do I do now? Don't just sit there and read. *Talk*. Actually, tell me. What the hell do I do now? What can I do now? Nothing. I have nothing now. I'm nothing.

✦

It's 11:00 a.m. I haven't slept at all, but I have to get out of here. I'll go crazy if I stay. I stand up and walk toward the door. I pace downstairs and head straight to my car. I start the vehicle and begin to drive to the beach. I don't want to listen to anything while driving; I just want to drive. I try not to think about poker, but how can I not? If before, the only thing that kept me sane was the money, imagine what I feel now. I feel so alone. I feel worthless; I push the accelerator a bit harder. I am not this immortal superhero I tried so hard to convince myself I was. I am mortal, and I definitely feel mortal. I push the accelerator farther in; the dashboard reads 112 mph. My mind feels like my own personal jail cell. I don't want to feel so alone. I don't want to feel so trapped within myself. I don't want to feel this anxiety; 130 mph.

I keep my foot on the pedal until I reach the end of the peninsula that is Florida. I park in the first spot I find when I reach the beach. I get down and walk toward the sand. I sit down so that my feet can feel the water wash up every fifteen seconds. My anxiety calms down a bit as I look at the water. Seven hours ago, I had more than a hundred and a quarter thousand dollars to my name. I now have practically nothing. Isn't that weird? We prop up and fabricate these ideas in our society, but they can be taken away so quickly. And that has been my problem this whole time, and I even knew it—always putting my self-worth and meaning on something exterior, knowing those things could disappear. That's the whole problem with me, and life, and gambling—we never think about the possibility of losing. I'm starting to breathe a bit easier now. Accepting my reality is helping. Maybe music will help me too. I lie down and click shuffle on my phone and skip a couple of songs until I find a good one. I can't help but think how the universe can never be predicted. If you told me a year ago that I would be driving to the beach in my Cadillac CTS-V to cry after losing so much money, I would've laughed. And, as I start to close my eyes, I do laugh a bit, which is better than crying.

As I am about to doze off, my eyes open, and the song "Riptide" by Vance Joy is on. I feel calm, too calm. At first, I think maybe all this really is a bad dream, but I look around and I immediately feel that dark and empty feeling again. I'm so tired right now. I feel as if something has been taken from me, something that I have spent so much time working toward; I feel like the world has cheated me. But I close my eyes again and let the music begin to calm me. And maybe this whole journey isn't over yet. I look at my phone before dozing off: 2:00 p.m. What do I do now? I really have nothing to do. I have nowhere to go. I let the song keep playing and doze off.

✦

I wake up a couple of hours later to the voices of other people around me. Was it all a dream? I turn around. Crap. I'm still here. I look at my phone: 6:00 p.m. My skin is burning. I have to figure out what I'm going to do about all this. I can't just go back to my regular life; I have to do something.

I walk on the sand. I'm still very much heartbroken and angry, but I still have twenty-four hundred dollars. It's something. I can't just sit here and cry. I can't lie in this ditch forever. Yeah, I might be some lost kid, but I'm not the type to feel bad for myself. I can still do something; I just need to figure out what. I have to do something…Start playing small cash games again? No, I'm not going to do all that work again. I don't want to spend another year doing the same thing I did. Go back to UCF? No way in hell. I have no money. What do I do? Am I blabbering now? I just gotta do something.

✦

Okay. I have it. Here's what we're going to do—I only have a little bit more than $2,400 to my name, right? It's too late to start playing cash games again and building my way back up to six figures. I only have a couple of weeks until MIT decisions come out and then only a bit more than two months of summer. So there's only one choice—a jackpot. I have no time or energy to do this the right way; I need to put it all on the line. I have to play a tournament that has an entry of around a thousand dollars and payouts of six figures. Or something. I need to do something. I need to take a real gamble. All or nothing.

But where? Local casinos don't have those type of tournaments. Underground games don't have those either. But you know who does? The World Cup of Poker.

I had only heard of these six-figure guaranteed and "millionaire-maker tournaments" on TV. Not many people actually play these things, as everybody says they are way too risky or simply not worth it. What's the risk? These tournaments mostly only pay a first-place winner. If I lose, my bankroll will consist only of memories. But if I win? First place pays up to a million dollars. I've spent the last year getting rich on my risk analysis skills. It's time to let that go.

I go on my phone to check when the tournament is. WCOP.com, click. Events > 2016/2017 WCOP Circuit, click. Schedule, click. May, 2016 events, click. And there it is: all circuit tournaments in May—one in Florida and one in Baltimore, but the one in Baltimore has already started. Florida, May 13, click. World Cup of Poker circuit in Florida > different events, click. Main event, click.

"Tournament information: Event #10: $1,675 MAIN EVENT, millionaire maker ($1,000,000 to first place, only payout)." Info, click.

"Four-day event. Starts Friday, May 13, 11:00 a.m. at the Seminole Hard Rock Hotel and Casino, Hollywood, Florida. First three days are played in Hollywood, Florida, May 13–15; the final nine are flown out to Scottsdale, Arizona, May 20, to play on live Television on the 21st. Funds exceeding the $1,000,000 are used for promotional purposes, flights for the final nine, production, and other expenses. The World Cup of Poker circuit events only make money on advertisements."

That's it! What we're going to do is play this World Cup of Poker circuit event at the Hard Rock in Hollywood for $1,700. It's all or nothing now, baby. The rest of the money I have I can use to survive until then and to stay at the hotel. I will use everything I have learned this year, the math, the reading, the emotions, use it all to play the best poker of my life and win this thing.

The only way out is all in (I know that's the most cliché line in every gambling story ever, but it's true). After this win, I promise I'll stop playing, forever.

By the way, May 13 is tomorrow. So we better start driving.

THIRTY-FIVE

MEDITATION

I feel like my whole life, especially this past year, has been the same movie on repeat. I always seem to have the same problems, and I always seem to never deal with them. I feel like all I ever do is find different ways to be part of the same old story. This time has to be different. It's time to beat this devil once and for all. We're going to do this tournament right—I'll be the youngest player to ever win a WCOP event, and I'll move on to my real life. No more telling you about poker.

✦

I drive up to the Rock, take a deep breath, and walk in. It's time. The past year of my life—You know what? No. These past twenty years of my life have led up to this moment. It's time to finally get a big win and not look back.

I walk up to the concierge. "How can I help you?" asks a young woman.

I tell her I want the package that includes a room, food, and an entry to the main event.

"May I have your ID?"

I hand her my license.

"Sir, the tournament is a three-day event. Regardless of when you get knocked out, you're required to pay for the whole package, which includes three nights."

"I'm confident I'm going to be here for the duration of the weekend."

"Okay, do you also want a room for tonight?" I look down at my watch; it tells me it's 7:00 p.m. I could go home, which isn't too far away, but I decide it's better to get some rest here and mentally prepare for tomorrow.

"Sir, your total is going to be twenty-two hundred dollars. This includes your buy-in to the WCOP circuit main event starting tomorrow going on until Sunday, three meals per day, unlimited drinks for the weekend, a parking pass for the duration of your stay, your room for tonight, and a room for the weekend. You must keep this receipt to receive your initial chips tomorrow."

I hand her all my cash.

"Sir, you can pay for your room in cash, but you must register a credit card for incidentals."

"Right." I have forgotten how the world revolved around cards. I hand her my credit card, hoping it doesn't get declined. She hands me my receipt.

"Thank you," I say and begin to walk toward the elevator slightly tempted to walk the casino floor.

"Oh, and Charles," I hear. I turn around. "Good luck," the concierge says.

"I don't really believe in luck. But thanks."

✦

I get to my room and start to unwind. It's these moments of silence that I can't stand. I don't want to go into the biggest day of my life alone. I need to start getting my life back together. It would be too much to call my mom, as she would have a heart attack if I told her the reality of this past year and what's going to happen tomorrow. But I grab my phone; I dial Sandro. A couple of rings.

"What's up?" his voice still half-distant with me, half too hippie to hold a grudge.

"Yo, Sandro…I'm…Uh…I'm sorry. I don't know what happened to me. Can we talk about that later? Right now, as a friend, I need you to come to the Hard Rock. I have a room."

He says he's on his way and hangs up.

A bit less than an hour goes by, and I hear a knock on my door. I open the door to see Sandro, who's three months past due a haircut.

"I'm sorry, man," I say immediately.

"Don't even worry about it. That wasn't you. I've said some messed-up things too. But we don't pick our friends for the wrongs they've done. We pick and stay with our friends because of everything they've done right."

"Woah. That was deep. Are you high or something? But, no. I really am sorry. I know it wasn't me, but I'm still responsible for everything."

"I have to ask…What happened that made you realize all this?"

I take a second to think about it myself and then answer, "I'm still not sure. I lost a lot of money last night, and when it happened, it kind of woke me up instantaneously. It literally took my breath away. It was like a car crash, when you almost die—it makes you reflect on your life, only for me it made me wake up."

He starts to nod and answers, "That's good. Not that you lost money, but that you are coming back to reality. How much did you lose? Last time I spoke with you, you had around fifty thousand dollars. How much do you have left? Forty-five?"

I stare at him, wishing I lived in a world like he did, where I was actually careful enough with everything I did.

"I lost it all, man. I don't know. If I think about it, I get mad."

He gives me a hug and tells me it's not the end of the world.

"So what are you doing here? Here to relax? Did you use the spa or something? Do you still get free rooms from playing here so much?"

"Listen. I'm here for the World Cup of Poker circuit event tomorrow. I'm using the little money I have left to buy in. I'm going to play for the first-place million-dollar prize, and I'm going to win it. Then I'm going to be done."

His expression instantly changes. "Are you kidding me? What's wrong with you? You finally realize and acknowledge that this lifestyle isn't good for you, yet you're here, at the Hard Rock. What does it take for you to learn? Maybe you do need a car crash!"

"Listen, man, tomorrow morning I'm going to start to play for a million dollars. I already bought in. I'm madder than you right now, trust me. I'm heartbroken; I have nothing left. I feel alone. I feel anxious. My mind is going crazy. I don't know what's happening to me, but what I do know is that I don't want to be alone anymore. I want to have my friends back. I miss you guys. I want my family back. I'm sorry I'm not the person I should be. I'm sorry I can't live up to my potential. But I need to know if you are with me or not? I need to know."

"Of course I am. You just can't keep doing this, though."

My heart is starting to beat fast after hearing myself talk about how I actually feel for the first time in what seems to be decades. I start to think about the game tomorrow and then as my heart accelerates simply by acknowledging my anxiety, I want to run. I want to get out of here. I want to get out of my body. My hands start to shake.

"Thanks for coming, man, but you should get out of here. I don't feel too well anymore. I'm getting anxious."

"Wait. Relax. Your problem is you think too much. You think you are responsible for everything negative that has ever happened to you, but that's not how life works. You're going to mentally kill yourself like this. Slow down, breathe. Literally, take ten deep breaths; close your eyes."

"Uh."

"Bro just listen to me."

I do what he instructs me to do, open to anything at this point.

"Okay, what now?"

"Just keep breathing. Slow down your breath."

I close my eyes, doubting his methods.

"Do you feel better?"

"I guess. Is this some type of placebo?"

"No. It's meditating. Focus on the breath. It will make you feel better— bring you back to a safe place. Are you feeling calm?"

I try to focus on the breath for a minute.

"I actually am, a little bit."

He tells me to lie down. "Okay, now get in a comfortable position. Be conscious of your breath. Think about everything on your agenda; think about everything that has happened to you. Think about the money you lost last night. Think about your tournament tomorrow. Be aware of everything on your mind. Now let it all go. You can't go back into the past or jump into your future, so worrying about it is useless. Focus on the only thing that matters—this moment, right here, right now. Let everything go, just be aware of your breath and of this moment."

I feel slightly better, taking long breaths.

He starts again. "Your mind is your best friend. Not your worst enemy. Whenever you feel anxious, you can always return to this state of mind; simply close your eyes and breathe."

I open my eyes slightly to look at him and answer, "This actually works. I feel like I can fall asleep for once. Is it always this easy?"

"That's a good question. It's very hard, actually. But like everything in life, it'll be easy at first. And then it will get hard before it gets easy again. You're not supposed to fall asleep, though. You're supposed to be conscious of your thoughts and focus on what's happening. If you want, you can meditate for some time and then gradually let yourself doze off, but try to clear the mind before it sleeps. What time is your event tomorrow?"

"I have to be downstairs by 10:00 a.m."

"Okay, I'll let you focus on your meditating. I'll stop by tomorrow morning before you go in."

"You know you can just sleep here if you want."

"I need to go home but I'll be back tomorrow."

I open my eyes again and look at him, and I really look. For the first time in months, I can actually look at someone and actually *see*. "Thanks for coming. I needed it."

I close my eyes again and focus. And it would be a lie to tell you that everything is fixed, just like that. But it wouldn't be a lie to tell you that my mind is clearing. I hear no voices.

This past year I have created a reality where I could lock myself in a poker table for weeks at a time. My days outside of the game went in double time because what was outside of the table was irrelevant at that point. Poker was everything to me because I didn't like what I felt outside of those rooms where I gambled thousands of dollars. My whole life, at least the part of my life I gave any attention to, was becoming the One Knight Stand. I wanted to live up to the faith some part of me had of becoming something better. Now I am going to play one last time to actually become better.

THIRTY-SIX

DAY ONE

I wake up at 9:00 a.m., and I realize I have slept all the way through the night. It's been a while since I've gotten a good night's sleep. I wake up actually feeling rested. Today is the day; today is the beginning of the end, hopefully leading to a new beginning. Got that?

I sit up on my bed and close my eyes, trying to remember what Sandro taught me. Long deep breath in, hold it, then exhale, repeat. I vocalize my thoughts in my head: *Today I want to finish the day in the top ten percent of the tournament. Today I won't feel anxious when playing. This tournament is the last time I do this. Today is my day.*

I eat something, shower, go to my backpack, and pull out the gear for the last time. The One Knight Stand classic: my black UCF hoodie, earphones, and some gum. It's time. No turning back. I look in the mirror, and I actually look at myself. I raise my chin a bit and take a second to pause. I'm ready. Two days ago I was only the One Knight Stand. But today, today I'm Charles Marquez. This tournament will be the end of my alter ego. I step outside and close my eyes one last time. Deep breath. I make my way downstairs and head to the room where the event is being held. Let's get this.

As I'm walking toward the event room, I feel a hand on my shoulder. I turn around to see Sandro. "How are you feeling?"

I had forgotten he was coming to see me before I went in.

"I'm okay. I'm ready; it's time."

He shakes my hand, pulls me in for a hug, and gives me his blessing. I walk toward the tournament sign-in.

"Good morning, sir. Player? Spectator?"

Player, baby. I'm a fucking player.

"What's the difference? Just kidding. Player."

I give him my name, hand him my ID and receipt before he tells me where my seat is. There is a ten-foot wooden door that leads to the tournament. This door in front of me separates sanity from my other world. On this side of the door I am Chuck, but as I walk in, I will be the One Knight Stand. If all goes as planned, I will be in there for the whole day. I stop right before I go in. Long and deep breath. *I can do this.*

As soon as I place my first step inside, I notice there are cameras covering every corner of the room, following players as they walk in. There are spectators, all behind ropes, trying to get a spot behind the tables where their favorite famous players are. I go to table eleven. Seat six. I sit down. Deep breath. The dealer gives me my chips. Twenty thousand to start. I look around the room a final time and then zone in to my table. You already know what I do—looking, hoping that I can spot the sucker within minutes completely terrified at the possibility that I don't find him like I haven't been able to in the last couple of weeks.

The tournament director gets on the microphone. "It's ten a.m., players. Dealers, shuffle up and deal."

The tournament has officially begun as the dealer distributes the first hand. Deep breath. The action gets to me, and I look at my cards: ace, nine of hearts. *Let's go.*

I don't know what's going to happen, my friend. I can be a millionaire in a week, or I can get knocked out any minute; I just have to play the cards the way I know how to. The only thing I can do is play my best poker and see what happens. I raise to five times the big blind. Everybody folds except one player. Flop: ace, king, king. He bets, I raise. He folds. It's going to be a good tournament. I need to focus, so I won't be talking to you much throughout the tournament. I'll make sure to give you live updates, though. Wish me luck (or don't)!

✦

It's two hours in, and I'm still here. I have a healthy chip stack, but that can change any second in a tournament. As I stretch my back and look down across the room, I see a familiar face. It's Lally. Remember that asshole? It's not uncommon to see professionals at these events. In fact, most people here *are* professionals, but I didn't expect to see him. But there he is, playing his game.

I can't help but think of all the different type of people here. And even though everybody at the table believes they are the best, here's the funny thing—players will play against each other, and in every move, there are at least two players. Meaning, every time two players are in a hand, and one makes a move, while the other responds, both believe they're move is astute. At least one has to be wrong. Everybody here has a different background, a different story. But everybody has the same goal—first place. Everyone thinks it'll be them but only one can do it.

✦

My stack is still strong. I'm playing conservative and taking care of my chips the best I can. I'm *conscious* that any move can very well be my last. But soon enough, it is 2:00 p.m.—time for the break. I get up and head toward the bathroom and then the buffet. Remember when I was first starting out, and I told you I had dreams of playing with the best players in the world? Well, they're all here. The moment has come. I eat slowly, taking my time. No earphones, I need to focus. I finish my food and find myself a quiet spot for a quick meditation. Deep breaths.

When I get back inside, they announce there are 556 players left of the original 650 plus. Only 555 players left to beat. Thirty minutes in, and I'm on the leaderboard—seventeenth place in the whole tournament. My table breaks eventually, and we are each assigned a new seat at one. I'm told to go to table nineteen, seat three. I walk my way over, and as I'm sitting down, on one end of the table, I look in front of me and see Daniel Ungur on the other end. "How's it going, kid?" he says to me as he notices me staring at him.

Another reminder of the intensity of this game, the best player in the world is on my table, directly in front of me.

"Going well."

I try to continue playing my game and focus on the cards and what I have to do. I know eventually there will be a hand where I get into it with Ungur, but for now I just have to focus. After a couple of hands of me sitting down, I look at my cards and see six, eight; I raise to six times the big blind in an attempt to steal the pot but get one caller. On the flop comes five, five, deuce. The one caller checks; I bet. He folds.

See, poker is easy. I look over to the leaderboard after some time and see my name has disappeared for the top twenty-five players of the tournament. But the thing with these tournaments is they're said to be a marathon. Tournaments take a long, long time to win. Big hands can essentially mean nothing. They seem glamorous on the outside and that's what you'll see on TV, but it's going to take hours and a lot of boring hands to win this one. And that's one more thing most people don't understand about poker.

The dealer deals a new hand, and I look down: king, nine, suited. I'm the third to act, and I call the blind. There's another call after me and then everyone folds until it gets to Daniel, who raises—this is what I was talking about; it's time. Everybody else folds, and it gets to me, and I think about it for a second—he's probably just using his name to scare people. I reraise him by tripling his bet. The next guy folds, so it's back on Ungur, and he just calls, staring at me like I've seen him stare at other players on TV. The flop ace, nine, three. I check; Daniel checks back.

There's a small possibility I'll be a millionaire in a week, and there's an even better possibility I'll be broke soon. But whatever happens I get to say that I played a hand with the best player in the world.

The turn: another nine; I bet fifteen thousand into a twenty-four thousand pot. Daniel raises to thirty-three. Here we go. What do I do? I'm pretty sure I have the best hand, but I'm playing against Daniel Ungur—one bad move, and I'm out; I have to tread lightly. I just call. The river: an ace.

I need some time to think. Daniel can very well have an ace, but if I check, I'll indirectly show I don't have one. If I bet, he can raise me, and I will have to call for my tournament life. If I make a big bet, maybe he'll just call. I slow down. Deep breath.

Or I can do this: "I'm all in."

Maybe this is a bluff, maybe it's a value bet, I'm not a hundred percent sure, but I guess we'll find out. Daniel steps out of his chair with obvious frustration.

"I know I am ahead until the river; of course another ace comes out!" he semiyells.

He looks at me trying to get a read. "Years ago, I would've have called instantly, saying that I'm mathematically already priced in. But I'm a different player now," he exclaims, still trying to get a read.

I look at him now. "What you got? King, nine, or something?"

He smirks, and he flips over his cards while folding. His cards: king, nine. Should I show my cards? Nah.

I keep playing my game, feeling confident. The table is mainly men around forty years old, Daniel being the oldest at the table, and next to me one of the few women in the tournament. It's been a couple of hours, and I find myself constantly around the average chip stack of the tournament. The board says there are 463 players left, and the dinner break is in twenty-one minutes.

✦

When I start to head to the bathroom, I am stopped by a woman with a microphone. "Hey, do you mind a quick interview?" she asks, her crew already filming.

"Sure."

"We're here with Charles Marquez, the youngest player at this circuit event. Charles is still in the tournament here on the second break of the day. Charles, how are you feeling? Is this your first tournament of this magnitude?"

"I'm doing pretty well. My goal is to always be above the average chip-stack size, and I've been doing that for the most part throughout the day, so I'm feeling good. And yes, this is the first WCOP tournament I have ever played—I usually play cash games, so I'm trying to play the best poker I can."

"Charles, we saw you were involved in a big hand with Daniel Ungur earlier, one of the best in history. How does that feel at your age? We don't know much about your history, but being just twenty years old, barely even legally allowed to play in this tournament, how did it feel to clash with one of the best?"

"It felt like a dream. When I first started playing poker, I would look at videos of Daniel playing and try to learn from him, so playing a big hand heads up against him was a bit surreal. Despite that, I had to ground myself and focus in order to really make the right move. It was a tough hand, but I ended up winning it. It was important for me to win, because if I can win a hand against him, I know I can win this tournament now, one hand at a time. But I'm not here to focus on him or any other names; I'm here to win."

"Thanks for taking a moment out of your break to talk with us, we hope to see more of you throughout the tournament."

"Thanks."

I make my way over to the buffet to get a plate of food and then go to a quiet spot, close my eyes and slow down my heart rate. Deep breath. I can do this.

✦

It's 9:00 p.m. now. It's been a full day of pure poker. One hour more to go. I look over to the board—just under four hundred left. I'm not on the screen, but I'm above the chip average by 15 percent. There are only around forty tables, and there are cameras around the room. I look down at my cards: seven, four. I'm ready to call it a day.

The tournament director announces that this will be the final hand of the day. I look at my cards: pocket deuces. I raise to six times the big blind; somebody with a short stack pushes all in. I fold.

Made it past day one.

You would think that the best part of winning all this is the satisfaction content one feels when they've had a good day playing poker—the going home and then being able to go out and celebrate all the money and being able to buy anything you want, eat wherever you want, drive any car you want. You would think that's the best part. You would think that I'm happy that all this stress is over at the end of the day. But going to my room for me is the hardest part. Because when the cameras are gone, when the huge stacks of chips aren't in front of me, when I go home—that's when I realize how alone I have been this past year.

Deep breath.

THIRTY-SEVEN

DAY TWO

I wake up on Saturday morning and immediately take ten minutes to meditate. Deep breaths. I can do this. I shower, grab my gear, and make my way downstairs, heading to the same table.

The tournament director comes on. "Players, it is now ten a.m., Saturday. Three hundred and fifty players left. There will be two breaks today like there were yesterday. Day two will continue until there are a hundred players left. In the unlikely event that there are only a hundred players before 10:00 p.m., the tournament shall pause and resume tomorrow morning when there will be cameras on each table. Good luck everybody. Dealers, shuffle up and deal."

Deep breath.

I am big blind on the first hand of the day. Ungur, under the gun, just calls; there are two more callers including the small blind. When the action gets to me, I look down at pocket aces. I take my time, observe the other players, and raise to five times the big blind. Only one person folds, three to the flop. The flop comes: two, three, ten, rainbow. Perfect flop for me. I look around, and after the small blind checks, I bet the size of the pot. Action gets to Ungur, and he raises me all in. Everybody folds, action back to me. *What do I do now?* If I make this call and lose, I will be down to only about fifteen big blinds. I don't have much in the pot, but the board is pretty dry. Only thing that really beats me is pocket tens. Unless he has pocket tens or two pair, I think I'm good. I started with the best possible hand in poker, and got a really good flop. I *should* make this call, straightaway. If there's one player in the world that called with two, three suited to my big blind raise, it's Daniel Ungur, though. Deep breath.

I shake my head and let the cards go. It's not worth it. I have no room for mistakes; I have to be sure of each one of my decisions. I'll get the chips back soon.

I just folded pocket aces on a two, three, ten rainbow flop—something I wouldn't have done a month ago. But a month ago, I wasn't ready; now I am ready.

As time goes by, the room is slowly but surely shrinking. I look over to the leaderboard: eleven thirty, 291 players left, two hours until the next break. My hand: pocket jacks. I call a raise, and so do four other players. Five players to the flop: jack, queen, three. I check, trying to slow roll, and to my shock, everybody else does too. Next card: king. I make an oversized bet, trying to get anybody on a draw off the hand, but I get two callers. The river: ace. I have to check; someone bets, and I flex my whole body in disgust and throw away my hand. Another big hand I have to fold. My chip stack is now well below the average.

✦

I am able to make it to the break, and as I am leaving the room, I'm asked for another interview. I nod, feeling a bit discouraged at this point.

"Here again with Charles on day two, still the youngest player in the tournament. As there are fewer and fewer players here, others are forced to take you more seriously. How does it feel to be the youngest player at a tournament like this?"

"It feels okay. I'm not really focused on what others think of me. When the cards are dealt, it doesn't matter who's sitting across from you or what their story is—you just have to play some top-notch poker. If I can, I try to use their perception of how they think I play and use it to my advantage. But, for the most part, I'm simply trying to play my cards right, and every hour I'm thinking about making it to the next."

"You're twenty years old. There's still two hundred and forty-three players left, but if you do win, you will be the youngest player in history to win a millionaire maker. It's still a very long road, but if you do win that payout of a million dollars, how will you use it?"

"You're right, it is a very long way down the road. Like I said before, I'm just trying to focus on getting to the next level every time. To answer your question though, I would use the money to right a lot of wrongs I have made and probably stop playing. But right now my goal is to make it to tomorrow to the final hundred players."

"Charles, Marquez, currently two hundredth place of the Hollywood, Florida, World Cup of Poker circuit event. Thank you for talking to us."

"Yep."

I get some food and skip the meditation this time. I sit down and think to myself. The competition is starting to get tougher and tougher. Players are getting eliminated at a faster pace, as people want to make day three with a healthy chip stack.

I hear the warning alarm and return to the table and put my earphones on, trying to focus. I need to get a big hand quick. But after I have a couple of small wins, I look down: *bullets* (and by this point I hope that you at least have done a bit of poker research. I mean, this book isn't *about* poker, but it makes it a lot more fun to know what I'm talking about. Or are you reading this part and not understanding what is happening? Anyway, bullets mean I have pocket aces). I raise to three times, trying to get a reraise so that I can push all in and collect the pot preflop. But a smaller stack reraises me his all in. Everybody folds, I call. He shows his cards: jacks. The flop: eight, three, queen. My heart is beating a bit faster. Turn: nine—making me sweat it. River: four.

✦

It's hours later, and I've been going slightly up and down but staying within a healthy range. There's an old guy with round eyeglasses and a curled mustache to my right who looks like he's played enough to write fifteen of these books. He looks like he's been rich and poor. He looks like he's fallen in love twice but been married three times. Synonyms. Anyway, he's being the table aggressor and winning the most hands. I'm waiting for the right moment to get him, like always. A couple of hands later, he raises to three and a half times the big blind. I look down at my cards: four, five of diamonds.

Let's have some fun. I call, out of position. Heads up. Flop: seven, eight, jack. Two diamonds. I check; he bets. I raise without thinking twice. He looks flustered, hesitates, and makes the call. The turn, another jack. I check immediately; he checks back. The turn: three of diamonds. Bingo.

I bet the size of the pot. He takes a second but calls and shows: ace, jack. He's not going to like this one. I show my flush. He looks like he just caught me fucking his girlfriend. He loses a good portion of his stack, and, as you can imagine, he is not happy.

He instantly becomes aggressive in the next hand. Here I am, thinking this guy was good, but he's on tilt now. Meaning, he's making the most rookie mistake you can make as a player—letting your past affect your future. He is making stupid decisions now, as he's mad at getting unlucky. And just like that, he becomes the sucker at the table. I just have to wait for the right position again. I try to be patient and focus without depending on him. But he's the sucker. I know it.

More bad, stupid moves, and he's down to thirty big blinds. He eventually goes all in; I look at my cards: pocket eights. I call. He shows ace, king. Flop: all low cards. Turn: still nothing for him. And on the river, he stands up and walks away.

Playing against this old guy, who was the only major threat at the table, I know now it's a good thing I'm not going to play anymore once I win this tournament. I don't want to be that old guy at the table when I'm his age. It's like being the only twenty-something-year-old at the high-school party. We've all seen that elderly person at the poker table trying to win back what he's lost his whole life. And I don't want that to be me because eventually the old players will resort to their younger ways—they will complain about bad beats and make stupid plays. Just because poker isn't a physical sport doesn't mean you can play forever. One's game will always get saturated. But here's the funny thing—we're all the same at the table, in terms of poker. We've all gone through the same stages—playing aggressive when we first start, then chasing, then being naïve, finally being conservative, and eventually back to being aggressive; a mature player has done the same mistakes as most at the table; some people just never learn or outgrow some stages, so they stay.

✦

At the second break of the day, there are 160 players left. The closer I get, the more nervous and anxious I start to feel. But I can also feel the money! After the break I get back to my table and take my earphones off. I'm ready to make it to the final day. I look around, and everybody seems to have the same determination as me. How do you win when you're playing against players who all want it as much as you? My first hand, I make a bluff and get called. Crap.

These are the best players I've ever played against, and my normal strategy isn't working that much anymore. I have to play even better than what I'm used to. I need to know what they think I know and then use it to my advantage. Because at the end of the day, poker is about doing what you know will work considering what your opponent thinks he knows about you, because of what you know about him that he knows you know. You know?

Everyone left here has been training for a while and wants to become a millionaire in a week just like me. Some are already millionaires who just want more. I want to win this, but the reality is that it takes more than skill to win these things. I'm starting to doubt myself. I'm getting worried. The rest of the players here are the best in the world. I don't know if I can do this. What if I don't win? What if I really do lose all my money in a week? What will I do? It's all on the line this time, and I really don't know what to do anymore.

A couple of hands down the road, I turn to the leaderboard, hoping the day ends, as I desperately need a break. My mind is entirely drained. I start to look around the table and spot a sucker. I start to bite down. My heart is starting to race. *No! This can't be happening right now. I love my mind; it's my best friend, not my worst enemy,* I tell myself. *Take a deep breath.* I don't know if I can do this. I'm having a hard time controlling my breathing. I can't seem to focus on the cards. *How am I going to do this?* Should I try to be aggressive and hope for the best? I don't know. I'm starting to bite on my knuckle. I need to get out of here. I can't sit here and pretend that meditating has completely healed me; it has helped, but I'm starting to fidget. The truth is that my biggest problem is my mind. Part of me wants to stay true to myself, but I have two different voices constantly arguing inside of me, and I can never seem to just listen to one. And each time I feed one, the other suffers. I can't be at peace.

I hate my mind; I feel trapped inside. The stress is so heavy. It's tough, you know, with your emotions going up and down for hours without end. I'm just a kid. Is it normal to be afraid of my own thoughts? God, I wish I had never started this stupid life. But the prize is so close. Fuck this shit.

I don't think I can handle this right now.

THIRTY-EIGHT

ALL OR NOTHING

"Charles? Charles, are you there?"

I focus my eyes on where the voice is coming from, my heart still pounding.

"What? Yeah. What was the question?" I ask the woman with the microphone.

"You've made the final day of the tournament. How does it feel to be part of the final hundred players?"

I am trying to understand what has happened within the last couple of hours.

"Yeah."

"Okay, the tournament is going to be live on television tomorrow— how will this affect the way you play?"

"I'm not sure."

"Cut the interview," she says, turning to the camera guy.

"You okay, Charles? You look like you're about to faint."

"Sorry, I'm just a bit tired I guess."

I find myself opening the door to my room and heading straight toward the bathroom, opening the toilet, bending over, and throwing up. I can't do this anymore. I don't want to. I knew this wouldn't be easy, but I thought the pain endured would at least make sense. Fuck this shit. It's not worth it. I thought I could look ahead to a brighter point. I walk to my balcony and open the door and stand outside. I look down at the pool from my nineteenth-floor suite. I take a step onto the railing and position both my feet over it. My heart starts to beat even faster. Tears run down from my eyes without me being able to do anything about it careful not to move my hands. I think about slowly letting go, wishing I never played poker. I wish I had never started this. I never thought it'd get this far; I never wanted this. I never pictured success to be alone in a hotel room. I never thought I'd be so fucking emotional. What did I do wrong?

Maybe I shouldn't have been the funny kid growing up. Maybe I should've been honest not only with other people and the possibility of not really being *okay* but also with myself and my own incongruences. Maybe I seemed to be glowing throughout school and was always able to say something witty and funny, but in reality I was just a self-conscious nerd who never understood what it meant to be cool. And maybe now I am starting to think about where I went wrong—what decisions I made in my life that led to this moment where I see the floor and am attracted to the possibility that loosening my grip would bring, while consciously admitting that only fucked up people dance with the idea of being more depressed or fucked up in order to relieve their immediate pain and realizing this only starts the hamster wheel again.

I think about this as the rest of the world continues because nothing in the universe was ever or will ever be waiting for me. I think these thoughts, that in themselves are already killing me, while Macoa is happy without me, while Sandro is in his room meditating, and while my mom is walking my dog. I think about my past and my future in an attempt to make a decision about my present while the writer stops writing this book toward the middle because he realizes that even though he worships honesty and transparency he hasn't figured out how to be honest with himself and ends up feeling like a fraud. One day *he* realizes he likes the idea of who he is but not really himself because he is almost a good writer but not one. I am almost good with girls but can never talk to the one I actually like, and I am almost funny and cool but definitely not, because how could I be funny if I'm never smiling when I'm alone and people think I'm weird, and how could I be cool if I'm busy telling you a story about never being happy? I am almost a real person, but in reality only an outline of my own vivid imagination that doesn't have any value outside of my head. Maybe I knew from the moment I could actually think that something deep down was fundamentally off about me and have spent my whole life trying to silence the voices in my head as I imagine that I have to be part of some type of science experiment and later in life realized everybody in the world thinks they are different, making us all part of a universal club or egocentric, unwise, nonprofound, one-grain-of-sand-in-a beach type of people who lack the ability to come to grips with being wrong. Maybe I feel like I can never please anybody, especially myself and have spent my whole life playing catch-up. Maybe I wish that for once in my life my mind would just be quiet, if I could just once have a regular thought, not a *how do I prove to myself that I am better than everybody else.* And, maybe, just maybe, I try my best to either be a really funny guy who gets along with everybody, or that guy who plays poker and is an asshole, but can't seem to do either. Maybe I realize this now and think it might be too late, that I'm so in tune to change because that's all I have other than the other ugly possibility.

I carefully put my feet back onto the safe side of the railing and make my way to my bed, crawl up into a ball, and try to breath slower. I look up at the ceiling as my imaginary reflection looks down at me, almost as if to say "How did we get here?" I grab my phone and set the alarm clock for tomorrow morning and close my eyes.

✦

I wake up short of breath and panting. It wasn't just a dream. It has never been a dream. Thank you for listening last night. I'm happy I still have you.

I try to breathe again and get ready for the third day of this tournament and make my way downstairs. Same thing as the other days—sign in, head to my table. Take deep breaths, tell myself I can do this. Only ninety players left to go until the final table. There are cameras covering every angle of the room now.

Cards are shuffled and dealt. First hand: nothing, fold. Second hand: nothing again, fold. Third hand: something but too much of a raise before me, fold. Then, ten, jack, suited, I just call, small hand, win. Nothing too exciting happening, just playing my game waiting for this to be over. I don't like doing this anymore. I want to go home.

I make it to the break. Seventy-eight players left. I'm in second place of the whole tournament; they want an interview again.

"Charles, you seemed to be out of it last night after the grueling, full day of poker where you had some ups and downs and were even short stacked and close to being out at some points. But you were able to impressively recover after everyone thought you were gone. After getting into your zone and hitting a hot-streak, you managed to end the day as one of the top ten. So we're wondering how does yesterday's roller coaster of events affect you today?"

"Look, since the moment I knew I was going to play this tournament, I had one goal—first place. I'm not here to have fun, I'm not here for the experience, I'm not here for the cameras, and I'm not here to make the final table. I'm here to win, and I'm going to do that regardless of what is thrown at me."

"What is your strategy coming into the final day here?"

"Well, like I said, I'm not here to get camera time or even to get to the final table. I came here to win. I will take advantage of players who are playing tight, and I will put myself in a situation where I can constantly be well above the average chip stack. I just hope the day goes by quick. It's been a long weekend."

I make my way toward the buffet area and try to meditate and get my heart rate to slow down. I'm pretty sure if I have another episode like yesterday, I'll have a heart attack. When I hear the announcement that the break is over, I go to the bathroom and then make my way back to my table.

By now, there are only eight tables left, and seventy-eight players total—hundred and ninety thousand chip-stack average. There are three featured tables, where there are actual sitting areas for fans, and five regular tables. The featured tables are the ones that hold the most famous or notable players. These include characters like Daniel Ungur, Phil Lally, Daniel Coleman, and one I don't know, all of whom I actually like except for Lally.

I still remember trying to meet Lally and what he said to me.

Give up now and don't waste your time.

Of course, he doesn't remember me, but I remember. To finalize the last thought, notable players include any that the cameras liked to be around. These players include big trash-talkers, the only girl left in the tournament, the youngest player by far (yours, truly), etc. I am still on the leaderboard at ninth place and am trying to play small pots to not get into too much trouble. I don't have any pros at my table, but the girl and one of the trash-talkers are here. You can never tell what's happening with girls when they play; I won't explain why, but you can never be sure with the females.

Next hand: king, five of diamonds. Most players play really tight toward this part of the tournament, as they want to secure a spot at the final table. Consequently, I am trying to abuse my big stack by opening most pots in an attempt to collect the blinds that are at thousand, two thousand with a hundred ante. I raise to thirty-five hundred. Only the girl calls. Here we go. Flop: three, six, jack. She checks; I check back. Turn: queen. I still have king-high. She checks; it's time to pull the trigger. I bet thirty-seven. She raises to nine thousand. Fuck, didn't see that one coming. I take a few seconds and try to read her. I can't call here; it's fold or reraise bluff. On this board, she is probably thinking the same thing I am. Either she had a big hand preflop and didn't hit or she has nothing.

Let's see what she's got. "Raise to twenty-eight thousand," I announce.

She takes a second and eventually folds. And as soon as she does, I hear a roar from the fan section. *Who could possibly be cheering for me?* I look over to see who's making the noise. And to my surprise, I see some familiar faces—my parents, my brother, Sandro, Charlie, and other friends. *Why are they here? Am I seeing things?* I haven't seen Charlie or my family in months, and only Sandro knew I was here.

I can't do much about it right now, though, as the cards are still being dealt. I have to wait for the break, which is in a couple of hours. But I look over to them and make a heart with my hands. It's incredible how some people don't give up on you. What am I going to tell my mom, though? How can I explain all this to her? I can't think about this now, I have to focus the next couple of hours.

✦

Players' chip stacks keep getting bigger as they eliminate others. Eight tables turn into seven and then seven turn into six. I look over to the board. Forty players left in total, break in twelve minutes. I'm not in the top nine.

I play some hands, and right before the break I climb to ninth place. The tournament director gets on the microphone. "Players, you will have an hour for the break. This will be the last one of the tournament. When you come back, we will play until we have the final nine."

I head straight to the rail where Lance and Brent have joined the rest of my fans.

"This is why you have been so quiet lately?" my mom asks as I near the fan section.

"I'm sorry. It's not what I meant to do. What are you guys doing here?"

My dad answers now saying, "Your brother saw you on TV. We came to support. You have some explaining to do later, but right now just focus on winning."

I am starving so I tell them to follow me to the buffet.

"I'm sorry, guys," I say.

"No time for that right now. Like your dad said, focus on winning. Besides, when we each get ten thousand dollars, we'll forgive you," says Charlie.

"Ha."

It feels good to have my family and friends with me here, makes me feel as if I'm not in this alone. Like the weight isn't all on my shoulders.

But it also adds to the pressure, as I want them to see me win. It's time to make it to the final table now. Once I make it, I can take a week's break to analyze my life and meditate on this last year.

After the break, which I use to mainly clear my mind, I sit down and take a deep breath. The final push. Still forty players left, five tables.

✦

It's 7:00 p.m. now. Three tables left. My stack is a bit below average at about four hundred thousand chips. Every time I'm in a big hand, I can feel my supporters looking on anxiously, and when I win hands, they cheer from the bleachers. Now, the girl is still at my table, but Ungur has joined. Lally is still in, but Coleman has been knocked out.

I can't afford to lose a big hand. In fact, I'm in desperate need of a big win to push me back above average. Next hand: two, three. I fold. Not the time for me to be getting garbage. Next hand: more garbage. I really need something now. The blinds are going up, and the antes will eat my stack if I don't make a move. Next hand: five, six, different suit. I have to take it. I raise the five thousand blind to twenty-five thousand. Only the girl calls. Flop: six, six, ace.

There we go. I need to extract the most chips I can from her. She checks; I check back, slow playing. The turn: jack. I hope she has an ace and a jack or at least one. She checks, I bet, she raises.

Déjà-vu?

I reraise. She pushes all in. I call, with my slightly bigger stack. I know she doesn't have a six or a full house—she wouldn't have gone all in otherwise. She flips over her cards: ace, jack. I show my cards. *Sorry, buddy.* River: king. Good-bye, girl. Hello, above-average chip stack.

✦

Ten o'clock now. Eleven players left. Average chip stack is 1.2 million; blinds are ten and twenty thousand. They have us all on one table now. Me, one trash-talker, Ungur, and Lally are the most notable players left. My stack is below a million, but I'm only two players from getting to the final table. Wait. Somebody just got knocked out—ten left. My heart races, not from anxiety this time, but out of excitement. One more player, and I will be in the final table.

Next hand: ten, eight of clubs. I raise to thirty thousand. Trash-talker and one more player call. I'm in midposition, trash-talker acting before me. I know I don't do a great job in describing the people who are around me, so here you go. Trash-talker is a darker-skinned older guy. He looks like he doesn't give a crap about you and has big black headphones wrapped around his head, which is a bit inefficient, as he spends most of his hands talking. He is bald, and he just sees the flop: ten, seven, eight. I have the best two pair, and he just bet twenty thousand. He probably hit a ten. I raise to fifty thousand. The other guy folds. Back to the trash-talker, he takes his headphones off and stares at me. "What are you doing, kid? You don't want to reraise again, trust me."

I stare back. "This is your moment to shine. Your buddies are over at the bleachers looking at you. You hit you ten, right?"

And then I hear the two words that make me instantly shut my eyes; the only two words you don't want to hear when you don't have the nuts in a tournament, especially when you are inches from the final table; the two words that mean everything in this game— "All in," he says.

My eyes remain closed for some seconds. I have too many chips in the pot to fold this hand. Time for some analysis. I'll let you hear what's inside my mind when I do this: *Let's see, he's the big blind, so he can essentially have any two cards. He's a wild player, which makes the situation a bit tougher. But he didn't raise preflop, he just called. No pocket pair. What beats me in this hand? Only trips or a straight. There are no flush possibilities on board. So why did he make the initial raise? If he flopped a straight, he wouldn't have done that. Now, he might have trips. But which trips? He doesn't have pocket tens; he would've reraised preflop. The probability of him having the last two eights in the deck are slim. Sevens? Would he reraise me with a set of sevens? That doesn't make sense to me. What does he think I have? I raised preflop. He can never put me on ten, eight. He thinks I have ace, ten, maybe? Or maybe he's the one who thinks I have pocket sevens. Making this call is for my tournament life, if I have a better hand, I put myself on the top of the leaderboard with a pass to the final table. If I lose, it's over.*

I look over to him; he looks back. "I'm ahead of you; I got it," he says.

I take a deep breath. The dialog in my mind continues, *This can potentially be the biggest decision of my life. What is he representing here? He's representing a straight, maybe a set, but I doubt he has a one. It's a semibluff; he's either open ended or he just has one pair. Or he has bottom two.*

No!

He has ten, seven: two pair. That's it! I know it; he has to have that. He went all in because he was priced in and wanted me to fold, knowing most players are playing too tight. It's not a bluff; it's a value bet.

I look at him and grin. I think I have him. I'm still nervous, even though I'm fairly certain I have a better hand. I can still be wrong. But you know what, I'm not here to survive; I'm here to win. I push my chip stack in front of me, indicating a call. He flips over ten, seven.

"There we go!" I yell out.

I slam my cards on the table. My heart is about to jump out of my throat. I jog to the railing where my family is, and Lance grabs my shoulder. "Whatever happens, that call was sick."

Turn: not a seven. One more card to go.

River: not a seven!

This one is for everybody out there who says poker isn't a game of skill. My mom hugs me as she cries tears of joy. Every single fan except for trash-talker's is now cheering and hugging as everybody else realizes they've made the final table. Everybody's family and friends are hugging their players, some are crying, and some are taking pictures.

We did it; the final nine is set.

My name is Charles Marquez, and in one week, I will start the final table of the South-Florida WCOP circuit event where I will have a chance to become a millionaire at the age of twenty. Oh, and by the way, I'm going in as the chip leader.

Anxiety is the worst of all. It demands to be felt and doesn't let you live your ordinary life. It makes you want to throw up whenever you can feel your heart. You feel as if you can never live in peace; you feel as if there's always something to worry or be scared about. It's like always being chased by something but never having time to turn around and see what it is. You go to sleep with your mind racing, and you wake up the same way—it restrains you from resting. It's something that seems to follow you throughout the day. It's a literal cold feeling in your chest as your heart is always trying to catch up with something that doesn't exist.

PART V
MEDITATION

THIRTY-NINE

AMENDS

SIX DAYS UNTIL FINAL TABLE

Following the tournament, I'm being asked to give a quick interview. For the last time in South Florida, I speak to the woman with the microphone and head back toward the lobby. I step into the elevator, walk to my room, and race to pack my bags and get ready to rest for a week at my house. I don't want to go out and celebrate; I want to relax and try to fix my life this week. It's time to start apologizing for the monster I have been to people. First off is my family.

I drive home with my dad coming in my car with me. When I get home I immediately collapse on my bed.

Next thing I know, it's morning, and I walk downstairs for breakfast; my family has already been awake for hours. I get to the table; my three-and-a-half (don't forget about my dog) family members are all looking at me.

"Time for some explaining," my mom says to me.

"What do you want to know?"

"Don't be a smartass."

"Well…it all started during the summer when I used to play the twenty-dollar entry tournaments. Remember those? Well, I won the first one…"

I tell my family the full story, leaving out unneeded details and they obviously forgive me and take me back in with open arms, but it will take a while to get my friends. I am going to spend the first two days inviting Charlie, Sandro, Brent, Lance, and others to lunch and apologize, explaining to them that it was never my intention to do the things I did. It will take some time, but they will eventually be understanding, I hope.

✦

Tuesday night now, I and the same friends and more are going out to celebrate the win. We start at 10:00 p.m. at Sandro's house, where we begin to drink with some girls. It's me whom we are celebrating, but I have no intention of getting drunk. Drinking right now is probably not a great decision. I am just sitting here, thinking. *I have made it to the final table, but the biggest test of my life is still waiting. I have to beat Lally, Ungur, and six other hopefuls to be a millionaire.* I know I have some days before I play, and I know I'm supposed to be focused on my friends right now, but I can't help think about what's to come.

At around midnight we get into an Uber and make our way to Fort Lauderdale. Once we get there, we find our way inside a packed club where everybody drinks, talks, and dances. Everybody makes their way to the densely packed dancefloor while I stand in the edge of the crowd because all I can think about is the storm that's to come next week. Don't worry, no table or bottle service this time. I also can't help but think that about a month ago I had a hundred grand to my name; now I have virtually nothing if I don't win in a week. I know I've said this before, but this is a whole new level; I never would've thought I would make it here. Not in my wildest dreams did I ever imagine playing for a million dollars.

My heart rate speeds up; I start to sweat. Have you ever been to a crowded bar while sober? Not the most fun thing in the world. I'm trying to relax, but I don't want to be in this bar right now. I'm feeling anxious being in the middle of so many people. I want to get out of here and run; the last place I want to be right now is in the middle of this crowd with people looking at me not doing anything. I know nobody actually cares about what I'm doing, but I feel as if I have a million eyes on me right now. But for the first time since my anxiety has started, I just kind of laugh. I guess I acknowledge that my troubles are very real to me, but I am alive; I am doing what I wanted to do since I was kid. Yeah I'm fucked up, yeah I'm going crazy in my head, but at least I'm doing me. I'm at a bar in South Florida a week away from playing with the best in the world—I got nothing to complain about.

I decide one drink won't hurt. I walk over to the bar and ask the bartender for some rum and coke and lean against the edge observing the crowd. And as I'm looking out into the rest of the dancefloor, I notice in front me is some kid handing over a car key and a bag of cocaine to his friend.

"I've never done this before, man," the kid's friend says as he looks at the key with white powder.

His friend shrugs his shoulders.

I look to my right, and some other guy can't shut up and keeps offering his opinion on the stock market to the people he is with. To my left is another douche trying his best to talk to a brunette girl. I guess everybody has their own problems, but we all come to the bar in an attempt to relieve them.

Soon, one of my not-so-close friends comes up to me. "Why aren't you with us, over there?" he asks.

"I'm just trying to take a break. I'll be over there in a second."

"Hey, man, I know what it feels like, the position you are in."

"What are you talking about?"

What is he talking about, though? He doesn't *know* about the position I am in.

"No, you're not. You were never like this, standing by yourself. We were talking, you know, me and everyone else, and we thought that you shouldn't stop playing poker. The solution isn't to just cut it off from your life. You should just know how to control yourself, how to be disciplined…"

I zone out as he keeps talking. When I realize he's finished, I say, "I'll be over there in a second."

Then the guy beside me who is trying to flirt with the girl grabs my shoulder. "Hey, I am trying to bring this girl home. Do you think she's interested? I'm too drunk to tell."

I look over to the girl, who smiles back at me; I half smile back. My heart starts to race again. I wasn't used to even looking at girls with confidence before becoming the One Knight Stand. I zone out again.

I think about what is to come. *Can I do it?* More importantly, what if I don't? I don't want to go back to being broke. I don't want to do other things for money. I don't want to be evil again. Without giving too much thought to it, I take out my phone and open the Internet to search "Mexton therapist." I need somebody to just listen to what's going on inside my brain, I decide. I get too many results, so I search "addiction, therapists, Mexton." I get more specific results; I look at different ones, but I try to find a female. A woman therapist would be more cliché, right? I find Dr. Tavoularis. Click. "I specialize in addiction therapeutic counseling…" click. Send inquiry, click.

"Hello, Dr. Tavoularis, I found your contact information online. I would like to schedule a session if I could. I've always been one to run away from my problems. Before I would do it with humor; now I do it with poker. I've had a rough year and need to talk to somebody. I keep overthinking this, so I'm going to send the message before I change my mind. I need to see and talk to you. Are you available tomorrow morning? This past year..." I try to include details including Macoa, drugs, and poker. Send.

Again, the guy next to me grabs me, too drunk to be trying to take anybody home. "What do you think?"

I look over again to the girl, who for some reason is still here. She laughs this time. "You got this," I confirm.

I take another sip of my drink and walk out of the bar.

Everybody around me keeps offering his or her opinions on my problems, and everybody around me has problems too. But I acknowledge that this mess is mine, and their mess is theirs.

FORTY

ELLA

THREE DAYS UNTIL FINAL TABLE

I open my eyes, grateful I didn't drink last night, and reach over to my phone to check the time—10:09 a.m. The first thing I do is check my e-mails for a reply from the shrink. I find one. "Hey, Charles. I think I can help with your situation. I'm booked in the morning, but I have an opening around three in the afternoon. Answer to the e-mail before noon, and I'll be able to squeeze you in."

I know I can't continue shutting down my thoughts. I need someone to tell how I am feeling; I need someone to know what is going on in my mind and be able to explain some of the things I can't. It's time to understand what this all means.

♣

Fifteen minutes before 3:00 p.m., I walk into the therapist's office. I think about turning around. *What am I doing here? Do I really need a shrink? This is ridiculous, being in this office.* I have been sitting down for a couple of minutes, but I'm leaving. I don't like the idea of this anymore. This feels weird. I'll just tell her I couldn't make it. I head toward the door. But just as I am about to tell the receptionist I have to leave, a beautiful woman walks out. "Hello, Charles?"

"Yes?"

"My name is Ella; you can follow me into my office."

She looks European, like a girl who has spent her life eating the best foods, traveling the world, and lying on the beach, like she has the superpower to make anybody fall in love with her but has never used it. I don't know if there's a God, but if there is, she was created in God's image. Okay, you get it. I am going to stay.

I sit down as she welcomes me in.

"So, Charles, I read what you sent me. It seems like you've had quite the interesting year."

"Yes. I really appreciate you seeing me on such a short notice. I know you're busy so thank you for squeezing me in. Also you can call me Chuck."

"Yeah. No Problem. Okay, Chuck. Your year. Eventful?"

I have forgotten for a second why I am even here. I don't feel like opening up to this woman I have never met right away. She is beautiful, but I am not ready to talk yet. "You can say that," I finally answer.

"Do you want to tell me about it?"

I was so sure I wanted somebody to talk to last night. But being honest becomes much harder during the daytime.

"Uh, well, I made more than a hundred thousand dollars playing poker in less than a year; then I lost it all in less than a week. I've been thinking about writing a book about it; maybe you can buy my book when it comes out next holiday season."

Why am I being an ass right now?

"I'm sure I will, but I need you to tell me how you're feeling now, about all this."

I am so used to talking to people the same way I have these past months; I don't mean to be a smartass. She is a therapist, and I assume she can see through me, but I am still not even sure where to start.

"I'm not sure how I feel; I don't know what you expect me to say. I want help, but I don't know exactly what I need."

She then asks me to tell her what I have learned from this whole experience.

"Well, Ella, I learned that poor people usually don't have any fun stories to tell," I reply as I chuckle.

What am I doing? She cleared up her schedule to see me and I am being an idiot.

"Okay…Well you said you wanted me to help, so here it is—I think you joke around because you don't want to be serious and have to face your reality. You're scared of who you really are sometimes and of your real thoughts and real pain, so you put on this persona as an attempt to escape all of it, or at least ignore it. It started off with being a clown when you were younger; now it has transitioned to poker and other activities to keep your mind off what's real."

"What are you, a therapist?"

She stares back at me, pretending she doesn't think I am funny.

"What do you want me to say? I just want to feel something when I go home rather than feeling empty. I don't know what you want me to tell you, I really don't. This is why I'm here. Aren't you the one who's supposed to do the talking? I feel alone, and it's an intense and cold feeling. It's getting better, because I'm starting to feel like myself again, after I'm back with my family and friends. But I'm terrified that regardless of what I do, I'm going to feel alone and sad. I feel so much anxiety when I think about being alone; it's a cruel feeling that builds on itself. That's all I got to say; you read the e-mail I sent you, so I guess I'm just repeating myself."

"I understand, Chuck, but saying it aloud will help you analyze this. Just tell me what you've learned; let's start there. Tell me how you have changed, what this whole experience has done to you. Focus on what you learned."

"Sure. Well, I guess I learned a lot about myself and the world through this beautiful and incredibly ugly experience."

I am taking long pauses between all my sentences. I am talking slow, trying to figure out what to even say.

"I've learned that you always have to account for change in life. Nothing goes as planned. Nobody asks for their life to change like this, but it does.

"I've learned that everything is temporary; nothing is forever. And that being attached to something and relying on your happiness on anything exterior is dangerous. I know all this is very cliché, but it took me a while to learn. I've learned that I am as lonely as I let myself be, and being lonely is my choice. Even though I still feel this emptiness at times, I know it's up to me to change that. I have myself, and that's all I'll ever have, and I need to learn that that's all I will ever need. Regardless of where I am in the world, and what situation I am in, I will always have myself, and I need to get to a point where that should be enough."

She isn't saying anything, so I keep going. "I've learned the true meaning of making a mistake and the consequences that go along with it. I've learned that every action has an effect and causes another action, and that I am not the only one affected by my mistakes. I've also learned that some who were closest to me were the ones who didn't want me to succeed the most, at times which really confuses me."

I pause and look at her, and really it's been sometime since I actually just watched someone. For the first time in about a year, I look at a person, for a person. I'm not looking at a player trying to decipher what his or her hand is. I'm not looking at a girl in a club trying to get in her pants. I am just looking; you know? Maybe I *am* done; maybe I *am* back to being Charles Marquez. And damn do I look at her.

"Ella, your hands are the most beautiful hands I've ever seen."

I can't tell if I actually think this, or it is the fact that I haven't actually tried to genuinely see a girl in some time. She is beautiful, though, everything about her. Her hair, the way she talks, her skin, especially her hands—something about her hands. It's refreshing.

Before she can say anything, I continue, "I told you that I am as lonely as I let myself be, but I'm still alone. I guess I've learned that I'm, well, *alone* in this world. You know? Nobody *actually* cares about me. I can die tomorrow, and the world wouldn't change. Maybe my friends would talk about me for some days or a week, but that's it. Their life would go on; the world would keep spinning. The universe isn't waiting for me, and I'm just one of billions of people on this planet, not more important than the next. I'm such an insignificant part of something much bigger. The universe wasn't ever talking to me specifically through this whole experience. Any push or pull I felt was just a reaction of a push or a pull I put out into the universe.

"I've really learned that we, or at least I, romanticize things too much. As a teenager I had this big problem where I would romanticize and plan most of life and was really good at planning how I wanted my life to happen, but not very good at actually living. I was a victim of this way of thinking, and as a result, I was always disappointed and failed to live in the present moment. I also failed to realize that my life was perfect through the imperfections. I know I'm getting off topic, but, anyway, I paint this picture in my head about myself and life, and it's just not true. My life isn't a movie, and I'm only a main character in my own head, and I have to be okay with that. I'm insignificant to the rest of the universe. Sounds depressing and scary. But it's true, and it gives me a bit of hope, in a twisted way. I feel so scared yet free knowing this now."

"When do you think you lost sight of reality?"

"I'm not sure. It was a slow process. I didn't wake up one day and say I wanted to be an asshole. I was shaped into it by my surroundings. Being an ass was the only way that I would get the things I thought I needed. Having that money was wild, but that was the problem—I was an addict, nothing more. What made it worse was the fact that it was a sick type of addiction because I profited by doing the very thing that was hurting me. And the world around me began to paint itself prettier in a way. On the inside I was dying, but how could I have realized that? Girls were finally paying attention to me, and I was doing things that I had wanted to do my whole life. And if I think about it too much, I can look back now and go crazy knowing that I lost it all so quickly. Growing up, as a kid, I daydreamed about being rich, and I wasn't really rich when I had this money or anything, but I did manage to get a lot of it and buy a lot of things. I thought I was going to be happy and satisfied. I thought I had done it all. You grow up and the media shows you how it's so important to be successful and rich, so I thought that if I could get money, I would be happy. But what's funny is that once I got there, it meant nothing to me. Only once I had the money, I didn't need it anymore. I hate to be cliché. It's hard to describe. I'm still in shock and going mad about losing all of it, but the money only made my life worse, it really did. The outside is only glowing when the inside is on fire, you know? It's so cliché and I know it, but, Ella, in a world after I've learned these lessons, I just know I was lucky I ever had a chip in my hand.

"I don't know much about anything, at all. But if I know one thing, it is that this roller coaster wasn't worth it. Yes, the highs were awesome, but the lows were unbearable. I know that once you get on this roller coaster, it's impossible to get off—it's a ride for life. This relationship really was a prison to me. I honestly didn't wake up one day and decide to be like this. It's a slow process, and it's important to not start with one bad decision. Just like I wouldn't recommend a political rally to someone without education because they can get swayed too easily, just like I wouldn't recommend to somebody with low emotional intelligence to listen to love songs, and just like I wouldn't recommend to somebody with psychological issues to use drugs. Point is I wouldn't recommend to anybody to play poker, but much less those who don't have self-control. And guess what? None of us have self-control, as much as we tell ourselves we do. This really wasn't any different than other drugs."

"Well, Chuck, wouldn't you say that you beat the roller coaster, now that you can look behind at all this and acknowledge what happened? You're done with poker, right? You're no longer on this roller coaster."

She does have a point, something I hadn't thought about until now; I *am* done. I haven't played poker in these couple of days off. I haven't taken a break this long since I first started, and I didn't even realize it. It is only now that I fully acknowledge that the opposite of addiction isn't sobriety; it's acceptance, acceptance of oneself and not needing an outlet.

"Yeah, I guess you're right. I'm done with gambling. I didn't know it when I was doing it, but I was gambling this year. I let go of discipline and mathematics and was in it for pure greed most of the time. Even though my strategy did have an edge, I was still gambling in the end. But this last tournament, I'm back to mathematics and intelligent play. And after that, I'm done with it forever. So I guess maybe it *is* possible to get off the roller coaster. The point is that it's not a fun ride.

"I have lived outside of reality my whole life, either trying to fix the past or anticipating the future and painting what I wanted it to look like. I always told myself that once I was rich, or once I had gotten this girl Macoa, only then would my real life start. It took a while to see that these obstacles, these were the realities of my life."

"Well, that's good. It's important that you can look back and be different now. I thought the Macoa part of what you wrote to me was interesting. You have to understand you attract the type of people you want in your life. When it comes to relationships, people will only love you and you will only be ready for love once you love yourself. Like you say, it might be cliché, but like most clichés, they end up being true, and you should live knowing that. If you don't love yourself, then being with somebody else will make you worship them and the relationship. You have to find value in yourself first; that's your truest asset in life."

"Yeah, but the show is over now. That's the scary part. What now? You know? I don't know if I can simply go back to my life. My friends don't really like me all that much anymore, and I'm too ashamed to really talk to my family. The thing is, I did all this because I felt alone. This alter ego that I created, it really was my best friend. Because when I had no one and nothing, I always had pain, and being the One Knight Stand took away some of the pain. So I guess I'm scared now, now that I'm not going to play anymore. Will I just feel lonely again?"

"You just told me that being lonely is all up to you," she finally answered after taking some seconds to think.

"It is; I can accept myself or not, but I can't help if I get home and feel empty; that's what nobody understands."

"Chuck, do you think you're a good person?"

I pause.

"I've never asked myself that. I don't know; I think everybody thinks they're a good person because we're naturally the protagonist in our own story. But I don't know if I am. It's hard to analyze myself; I don't know. I don't know *who* I am. I've done so much cruel stuff this past year. It's hard to forgive myself and hard to even think I can be a good person. The reality is we're not who we think we'll be in our future; we are who we are every day. Does that make sense? I can say I want to be a good person all I want but what defines me is who I am day to day. Sometimes I think I am a fraud. I'm always trying to become something else because I fear I'm about to be found out and exposed. I'm not as smart as other people think I am, and it makes me believe I'm not anything sometimes. I never was good with girls; I just pretended to be. I never was confident or cool; I just pretended to be. I think I'm always trying to be something, but I never am. Even my depression; I try to sell that too. Like I was never actually anything and that haunts me. I know this doesn't make much sense, Ella, but the worst part is that I know everybody is unhappy. Many people feel the same emptiness and sadness I do. Having anxiety attacks is almost a cliché now. Like what the fuck am I supposed to tell other people? I'm a kid from fucking Mexton, one of the richest cities in the country; I got lucky, and I am still depressed? But I still lie to myself and tell myself I'm special. Like my depression is something worth talking about.

"Do I even want to be a good person? Maybe I just want to think I am. Sometimes I just want to be okay with myself, you know? I think all this time I was trying to paint a life that would make me happy. I was trying to do the things I thought would make me accept myself, you know? I just wanted to get home at night and be a fan of who I was becoming, be part of the audience that I wanted so badly to love me. What else did I want other than to think I was happy? I didn't want to be happy; I just wanted to think I was, looking in from the outside. Although I was painting my own story, I desperately wanted to be a satisfied audience member who would praise me, watching as I painted my own character; I did not want to be the artist who was alone."

I take a sip of water and a deep breath. "But I never really was me; I never took a step back and was conscious of anything. Part of me was being distracted not only from me feeling lonely, but also from myself in general. Maybe I just didn't want to be with myself; I didn't want to hang out with me. I didn't want to go home to the quiet and have to face who I really was. Maybe I'm not the good guy."

Every time I say a lot she just looks at me when I'm done, not knowing if I have more to say or not. But when she doesn't say anything; I'm forced to keep going.

"I just want to be happy, Ella. It's all I really want. I desperately want to feel okay. I don't think I can handle not being okay much longer. I've been trying for so long to be happy. And I'm worried nobody is happy. I'm worried I'll spend the rest of my life almost being happy I'm terrified I might not be capable of being happy. Are you happy, Ella?"

"I think so. Nobody is completely happy. There are good days, and there are bad days; the bad days make the good ones even better. The goal is to always have fewer bad days."

I take a long pause and then open my mouth again. "I became everything I hated," I say looking down.

I take a deep breath and pause again, look up to her and say, "I just want to be happy."

She hesitates for a second and then looks at me and then finally she speaks.

"Chuck, do you think you deserve to be happy?"

FORTY-ONE

RIPTIDE

TWO DAYS UNTIL FINAL TABLE

And now you're thinking, *I picked up this book because it had a cool cover and said it was about a kid playing poker. I didn't expect this life-lesson rant.*

I didn't expect it either.

The next morning, I find myself back in Ella's office for another session. When we finish, she walks me out of the room as we are saying our good-byes. But I hold the door and look back at her.

"I'm not exactly sure why I'm paying you. I have done most of the talking during both of our sessions."

"I helped you realize some things you already knew," Ella replies

"I know. I'm kidding. But I want to hear you talk more. Come out with me tonight."

"I do not have relations with my patients outside of my practice. It's inappropriate," she says, smiling.

I smile back. "I didn't ask for a relation, whatever that means."

"I really can't, Chuck."

"Being with you calms me down. Consider it part of my therapy. I leave on Saturday morning; I only have two nights left here anyway. Just spend one with me."

"I don't know."

"Just one."

"What did you even have in mind?"

"Dinner or a drink. Just to hear you talk."

She looks back at me and then pauses. "Just one."

"Nine fifteen good?"

I tell her I will pick her up a bit after nine, still having my Cadillac to show off. But she doesn't accept and says she will meet me at the bar.

I spend the afternoon trying to meditate and still restoring my relationships. I start to be able to breathe easier.

At ten I walk into a bar in Fort Lauderdale near the beach where we agreed to meet.

"You know I'm technically not allowed to go on a date with you," she says as I sit down.

"Who said this was a date?"

The waiter comes to our table. "What can I get you guys?"

We split a pizza. I order a rum and coke; she orders a mojito. We talk, casually. It is odd to be here—odd, but nice. I haven't ever really just hung out with a girl like this, on a "date." It's only when we don't experience simplicity for a long time that we appreciate it.

We stay in the bar until midnight and then we walk to an Italian bakery for dessert. She orders chocolate; I order gelato. We walk toward the beach, and once there we sit down and continue talking.

"Ask me something," she says.

"What do you want me to ask you?"

"I don't know. I feel like I know a lot about you; what do you want to know about me?"

"Uhhh, I don't know; how old are you? You're pretty young to have your own practice."

"Good observation. The office belongs to my dad; I'm twenty-four, just graduated from grad school."

"Nice."

"What about you? You never told me your age."

"Yeahhh. You probably don't want to know that."

"Okay, what else then?"

"Um…if you could be famous, would you be?" I ask.

"Probably not, maybe once I die. I kind of like the idea of people appreciating me once I am no longer here, in a way like leaving a legacy. What about you?"

"I'm not too sure either. You know, as a kid I wanted to be famous and all, but this past year has taught me how having status and power is at times the opposite of what one imagines. I definitely like the idea of people recognizing my work, though. Like I said, I am writing a book about my experiences with poker. It would be amazing for that to impact and touch people. So I guess, I'd like to be low-tier famous. But not famous to the point where I can't even go out."

"Yeah, I agree."

"Now you ask me something," I say as I lie down with my back on the sand.

I rest my body closer to hers so that we are touching as she thinks of what to ask me. She puts her head on top of my arm and lies on my chest. Ella smells like…like, well she doesn't smell like a perfume. She smells incredibly *good*, just not a smell that a perfume can provide. She smells like a flower. Like she bathed in a bath of French soap. I don't know how to describe it. I don't even know how you can smell like this, but she does.

We spend the rest of the night here, talking. Something about this girl, man. She's captivating. There's something special to her, something that can't be grasped. When I'm with her, she makes me feel like the most important person in the world. When I'm with her, it seems as if nothing else in the world matters. Only her and I exist. I can breathe now.

At 4:00 a.m., we walk back toward our cars.

"You leave tomorrow, right?"

"I fly out Saturday at three a.m. Tomorrow is my last day here," I say as I slowly nod my head.

"What do you mean your last day here? You're coming back after the tournament, right?"

I take a second. I realize for some reason, my mind thought I was not coming back to Mexton.

"Yeah. I meant my last day before I leave. Actually, I don't know. I guess I am. I have no plans. Literally. I didn't think about that, now that you bring it up. I have no idea what I'm doing a week from now. I kind of dropped out of school; I guess this tournament will dictate my future. You know? Being a millionaire will probably change some plans."

She stares into my eyes. "What are you doing tomorrow?" I ask.

She is still staring and softly replies, "I have to work, you know? Like a normal person. But come see me at night?"

"Yeah, definitely."

She continues to gaze at me, slightly tilting her head to the right.

Long and luscious hair, bright but not too bright pink lips, wearing a cute sundress that I can imagine she bought somewhere in South America, delicate and smooth skin, and those hands, something about her hands.

It has only been a couple of seconds in my head, but it has obviously been more. She ends her gaze. "Are you going to kiss me or what?"

FORTY-TWO

TIME

ONE DAY UNTIL FINAL TABLE

I t's my last day here, and I'm going to use it wisely. I wake up early and try to meditate. But as I am about to start, barely closing my eyes, I hear a knock on my door. I make my way over as my dog begins his usual routine of barking at whatever he assumes is on the other side of the door. I take a look through the peephole wondering who could be knocking on my door on Friday at 9:00 a.m. other than the mailman. My eye fixes on the girl on the outside of the door. You guessed it. It's Macoa. She's back.

"Macoa?" I say, as I step outside.

"Chuck!" she exclaims, giving me a hug before I can process what's going on.

"Hey! It's good to see you," I say, excited but confused.

"How are you?" she asks.

"Wait. I see you don't believe in the common 'Hey, I'm going to your country' text. What are you doing here?"

"I'm interning here for the summer and just landed last night, wanted to come say hello."

For those of you who are just now joining us, Macoa is a girl I had chased my whole life but later forgot about; she then kissed me, making me fall for her again during that summer, asked her to be my girlfriend to which she said no, later hooking up with my best friend at my own party. Some other stuff happened in between all that, but I have to admit, I am still happy to see her. I'm not the One Knight Stand anymore, and I miss my best friend.

"Come in. Say 'hi' to Bruce so that he'll stop barking."

She steps inside and accepts a cup a tea (typical Macoa). We sit down and begin to catch up. I notice how pretty she is, as she has always been.

"Listen, I owe you an apology, Macoa. I've done some messed-up shit this past year. And even though I meant a lot of it, I still want to apologize. Not because of what I did but because of what it made you feel. The things I said and did to you were just a reflection of my own insecurities, so don't take it personally. I'm sorry for any pain I've caused. I'm happy to see you now."

"It's okay. I owe you an apology as we—"

I hold my hand up, trying to slow her down "No, let me stop you there. You didn't do anything wrong. You have nothing to apologize to me for. You don't owe me anything; you never did. I'm just happy things between us can be normal for once."

"Me too, Chuck. I'm happy we have a chance to sit down and talk. I think this is what I missed the most. I actually want to tell you something."

I roll my eyes, expecting her to apologize for the party situation. But I want to forget about that, pretend it didn't happen. I don't want to think about it again.

"Just listen to me, please," she continues, "listen. I think I want to give us a chance. There. I'm finally saying it. Chuck, I do have feelings for you. I knew it then; I knew it when everything in my body told me to kiss you last summer, and I know it now. You've continually been there for me."

"I haven't been there for you. I've been an ass this past year."

"Well I want you because of everything you did right since we were in elementary school together despite this past year. You're what I want; it just took me a while to notice. I know this is out of nowhere, but the time away from you made me realize this. I don't know; I guess I was scared to actually be happy before. But when I saw you with my friend going upstairs during the party, I realized how I really felt." She pauses for a second and continues before I can say anything. "I'm going to be here all summer, and I want to give this a try. I'm finally ready."

Is this a dream? Is this really happening? Because if it is, this is some messed up world. Well, there it is—what I had wanted to hear for years, she just said to me. I take a second to think. A shock of happiness runs through my body as I process what she said. But the happiness quickly turns into disappointment as I realize everything that has changed.

I feel like my life is cursed by always having the wrong timing with things I want; It's too late. I have to let the past go. Why, you ask? Part of me wants to grab her and kiss her right now, but I can't. Part of me wants to not even show up to the final table and run away with her, like I dreamed for so long, but I can't. You can't imagine how badly I want to kiss her right now. How badly I want to grab her and do everything I have dreamed of. I wish I could but I have to go. Being with her won't allow me to let go of the past. I know I should at least give her a shot, like I always wanted her to give me. But I can't—because I waited the ninety-nine days, but she never did. I chased her for more than ten years, but she never realized it. Friend, you shouldn't chase someone, not if they don't realize who you are, not if they don't appreciate what you do for them. You have to live life on your clock, not others'.

"God, Macoa. I don't know what to say."

"What are you thinking, Chuck?"

"You know I adore you. I really do. You're everything to me. But I don't want you anymore, not like that at least. Aren't you happy we can just be friends again?" I say in a low voice as I shake my head, partially regretting what's coming out of my mouth.

I say all this thinking that I have Ella now. But I just rejected what I had wanted my whole life, what I spent hours at a time dreaming about.

"Why? What do you mean, Chuck? You spill your heart out to me over the phone a couple of months ago and then you ask me to be your girlfriend when I'm in France. And now when I'm finally ready, you're not?"

"It's not that. I do want you—a part of me will always be yours. But I have to grow up; I can't be a kid trying to live a fairytale forever. It's my fault for holding you in this fantasy with me, because I always saw you as some perfect girl. But you didn't see me that way then. You only want me now, when I'm a more perfect version of myself. I don't think it's a coincidence you're attracted to me now. I was on national TV last week, and in twenty-four hours I'm going to be a millionaire. *Now*, you want me? That's not how this works. I'm not going to lie to you and say that some part of me isn't still very much attracted to you. But I need to let go of this habit of trying to romanticize my life."

She starts to reach for her purse. I think she's going to walk out. "What about this?" she asks as she pulls out the queen card I gave her some time ago.

"Don't you understand? That's the whole problem. I gave it to you and told you to always keep it, and when I asked you to see it, you didn't have it. Now you have it, but now it's too late. I left on this long journey looking for a part of me that was better than wanting you, and I've finally found it."

"I understand that," she answers. "But part of my journey was being ready to be with you. It took me sometime to realize that I was ready for a guy like you. Why can't you give me a chance to fix everything?"

"I think it's too late. I have let you go. If I don't, I never will. I always told you that I saw you as a queen. And even though the whole universe had led me to you at times, I realize now that even the universe can be wrong. Now, it's time for me to see myself as the true me. If I don't let you go now, I'll never wake up from this dream, and I don't want to be an old man and realize I've been sleeping my whole life."

"But you're doing it again, Chuck. You're even being cliché about not being cliché. You say you have to get rid of this fantasy of you're still living your life in quotes. This is the last thing I expected you'd say, Chuck."

"I know. And I'm sorry. I'm sorry for all the confusion I've added to your life. I'm sorry for idolizing you and holding you to such a high standard. I'm sorry I'm so complicated too. I just think there's too much history here, and I think I need to start fresh if I want to become a better person."

"You're giving up on us."

"Maybe. Maybe there's a future for us. But I need to focus on the tournament right now. I can't be thinking about this."

Macoa tears up.

"You should go," I say.

I can't help but think about telling Ella about this; she would be proud that I did this. But it is weird because she is half my therapist, half my preferred future girlfriend.

I call Ella but she doesn't answer.

FORTY-THREE

KARMA

HOURS UNTIL FINAL TABLE

t's reaching late afternoon, and Ella finally responds to the text I sent her hours ago. "Hey, come by my apartment at seven p.m. when I get off, and we can do something."

I smile as I read the text, but I want to see her now. It's my last day in Mexton, and I want to spend it with her; for some reason she's all I can think about. So instead of waiting until night I'm going to surprise her with lunch now and then I can pick her up at night.

What do you think?

Nice. Let's go. But before I ride to her office, I need a haircut. I haven't cut it since last summer, and doing so will mean I can finally leave half of my persona behind. It's time for a new look.

♣

It's one thirty, and I'm leaving the barbershop. Finally, some minutes later, I'm walking into her office. I ring the doorbell, but nobody answers. I ring again, and, finally, her receptionist opens the door.

"Hey, I'm Chuck, Ella's friend. I don't have an appointment; I just need to give her something really quick."

She looks a bit confused. "Ella isn't working for the rest of the day. Are you one of her patients? If it's an emergency, you can see another psychologist now."

"Uhhh no. It's not an emergency. Give me a second."

I step away from her desk. I thought she was working until seven…I call her, no answer. I call again, still nothing. I text her, "Hey, where you at?"

She *does* answer. "I'm with a patient. I'll call you when I'm done."

Hmm…I walk toward her receptionist again. "Are you sure she's not working today?"

"Positive."

"Would you happen to know where she is?"

"I'm not sure I'm supposed to share that information with her patients," she tells me.

"No, I'm her friend; she's just not answering her phone. I just need to give her something. It's a gift actually. Is she somewhere near?"

"Yeah, she just left for lunch at Town Center; I think she mentioned something about pizza."

I thank her and walk toward my car. Town Center, by the way, is an area where there are some restaurants and coffee shops in the middle of Mexton. I jog down the stairs of her office and pace quickly toward my car. I drive off to Town Center dying to know why she lied to me.

I pull in near where most of the restaurants are and start looking around to see if I can find her. Is this creepy? I don't think so. I really just want to give her lunch, and I'm wondering as to why she told me she was working. I drive around seeing if I can find her outside. I do two laps around the block but still don't see her or her Jeep. I'm finally able to spot her outside the pizzeria, on her phone. She's sitting at a table outside, alone. I park my car in the nearest spot I can find. I start walking toward the restaurant but leave the lunch in the car as I don't know why she lied to me, and now I'm uninterested in her food at this point. And as I'm crossing the street, I see somebody walk up to her and greet her. I pause at the other end of the street, still some shops away from her. It's a guy; he gets closer and kisses her. *What? Is she on a date?* I try to fix my eyes to make sure what I'm seeing is real but can only see the guy because Ella's back is toward me.

I think I actually know who that is. He looks like some guy I've played poker with before. He's a frequenter at the Hard Rock, I think. I can't believe what's going on in front of my eyes. I step a bit closer and try to get a real sight of what's going on. It really looks like they're on a date. He seems to be drinking a beer. They're laughing.

Why is she with him? What's going on?

I wonder if he is one of her patients too? Is he also leaving poker? Did he also see her because of an addiction? Did he also fall for her as he was vulnerably opening up? Did he also try to take her out on a date? Did she also tell him, "Having relationships with patients is inappropriate?" Did he also talk his way into a date with her? Did she also agree, a bit too easily? Did they also go out for pizza? Did they also talk about each other all night? Had he also kissed her and stupidly, like he always managed to, fall for a girl just like that? Had he not learned that girls don't think he's special like he thinks they are? Is he unable to understand that he's just the type of guy who shouldn't get invested?

I continue walking toward them to make sure it is one hundred percent her, and as I am close enough, I can confirm that it is in fact Ella and some guy I had played poker with before. But I don't say anything; I just continue to walk past them. There's nothing to say to her. I'll walk around and then come back to my car. And as I am a few yards ahead of them, I hear somebody yell, "Chuck!" but I don't turn around. I continue to make my way toward my car.

It breaks my heart to see that I wasn't really special to her. I mean, I know it was just one night. But it was just hours ago. It's embarrassing for me to be thinking about her while she's on another date. The night we had shared managed to captivate me and her too, I think. But the difference is she was able to wake up out of the dream state and continue with her life the next morning. Compared to me, always managing to stay in the dream. Why do I always fall for girls so quickly? Why do I feel so much? There she is, giving another guy her full attention, and most likely, she will give it to somebody else tomorrow. A wildflower. She can do and say what she did with me with anyone else. I was just something temporary to her, something that she could forget about the next day. And as I make my way into my car, I hear a louder and similar "Chuck! Wait!" or at least I think I hear it. But I'll never know because I don't turn around and drive off.

My mathematics would tell me to let her go; she isn't worth the investment. My poker knowledge would tell me I might be reading the situation wrong; I'd have to factor in other variables and give her a chance to explain. And my experiences would tell me this was bound to happen, as I, again, romanticized a girl without even really knowing her. But I follow my gut this time, driving off. There's that saying "Go with your gut feeling. That will always be the right choice." I hate it when people say that. Me following my gut is the reason I'm here; it's been wrong time and time again. And that's all I have to say about that.

I haven't managed to get much sleep as my flight is leaving at 3:00 a.m. Actually, I don't know why I said that. I didn't get any sleep. Everybody shows up at my house at midnight to wish me luck and then I make my way to the airport at one with my parents. Nothing special to talk about. I check in and get my boarding pass. I'm exhausted. My mom gives me a big hug and says, "Dio ti benedica," as she moves her hand up and down my back, her eyes starting to water. Yeah, if you forgot, or I forgot to mention, I'm Italian. I make the security line and look back to get one last look at my parents before I leave. I wait at the gate for the plane. The girl at the desk announces it is time to board. I board the plane and wait a couple of minutes until I am finally in the air.

And as I try to look out from the window but only see darkness, I can't help but remember how I was scared of planes when I was younger. In fact, I was terrified and wished that I could avoid them each time I travelled with my family. And now, I am on a plane for the first time in some years and realize I'm not scared. Maybe it has to do with the fact I'm not a kid anymore and can see things rationally. Maybe it's that I have been so close to death that I don't fear it anymore. Maybe I am at peace with my circumstances.

I start to think about my situation, start focusing on what's to come. Deep breath. You know, the way I see it, there are two possible outcomes tomorrow: I either make more money than I ever have, or, I lose it all. If I turn into a millionaire tomorrow night, there's a possibility I go back to being this insane poker player who's dead in the inside and is entitled and treats people like garbage. Or two, I can lose it all and will probably go into a severe depression battling my issues with nothing. With both options I can *die*. But I can also die here on this plane. I can die on the way to the hotel, and I can die by some random heart failure. But there's no reason to fear death; I have made my peace. There's also the reality – I probably won't die. I'll get off this plane and make it safely to the hotel. And I'm done living not knowing that. I'm done living as I will live forever. And that's what we owe the universe. Every time that plane doesn't crash, we have to live life knowing it one day can. I can be a good person. I can live a meaningful life. And you know what? Even if I do die, at least I'd die free. So if the plane goes down as I had feared as a kid, then tell my mom that I died okay. I'm all right.

I'm not scared, not anymore.

FORTY-FOUR

ONE LAST TIME

MOMENTS BEFORE

As soon as I disembark the plane in Arizona, I'm greeted by cameras. The World Cup of Poker coordinators drive me to the hotel where the event will take place. I have a camera on me the whole time, but I'm exhausted and just focused on getting to the hotel.

I look out of the window throughout the car drive. I see the few skyscrapers and I look at the different people and scenery. I look off into the new city with the curiosity of being in a new place. We arrive at the resort around eight in the morning where they give me the key to my suite and tell me I can do whatever I want until 5:00 p.m. I have access to every part of the resort. I can eat and drink whatever I want. But at five, I have to go downstairs to the event room where the interviews will start, and eventually I will become a millionaire.

I make my way up to my room, take my shoes and pants off, and try to get some sleep. When I wake up, it will be time to face my destiny.

♣

After several hours, I wake up, look at my phone, and realize it's go time. But I close my eyes again, and before I open them, I take a deep breath and smile. The last year of my life has had its ups and downs; it's been beautiful, and it's been ugly. It's taught me some stuff and left me confused about others. It's made me love life, and it's made me want to stop living. It's made me feel unstoppable, on top of the world, and it's made me feel the lowest of lows. Everything I've done this year is not only what I'm most proud of but also what I'm most ashamed about. It was all a sequence of really good and really bad decisions—one bad behavior after a good one. I never planned or wished that it would lead to this. But it doesn't matter anymore. It's in the past; it has all led up to this moment.

I put my bag on top of my bed and start to unpack it—I take everything out one by one. First, some jeans, then, a couple of pieces of gum, a small metal ring that was once given to me by a girl (for a different book), and finally, of course, my classic black hoodie. Here it is, my poker kit, the kit that made me be the One Knight Stand. This will be the last time I wear this. I do this one last time and then I put away the mask forever.

It's time to go.

I make my way downstairs to get a quick bite to eat as it's going to be a long night. I see a Japanese restaurant and ask for a table.

"We only have tables for big parties; do you mind if we sit you down at one of them?" the hostess asks.

I tell her it's fine. But as she's walking me toward a table, I see there are in fact empty single tables. Weird, but I don't think much of it as I am trying to concentrate for what's to come. I order sushi. I try to think about my strategy for today. I envision myself with the million dollars. I will be a champion.

After some minutes of sitting, I hear a voice behind me. "So are you ready?"

I turn around. And to my surprise, there is my family and all my friends just like last time.

I'm speechless.

Charlie states and asks, "You might become a millionaire today; did you think we weren't going to be here?"

I hug all of them as they sit down to eat with me.

"So how are you feeling?" Brent asks me.

"I'm okay. I'm a bit anxious, but not like before. I just want to start; I want to get out there and play my game. I'm excited. I mean, there's a good chance I'll be richer than most people in Mexton by the end of the day."

After everything I have done, they are all here, rooting for me. Wow. Like I said, I don't believe in luck; but I am blessed. These moments together help me as I can take my mind off poker before I go to play.

But they are short lived, as I look down at my phone and realize I have to make my way toward the interview session. Everybody gives me a last hug and wishes me luck.

"I don't believe in luck, but thanks."

Right before I walk away my dad stops me and takes to the side.

"How are you feeling, buddy?"

"I'm okay. I'm a bit nervous, you know? But how many people my age get to live this experience? I'm excited more than anything. It's crazy to think about. I'm about to play for a million dollars. When I was in high school, no one would've bet on me. No one would've thought I was going to be the one to make it. I don't even think my friends really believed in me, but I always did. This isn't how I imagined it would turn out, but here I am, about to play against the best in the world."

"Can I ask you something?" my dad asks, lowering his voice.

"You're my dad. You don't have to ask if you can ask me something."

"Hah. Right. Do you want to go back to your old life after this? You know? Do you think you'll be normal once this is all over?"

Both of us turn serious as our tones soften and stiffen.

"I was never normal."

"Yeah. You're right."

"No. I want to ride planes and eat breakfast alone for the rest of my life," I say sarcastically before I really answer. "Of course I do. It's just hard. I like being here sometimes. Even though I hate the anxiety, it keeps me alive. I created my own world here. Nobody can hurt me at the table. I can't get heartbroken like I can outside these rooms. That's what it was always about—escaping pain. But do you think I honestly *want* to be here? It's summer already, but I'm here. While everybody my age is at the beach or doing something fun, I'm in a city where I don't know anybody. I want to be eating breakfast with some girl right now in Paris, arguing about some stupid couple crap," I say as my eyes look away from him, almost as if I'm trying to find the answer outside of myself. "But then maybe I would wish I'd be back here, talking to you, about to play. I guess we're never really content with what our lives are. But I can't be thinking about any of this right now; I got a tournament to go win," I say, as I hug him and start to walk away.

"Wait. You need to understand something before you go. This world without pain, it's fiction. It's not real. Real life has pain, always. You know that, right?"

I step closer to him again. "Yeah, I don't know if I can accept that.

Maybe, I prefer the fiction to the pain."

"Well, you can't always have both. You have to choose sometimes. Fiction or real life?"

FORTY-FIVE

BREATHING

MOMENTS BEFORE

I make my way to the event room. As soon as I check in, they put a microphone on me and the interviews start.

"Chuck, you are the youngest player to ever make the final table at one of these events. How does that feel?"

"Chuck, will having your family and friends here affect your style of play in any way?"

"Chuck, you're coming in as chip leader, what exactly is your strategy to make sure you stay in this in this position?"

"Chuck. Twenty years old and most likely to win this tournament. What is going through your mind?"

"Chuck, what does a million dollars mean to you at this point in your life?"

"Chuck, you're being rooted for all over the world. Are you ready?"

♣

After an hour of answering questions, posing for pictures and other press stuff, they introduce each player into the final table in order of chip stacks, from smallest to biggest. I wait for them to do the other eight players before they finally get to me. The camera people tell me to walk toward the table.

Here we go! No turning back now.

"The youngest player to ever make the final table, a sophomore from the University of Central Florida, Mr. One Knight Stand, Charles Marquez!"

As I walk in I can hear people cheering and some booing. I spot my supporters and make a heart with my hands to them.

Now that we are all sitting, the tournament director is handed the microphone.

"Okay, here we have them. The final table of the South Florida World Cup of Poker Millionaire Maker. Congratulations to everybody who has made it here—you guys have passed a lot of good players and faced many obstacles along the way, a big accomplishment. The rules are as follows: we will begin in approximately five minutes after the dealer has shuffled and the cameras are all fixed on you players and your respective fan sections. We will play until there is only one player left, regardless of time. We expect the champion to be crowned at around ten p.m., but it can go earlier or a lot later. In the case of not having a winner by midnight, we will continue tomorrow. Only the champion will get paid in this tournament. Congratulations again for making it this far. Enjoy your night and good luck guys!"

The crowd cheers in anticipation.

I take a deep breath and close my eyes. I try to clear my mind and really focus. Long deep breaths. Complete concentration.

"Dealer, shuffle up and deal!"

It's time. This is what we've been waiting for. I open my eyes and look a last time at the railing where my family and friends are. I know that throughout the night my mom will be dying of stress, as I can already notice worry lines on her face. But because I need to focus and play as if no one is watching, I try to look away and concentrate, and close in on the table. But as I am looking away, my eyes fix on them, and I realize there is someone else there with them.

I look closer and there she is—Macoa, as beautiful as she was when I had first met her. Now, I don't want to be an ass, but when I see her and she waves to me, I don't wave back, not because I don't want to be friendly, but because I have to focus on what is to come. But I still have that millisecond moment, you know, when it sends hot temperature and freezing blood at the same time through your body? She is here to see me, after all this time of me seeing her.

I feel cards hit my hands, which take me out of my meditative state. I look at them, nine of clubs and nine of hearts. I remind myself that only one person wins; everybody else loses—my goal here is nothing else but first place.

Before I play my first hand, I have to admit something. I owe it to you. My relationship with poker isn't exactly what I've made it out to be. There's a part of me that enjoys playing, like when I began; it can be, and sometimes is, just plain fun. It takes me away from a harsh reality where I can just relax. Part of me really loves it. I love the statistics. I love the competition and the ability make money off of strategy. Not in some fucked up, deep crazy love way, but in a simple and sincere manner. The problem is it has cheated me too many times, so part of me can't trust it. It's not easy to be in a casino; knowing I can lose thousands of dollars is never a good feeling. Part of me hates it. I had become the best, but I was never comfortable—poker never made me feel like I was on the inside. There was always a bigger monster once I defeated the one that haunted me. Part of me fears it. But poker is what gave me value; it's the only thing I have had for a long time. Part of me needs it.

And here it is—what I've needed to tell myself this whole time. When we chase things in life, a lot of the times we don't actually want the thing we're chasing. Whether it is money, the girl of our dreams, or an ideal lifestyle, the rush isn't in achieving our goal. The rush of the game is in playing. When we imagine and fantasize about what it'll be like when it's all over—that's the magic. The fun in women wasn't actually sleeping with them, rather it was the *game* in chasing them and making them fall for me, not the actual closing.

The fun about poker is romanticizing the idea of what I'm going to do with all this money once I'm done and imagine this person I can be. This fake persona, you know? The alter ego I created. It wasn't necessarily real, but it was the only thing I had, so I wanted to hang on. Did I ever actually want to fully be the One Knight Stand? It's just that I lived my whole life telling myself that I would be happy once I got *this* or did *that*. Well, getting *there* wasn't in the distant future anymore; it was very near. I spent my whole life chasing this lifestyle that wealth has provided me. But now that I am so close to having it, I don't need it. What if nothing changes when I am a millionaire? What if girls still don't like me for me? What if I get into MIT and *am* able to pay for it but aren't happy when I get there? What if I get a girl like Ella, and I realize that it isn't her I want either? What if I one day I have to actually face the reality that I am the problem?

What if I sit in my Cadillac at the end of the day, and I don't like who I am? What if all my dreams come true—the money, the perfect girl, the school? What if I get all of it, but I am still depressed, lonely, and anxious?

I didn't want to find out the answers to these questions for the same reason gamblers who have already lost don't want to leave the casino and drive home. Because once they leave, the loss becomes real, and sometimes we don't want to live in the real world, but now I have to. It's like a dog chasing cars: the dog doesn't actually want to catch the car, which would end the game. And we don't want the game to end. But the only way for me to beat my game is to stop playing.

But, before I win, I'm going to make a killing.

I hope no one ever finishes their game, but it's time for me to. Let's do this—real life beckons.

"Raise."

FORTY-SIX

I HAVE HIM

My strategy is to slowly eliminate the short stacks one by one. This way, I do not have to risk most of my chips and can remain the chip leader throughout the night. Second place is a thirty-year-old darker guy, who shouldn't be too much of an issue for me. Third place is Phil Lally, and I want to make sure that I'm the one who eliminates him. He is followed by a trash-talker, who I'm pretty sure I have a solid read on. He asks questions, bluff—he just talks; he has a hand. Fifth place belongs to an Asian guy, who looks like he spent his childhood summers studying piano theory. Sixth is Ungur, who along with Lally, is the biggest threat here. Seventh is an older guy, who I can't discount just yet. Eighth place is a guy who looks like he loves telling girls he was in the ATO fraternity. And ninth place is a Hispanic older guy, who should be out soon.

Within the first ten minutes, the older guy in seventh place goes all in with pocket jacks and is eliminated by Lally, who calls him with queen, king. After half an hour of play, I eliminate the older Hispanic guy. The most dangerous player is Lally, and our chip stacks are repeatedly passing each other's, continually exchanging first and second place. After another half hour, I eliminate the Asian guy, who was down to only ten blinds. Lally then eliminates the frat guy.

"It has turned into the Lally and Marquez show," announces one commentator.

It has been three hours, and the players remaining are Lally in first, me in second, Ungur in third, and the darker guy in forth. The chip stacks are about even, with each of us having somewhere around three million chips. Then, Ungur raises the big blind to three hundred thousand. It's hard not to think that any action I do can be my last. I look down at my cards, nothing; I throw them away with a sigh of relief—I get to live another hand. Darker guy folds. Lally looks down at his cards and takes a second. He reraises to seven eighty.

It's about to go down! Ungur just calls. The flop comes seven, seven, seven. Ungur checks; Lally bets. Ungur announces he's all in! Lally calls! They flip over their cards: Ungur shows kings; Lally shows aces! The turn: jack, river: five! The crowd gasps in disbelief as most people here are cheering for Ungur. I stand up to shake the hand of one of my poker idols, who has just been eliminated from the tournament by one of the players I have hated the most. But my pity and disappointment are quickly turned into relief, as I am one person closer to the championship.

But just like that Lally becomes the overwhelming chip leader with more than six million chips with me only having a bit more than three, and the dark guy just under three. I continue with caution.

We continue like this, going up and down with no big hands for another hour. Finally, I get my favorite hand: ace, nine. I call. Lally folds; dark guy raises to four hundred. I call. Flop comes nine, jack, ace. I check—you know what I'm doing. Dark guy bets; I smooth call. I'm going to eliminate this guy right here; watch. Turn comes a three; I check. He checks back. The river: ten. I check again—a risky move, but he bets, just like we want him to. I think he has a good hand like pocket kings or queens, and he's not sure he has me beat. He's concerned about the ace on the board, but why would he be betting?

I raise.

"I'm all in," he says.

This was part of my plan, but do I want to risk most of my stack on only two pair? I still think he only has kings or maybe a jack and a ten. This can also very well be a bluff. I didn't come here to be scared though, I call. He flips over queens! I close my eyes and smile.

It's down to me and Phil Lally, heads up! He has me covered by only two hundred thousand. One more player I have to beat, and it's over. Just one more player I need to eliminate and then I don't have to play poker ever again. Just Lally and then this whole year is over, and I come out a champion. Hopefully, all I have to do is focus for no more than an hour and take the million dollars home. My heart is racing, and I can feel it wanting to come out of my chest. I'm nervous, but not anxious. Fuck that, I'm here to win. This is mine.

We play for thirty minutes with no significant hands; both of us are being cautious. There he is, right in front of me, about forty-five years old, wearing Ray-Ban black glasses and a long-sleeved shirt. It's always funny when you picture something for so long and actually arrive to it. That moment as a kid, or even a year ago, when I pictured myself playing on TV against the best players in the world—it's happening, right now, against the guy who told me I would never make it this far.

"Hey, Lally."

"Yeah?"

"Do you remember me?"

"What do you mean?"

"Hialeah, Florida. Last summer. You were playing a tournament; I asked you for tips to be a good player."

"I don't, to be honest. Were we playing at the same table?"

"Ha. No. Not even close. Never mind."

Next hand: six, nine—both diamonds. I call. He raises to a million. Huge raise. I think about it. It should be an immediate fold, but I've been here for hours, and I need to take this home. If I call and hit something on the flop, he'd never suspect I have this hand. Let's see what happens—I call, looking at him while I try to get a read. Flop: ace, king, jack; all diamonds.

Bingo.

Here it is; it can all end. This last year, this whole journey—it will probably come to an end right now. I bet a million, and Lally looks shocked. He doesn't know what to do; he checks to see his cards, looks at the flop, and then looks at me. I know what he has. This fucker has aces or kings. He just flopped trips. I know it; I really do. He looks at me again before looking at the flop one more time. I know his tell. I know he has aces or kings! I did it. I can read him!

He might put me on two diamonds, or at least one, though. Let's see what he does. All that needs to happen is for the board not to pair, and this thing can be over. He raises me. I have him just where I need him, friend! I look at him, take a second to thank the universe, smirk inside my head, and slowly push all my chips forward, hoping it's the last time I have to do this.

He calls. My heart is a roaring pound. I can't watch this sitting down but I almost fall as I try to stand. This is it.

No ace, king, or jack on the turn and river, and I win this; the board doesn't pair, and I'm a millionaire.

As he pushes his chips all in, I finally feel it again. Remember? That feeling I felt the first time I won a big pot. The feeling where you know you have the best hand. I know I have it; I know that all this suffering is over. I know I can finally go home and sleep peacefully again.

I have him. This can finally be done.

The crowd is in a roar as we both flip over our cards, nobody expecting me to have six, nine. My family starts cheering. Lally is in shock. The commentators are going wild. Daniel Ungur comes to hug me. Turn: four of diamonds—doesn't change anything. One more card, and it's done. One more card, and I will have 97 percent of the chips. Just one more card, and I'm a millionaire. The dealer is waiting for the announcers to commentate on the hand before putting out the last card; and although the pause is supposed to be less than a minute, it seems like an eternity.

And they say your life flashes before your eyes before you die, but that idea always seemed stupid to me because there really wouldn't be anybody to attest to that. But here time seems to freeze, and I can only think back to everything that has led me here. This last year, or even my whole life, everything has led to this moment. I think about that first tournament I played and won, I think about kissing Macoa outside of her house, and I think about all the other girls I have been with whose names I don't remember. I think about almost dying from pure anxiety and how now it is only going forward—it will be the start of my new life.

I can't help but smile—we did it.

I think about all the times I've lost just when I thought I was in the clear, but I snap out of my thoughts as I see the dealer hit the table twice with a fist indicating that she's about to put out the last card.

Here it comes.

Jack of clubs.

FORTY-SEVEN

FREEDOM

I can't believe what I am seeing. My heart skips a beat—I don't believe my eyes. I don't believe any of this—this can't be real.

It takes me a second to realize what has just happened. I put my face into my hands as I bend down. It's over. Everything—the ride is over. Done. Lally wins the hand and eliminates me. I am eliminated in second place. I have nothing now. A second ago I was about to become a millionaire. Now I don't even have enough money to buy a drink tonight.

Pain is something I have dealt with my whole life, both physical and emotional. When I was a kid I was playing soccer in my grandpa's backyard, and I slid trying to get to the ball and suddenly felt excruciating pain as I saw my foot bleeding, as glass had gone three inches inside the side of my foot. When I was in middle school, I got hit by a foul ball at a baseball game; I don't think I've ever felt so unconscious while still being awake. When my grandpa died and I had to see my mom in the worst pain, my heart ached, and I felt it physically. When Macoa told me she only wanted to be friends, it hurt so bad, sending me into this year-long downward spiral. But this moment right here, this tragedy is by far the most painful moment of my life.

As my eyes fix back on the room, I am just starting to regain my breath, and I look at Phil Lally as he is celebrating his million-dollar addition. I start to look around the room, and everybody is in the same disbelief I am.

And now I look up toward the heavens and yell; I scream at the top of my lungs, "Fuck this shit! You did this to me! Why do you treat me like this?" I don't know if I actually yell or I just did in my head.

I am furious at God, if there is one. I am insulted that he would do this to me now, now that I was on the good side. Where is he now? Where is God when I need him? *The same universe that gives you life and shows you heaven, also gives you death and sends you to hell.*

I continue to scream in the midst of the noise in the room, with half of the people celebrating, and half still in shock. When I am done, I collapse into myself and begin to feel tears running down my face. But before I break down even further, I try to compose myself and walk toward my fans where I make my way into my mother's arms and continue to fight back my emotions as she holds me. I can't believe it. For I too am one of those people who deep down believe that good things happen to good people. *I am a good person?* I too believed that maybe this time it was all over. I too thought that the gods and the universe had a plan for me. But that isn't the truth; I am back to where I began.

I stay in my mom's arms and sob. And I wait here until it is all out, all the pain, the huge amount of fear that is still inside of me, the anger, and even the pride. I let my entire collection of emotions out as I am in my mom's arms shielding me from reality.

When I'm finally able to compose myself again, I'm instructed by the tournament director to make my way into the tunnel to exit the final table. Right before I enter the passageway, I'm stopped by the same woman who had done all the interviews, asking me for one last interview to which I agree.

"Charles, thank you very much for doing this. Can you describe the emotions after a loss like that?"

"Not yet. I'm still taking it in. It hurts. It hurts a lot, but what can I say? The show is over. Pain is nothing new to me. I have been defeated many times in life; this is not the first."

I can see the disappointment in the interviewer's eyes. She looks embarrassed to be doing this right now. "It seems to be that the whole world was cheering for you. Everybody here held their breath for a second on that final hand and people from across the globe were and still are sending in messages rooting for you. It was a Cinderella story, and you were the people's protagonist. Will you be back?"

"Ehh, I don't think so. I don't want to be Lally, still playing this *game* at that age. You know, the loss is still very fresh, but hopefully I will be freed from this game eventually. I have nothing now; I was literally all in with this tournament. So losing everything is freedom in a way. I have no attachments now," I say as I realize what this loss actually means. "Hopefully, this will mark the end of my poker career."

"Thank you for everything, Chuck. From the World Cup of Poker, we can honestly say it was a pleasure to see you on this journey."

As I make my way out of the tunnel, I see Macoa waiting for me. I turn my head to her, but my body is still pointing toward the elevator.

"How are you feeling?" she asks me.

"I'm not completely aware of what's going on right now. I'm feeling so many emotions. I'm heartbroken; that's for sure. But for some demented reason, I feel unrestricted too. My breathing is a bit better, if that even makes sense. When I teared up and screamed, I felt liberated. I want to run and get out of here."

I look into her eyes. "Why are you in Arizona, Macoa?"

"What do you mean *why?* I came to see you. Like I said, I'm making an effort to fix this. Come get some dinner with me. Let's just hang out."

I take a second to process what she's saying to me. "Macoa. Stop. Don't chase me. Look at me. I don't know what I'm doing. Go for someone who has an idea of what he's doing in life. I wouldn't do you any good. There's no reason for you to want me. You deserve so much better. You should be someone you're more than a dream to. You deserve something real. You're still so beautiful to me, but a girl like you needs to be somewhere else, not with a gambler."

"Okay. I tried."

I kiss her on the forehead and keep going.

"Chuck!"

I turn around.

"I love you," she says.

"I know."

And as I leave the casino floor and leave Macoa behind, I feel as if I have left a war. I have left everything that has held me behind. I feel a huge weight lifted off my shoulders. I have no attachments, no commitments, no demons, nothing; I have nothing I owe any time to. I am free, free to do anything.

FORTY-EIGHT

FULL CIRCLE

Okay, we all know this can't end this way; there still has to be something left to do. As I get to the room, I pack my clothes and think about the final hand over and over. I replay the hand in my head. *Did I do something wrong? Fucking jack of clubs.* I can't stop seeing that card in my head.

You know, I'm not anxious or anything, but I can't help but think that there's not much to do now. *I should've won that hand.* I look around the room and realize I still have to be here until tomorrow morning as the plane ride back isn't until midday tomorrow.

Maybe I'm just not good at this game, at least not as good as I thought. Maybe I never was as good as I thought. Maybe I didn't even deserve to win. But why did the universe choose this path for me? How come the universe let him beat me, now that I am a good person? I have worked hard for all this time, for what? How come I don't get my happy ending?

This can't be over. This can't finish like this.

I know what I'm going to do. I have finished packing my bags, but I leave them in my room. I make my way down to the lobby, still wearing my black hoodie. When I get down, I see all the press and most of my family still discussing the events. I go straight to my mom. "Hey, do you have a hundred dollars I can have?"

"Um, what do you need that for? Didn't you go up to your room?"

"I want to go get a nice dinner, probably ask Macoa to come with me. I'll pay you back. I just want to get my head off poker right now."

"Why do you need so much money?"

"I want to take her to a really nice dinner. Okay, I'm lying. I want to take myself to a nice dinner. She's just an excuse. Also, I need to pay a taxi."

"Okay. Fine."

"Thank you."

"You're paying me back though, right?"

I nod as she hands me the hundred dollars.

As I take the bill in my hand, I know exactly what I am going to do. My feet are making their way to *the room*. I know I made a promise—but I can't let this end like this. I have to leave with a win. I have to make this right.

I get to the poker room. "Hey, can I get into a 1-2 no-limit table, please."

The guy at the front desk stares at me for an extended amount of time with a confused/shocked look on his face.

"Sure, you can go to table twenty-one, which is the one all the way down to your right," he says, pointing toward the back of the room.

I make my way toward the table and ask the dealer for a hundred dollars' worth of chips. He pushes the chips toward me as I sit down wondering whether I should be here or not. Because here I am, in a similar room I have been in this past year. My head is down staring at my chips. I put my head up as I look around the table, seeing who I'm playing against as I feel cards hit my hands. But before I look at my cards, I look in front of me to the opposite end of the table, and I see some kid. Seems to be about nineteen years old, Hispanic looking, no emotion on his face. Black hair. Dark brown eyes. Wearing a black bracelet on his right hand that is covering his mouth with a fist. He has a blue UNC T-shirt on with sweatpants and gray hat on backwards. He is sitting just like I would sit when I first started playing. I notice him staring me down after he is done analyzing other players—he's looking for the sucker.

I freeze for a moment. Had he seen me play at the final table and wants to read me? Might he be trying to be like me? Is it a coincidence? *Am I going crazy?* My mind flashes back to when I first started to play no limit and was in his position. I was this kid not too long ago.

What am I doing here? What the fuck am I doing playing at a hundred-dollar table?

I realize this game, which I thought only valued me and I thought only made me special, isn't exclusive. This game makes everybody think they're special. I wasn't one in a million this whole time. The game is pulling this kid in just like it had done to me a year ago. I was one of many getting sucked in. I'm seeing in front of me how another sucker is being made to believe he is special.

"Hey, it's on you," the dealer tells me as I snap out of a daze.

I look up at him. "Oh yeah, I'm sorry."

I look at my cards: two red aces. I pull my head up again and look at the kid in front of me, who has the most arrogant appearance on his face one last time. It breaks my heart to realize that I'm not different after all. I was just one who could be taken advantage of.

The biggest pride in my life was being a successful poker player who was good with women. But anyone could do it. Anybody could be sucked in, do simple math and make money. Anybody can hang around other assholes, buy tables at clubs, and take girls home. And I don't want to be just anyone anymore.

I look at my cards again, still aces. I throw my cards to the middle of the table indicating I fold and stand up taking my chips with me. As I get out of my chair, I turn toward the exit passing the kid with the UNC shirt on. "Here you go, good luck," I say as I hand the kid all my chips before I walk out.

I step out of the casino and start running toward my room. Don't ask me why, but I want to run again. I just need to leave everything behind, so I start sprinting down the casino floor. Every step I take closer to my suite is a step farther from the poker room; with every step farther from the poker room, I'm leaving the One Knight Stand behind a bit more.

I finally get to my room, short of breath, and sit on the bed. My mind running faster than I can articulate. As I do this, my eyes shoot wide open.

I remember.

I can't believe it. I remember about the account. Do you know what I'm talking about? The bank account I made in case it all went bad? The money I put aside in a different account to buy a plane ticket out! I go on my phone and log on to my bank account to check if it's still there. Of course it is. I then go on Google Flights and search different itineraries leaving today.

I find one and call an Uber.

Don't ask me what I'm doing, because I don't know.

FORTY-NINE

ESCAPE

As I'm leaving the casino and stepping into the parking lot, I turn around to see what I'm leaving behind. Back in that place I did everything I hated. I became what I thought I never would. I treated others the way they treated me, even after I told myself I would never turn into that type of person. But I did become everything I hated, and I did it all with a smile. And now it is time to let it go. Not for hours or days, not for a week or months, and not for you, or for the sake of this being a good story with a happy ending—it's time to let go forever, for me.

It is only after I am not one of them that I realize how stupid we looked. Being on the inside, I was blinded. I was blinded by something. Whatever you want to call it—greed, love, consumption, or something else. *But I was blinded.* I couldn't grasp not only the plainness but also the irrationality of this game: it was stupid; we just looked stupid. It was a world made by insiders, for insiders, and worshipped by insiders. And guess what—we all have that inner voice—we all think we have *it*. Of course it was impossible for me to realize this being on the inside, but I can't help but get mad at how stupid I must've looked.

I arrive at the airport and make my way to my counter.

"Checking in," I say.

"Where are you flying to today, sir?"

"India."

Yes, I'm going to India.

"Okay, you're a bit late for your flight, so you're going to have to move quickly and head straight to your gate. Passport please?"

I hand her my passport; she hands me my boarding pass, and I make my way toward immigration.

See, most kids from my generation have their plans in life, their backup plans and their backup for the backup. Our whole life is planning. But that now seems stupid to me. You make a bet on what you really want, not the things you don't. What's the point of having a backup plan anyway? I'm the type of person who goes for it all. Having a plan B just means you don't believe in yourself enough to get what you really want. You can call it gambling if you want to, but to me it's betting on myself. You have to be willing to lose something to truly have it—even if that something is your mind.

I made a bet on myself, and it didn't pay off. So what did I do? The only reasonable thing to do—a second bet. And here I am.

FIFTY

CAPITAL T—TRUTH

And you know what? For some reason, I feel really bad, but I feel bad for you. I feel terrible. This is such a disgusting feeling. I'm sorry I let you down. You, the one who never lost hope in me, the one who supported me through thick and thin, the one who felt when I felt and hoped when I hoped, the one who knew this was more than fiction the whole time.

I'm sorry. To the person reading this who wanted me to win; to the kid who has ever felt isolated; to the kid who has suffered with depression, addiction, or anxiety; to the adult who thinks he or she has *it*; and for the one who thinks he never will:

Hey. You're not alone. Tonight, I feel the same way as you. If you could see me right now, you could tell by the look on my face that something is more than wrong. You could tell that I've seen a lot and been broken. My eyes are open, but my focus is not anywhere physical. Tonight, I'm a bit quieter than what I like to normally be, and I've felt the same urge to cry that I imagine you have. You're not the only one. Today, I also thought that this time, we finally would reach the stars and leave this dark world behind. I also thought we were going to defeat Lally and for once we would finally be able to go to sleep with a smile on our face and have no worries about what's to come tomorrow. I thought we would look back at this time and smile now that the good had finally prevailed. You're not alone; you're not the only one.

Today, I've looked down at my watch and felt that this day would never end. I felt that same feeling you get when you count down the minutes for a boring class to end but then realized I wasn't waiting for anything to end. I'm scared to death thinking that maybe this feeling will last forever. Today I asked God to bail me out one last time, that maybe the universe had one more miracle and favor in store for me.

But here's the truth—I don't know what to tell you, and I don't know how to explain it. It's not a good feeling knowing I can't say or do anything to save myself right now. I have no more backup options. It's scary. And just as I, my friends, and my mom, just like Macoa, and like everybody else who was there to see me today. Today my heart was broken. Listen, life has moments like today's where we don't understand why the things that happen to us, happen to us. Why destiny denies us what we want, and what we've worked hard for.

The truth is that we can work for something all our lives, we can be honest, and we can put in all our time into what we want; but nothing is guaranteed. The truth is that the good doesn't always prevail. That truth is that sometimes the nice guy doesn't get the girl. The truth is that life is more than *unfair*.

Today I'm leaving Arizona empty handed, but I know I've left my mark on the poker world and my opponents. I'm leaving this country, but I'm leaving with a tranquil and free heart. I'm sorry, my friend. Like I said before, today I'm confused with the universe and why this happened to us. I really did think that the universe would help me now that I had made my peace with it. I can't say anything that will make this situation better and can't romanticize the situation enough for it to be okay. I can't tell you anything to take the sadness from you or make you realize how real it is for me. Because this isn't a movie or your typical book. This is real. And any words or some cliché quote won't take away the pain.

Remember I told you how all this happened? I was playing poker with my friends in middle school, and I wanted to be the best. Really, what if that had never happened? What if I hadn't been ambitious? What if poker and I had never met?

But listen to me now. This is the important part. We didn't win today. But this is what you need to take away from my story—I like to think we didn't win because the universe has something more special in store for us. I like to think that our suffering and pain will be cashed in later down the road, for something we will appreciate and want even more. I like to think that today I'll start to fight to be healthy and look back at this particular moment. I have a strong feeling this won't be the worst day of my life forever. I think it will soon be the best day of my life because it marked the transition for something better. This year has been the worst of my life, but I'd like to think that in ten years from now I'll be sitting in Italy with the girl of my dreams and we'll laugh about all this, because maybe I only met her because she listened to my story and wanted to get coffee with me. And maybe all this pain will teach me to really value the treasures of life.

Or, probably, most likely, none of that will happen.

And that's okay. Who knows what will happen. I just have to believe in a reality outside of mine. I have to believe that my decisions and future still have meaning despite my past. I need to trust that it will all turn out okay. And you also have to trust in something too. God, Karma, love, whatever. Listen, one last time, if we live our lives as if there's always one more thing to take care of, just one thing to do before real life starts, we will never live. You have to love what you have. Our lives aren't out there in the future, they're right here, right now. I know I said I didn't believe in luck, fate, destiny, or any of that crap. And I still don't. But our happiness is out there somewhere, or maybe inside of us; we just have to be in love with the path to find it.

Meditation is freedom.

EPILOGUE

FIFTY-ONE: HELL OF A RIDE

There was a time when I looked at people and judged them based off their character, not their chip stack. There was a time when I didn't understand what it meant to make a mistake—a time when my mistakes didn't mean I would lose sleep or have anxiety attacks. There was a time when my happiness came from living a sincere life, not from having temporary pleasures like money or women. All I can say is that it was a hell of a ride.

♣

I was excited to see that I had the whole airplane row to myself. I could have lain down and slept and just thought without having to talk to anyone. That's almost the last thing I wanted to do—talk. I had to get away from everything for a while. Not only from my friends and family, not only from

Macoa and all the other girls I had met that year, not only from Florida or Arizona, not only from poker, not only from my past, not only from school, and not only from social constructs that were ingrained in my mind from living in America. Rather, I needed to get away from part of myself, from the One Knight Stand.

I put my earphones on, closed my eyes, and waited for the plane to start moving. The first song to play on my phone was "Riptide" by Vance Joy. I couldn't help but smile. Although I had heard that song before, I had never really listened to the lyrics. But when I was on the airplane, I had all the time to really listen. It was just me, an unknown future, and the plane. I listened as I waited for the plane to move. I was anxious for it to get into the air soon.

I was scared of dentists and the dark,

I was scared of pretty girls and starting conversations

I started to think about me before I was sure of myself, how as a kid I was scared to tell Macoa how I felt and hid in my humor. How even though I pretended to be confident, I never really was.

All my friends are turning green

I remembered when I began playing poker, and my friends had shunned me when I turned into the One Knight Stand.

Running down to the riptide, taken away to the dark side…

Those lyrics reminded me of when I first took a bite of the forbidden apple and knew I wanted more. This song was telling the story of my life, and I couldn't help but close my eyes, smile, and wait for the ride that was to come.

I was at peace, or at least I was on my way to peace. And just as I was sure the plane was ready to back up, the last person made her way onto the plane, and the captain announced that the gate doors were now locked. It was real now, no turning back. I noticed the person who made the plane wait was a blond girl, about five feet tall. She had the cutest glasses on and was looking at her ticket trying to find where her seat was. As she stepped closer to my row, she kept looking for her seat, and as we made eye contact, my heart skipped a beat. Not the expression. No. My heart literally discontinued its natural rhythm when our eyes paired.

She seemed like she was smart but very lost. Like she wasn't quite *there* in life. But then again, is anyone? And I didn't think love at first sight was real. And I still don't. But now I understand—It's not that we ever fall in love with one glimpse. It's the fact that it sometimes takes only one glimpse to know we'll eventually love this person.

She finally realized that her seat was on the end of my row. I guess I wasn't going to use the whole row to sleep anymore, but I didn't mind. What did I notice about her? She was more gorgeous than I care to try to explain and had blue fingernails. She sat down and smiled. Killer smile.

"Hey," she said.

"We were waiting for you."

"Yeah, I'm sorry. This whole trip is last minute for me," she said giggling, pushing her glasses back up, trying to organize her things.

"What do you mean? We're going to India, not a Chainsmokers concert. Or are you getting off at one of the connections?"

"No. I'm also going to India."

I noticed that even though my decision to come here was also last minute, I still perceived others' actions in a different light. I realized that humans have a control setting installed in their brain—we can judge others, but never really ourselves.

She continued, "But I decided I was coming just last night."

"What made you decide?"

"Lots of things really. I just feel like I needed to do something different."

"Hmm. Like travel more?"

"Not exactly. It's a long story. It's stupid."

"Tell me. I'm curious. We have a lot of time."

"It's just, I've been the perfect girl my whole life, you know? I've grown up in the same city from childhood and gotten good grades throughout school. I've been exactly what my parents wanted me to be and have had the same boyfriend throughout high school. I graduated this week, and I was going to go to a good school in the fall. But…" she paused for a second. "Yesterday I was thinking about it, and I have never done anything for me. I haven't ever stopped to ask myself if I really wanted to be doing what I'm doing, you know? It's not my parents' fault, but I needed to get out—I just got really cold feet about this whole college thing." She looks at me, almost not sure of her decision of unveiling her life story to a stranger. "I'm sorry for rambling."

You know that feeling when you meet someone for the first time and hope they end up in your life somehow? This girl. I'll think about her for the rest of my life if I don't do something.

"I guess I understand. So what, you're just not going to go to school?"

"I don't know. I've been working this whole past year and have this money saved up, and I thought, I gotta get out of here. I've never done anything out of the ordinary, so here I am. School doesn't start until late August, and maybe I'll come back; I don't know. I don't know what's going to happen. And for the first time in my life, I'm okay with that…"

She continued speaking while I got lost in her. Her lips kept moving, but I was just mesmerized watching her speak. There was something about her; I couldn't help but look at her. I wanted to understand and be able to reply, but I could only stare at her lips as she spoke. I wouldn't have minded if she had kept talking for the rest of the plane ride. And when I realized she was done, I answered, "Well, that's good. I'm happy for you."

"Thanks. Means a lot."

"No problem. What's your name?" I asked.

"My name is Samantha. Your name is Charles, right?"

What? I was confused now.

"Yeah. How did you know that?"

"Your boarding pass is right there."

As the plane backed up, I couldn't help but think that although she was beautiful, she was far from perfect. She was insecure at times when she spoke, her fingernails weren't done nicely, and her laugh was more than a bit nerdy. And you know what? Those imperfections of hers, they were absolutely perfect to me. I didn't want a perfect girl like Macoa anymore. I didn't want the hot girls I had met at the clubs, and I didn't want a wildflower like Ella. All I wanted was to sit back and enjoy the ride with this girl who wasn't what I wanted my whole life. So as the plane started to drive on the runway, I put my earphones back in, and hit play so that the song could continue.

Lady, running down to the riptide
Taken away to the dark side,
I wanna be your lefthand man

And finally the plane took off, and I looked over to Samantha. She looked over to me, and neither of us smiled or said anything; we just both communicated through our eye contact.

The plane was now in the sky. Again, I understood that I needed to get away from everything. I needed to leave behind the social constructs that were ingrained in my mind being raised in a society like ours. My whole life I had planned for years down the road. Now, I didn't even know what I was doing in a couple of days. I contemplated the purpose of it all. Maybe this *was* better somehow. What's the point of studying for four years with little to no sleep or sanity? Only to get a job I don't really like to make money that doesn't really mean much? What's this obsession with becoming successful? The obsession with earning and spending money? People's journey to success is at the expense of everything else, especially happiness. Nobody ever stops to ask themselves if this is what they *actually* want to be doing. Maybe it was a good thing I was taking the road less traveled by, that I wasn't going to be a depressed college kid anymore.

"Wait. You never told why you're going to India. What's your story?"

"Not sure. Ask me again in a few months; I'm still figuring it out."

And here's the thing, the real and naked truth—I knew I wasn't going to marry that girl; I knew I probably wouldn't even be with her in a couple of weeks. We just have to understand that even though love is an energy that can and usually does transcend dimensions, it is not infinite. It's just that—an energy that comes and, also, goes as it pleases, respectfully finite. Because love is a *wildflower*. This, however, is not to say that what we feel now is any less significant knowing that it can, and probably will, end. The wiser among us might not even get over this fault in our stars. But what I do know is as of that moment of me sitting on that plane, that is the realest love I have felt. Call me crazy because I didn't even know her last name; I hadn't even kissed her yet. But I felt it.

I looked down to the clouds. I had done it; I was off. It was easy to get there. All I had to do was play a little poker and get a little lucky.

The funny part was, even when I thought I had made my peace with

God, I cursed the heavens because it had let me lose it all. Twice. Some ten hours prior to that moment, I was furious at the universe for what had happened to me. But in that instant I couldn't help but thank the gods for the broken road that had brought me to that seat, in that plane. Because that place in the middle of the sky was the only place I wanted to be, looking at that girl I had just met next to me, feeling completely free. It took me a while to understand that the truly beautiful moments didn't require a past or a future. They are so potent that they are absolute. Nothing else in the world exists.

Ecstasy. So I loved that moment because it made me forget about everything else.

I sat back and stared down from the window, and I closed my eyes and let everything go. I took a deep breath in and inhaled all the air I could contain. I held it all in for a second and then opened my eyes as I slowly exhaled and let go of all my past.

I opened my eyes to meet Samantha's. "So do you still have a boyfriend?" I asked her, as I paused the music.

But as her mouth started to move, and she gave me her answer, the music began to play again.

I love you, when you're singing that song and,

I got a lump in my throat

'cause you're gonna sing the words wrong

It was time to go. I didn't know where I was going, and I didn't really care. I just knew I'd be content where I'd end up because I was going with myself. I was healed and didn't need to do something so dramatic, but I wanted to. I wanted to get out in the real world. It would be a lie to say I wasn't a bit scared. I didn't know anything of my future, but I didn't care that much anymore. I don't want to sound like a hippie, but the cliché always ends up being true. The materials I had set value to were just a trap; I never ended up owning them, they ended up owning me.

Had I never realized that, I wouldn't be here right now, in India, telling you this story, on July 31.

FIFTY-TWO

CHARLES MARQUEZ

As the plane was landing in New Delhi, my phone began to blow up with notifications—a bunch of people asking me if I was okay, more people asking if I was even alive. I answered my mom first, initially apologizing but then telling her I had to get away, but that I would be back soon. I looked at other messages but felt overwhelmed and proceeded to block all future messages.

I then looked at my e-mails, something I hadn't done in months. Many were from UCF telling me about exams; others were usual mails I received. And as I scrolled up, they became more and more intense, from, "possible school probation" and "missing attendance" to "no show for finals" and "GPA dropping below accepted level." I opened a few but again felt overwhelmed. I deleted all messages from school and junk e-mails.

I began to get off the plane, Samantha behind me, and as I stepped down I looked at this unknown land that would be my home for an undefined amount of time.

But as I was stepping out of the plane and into the airport, still scrolling through e-mails, one seemed different from the rest. It was from MIT, the subject being *decision*.

Crap.

I opened the e-mail. "Dear, Charles, your decision is now available online. Please click on this link to view."

My heart accelerated like it used to.

I had forgotten all about MIT, but I couldn't click on the page fast enough. My phone was still a bit slow, but I got to the page where my information was. "View decision." Click. My phone loads once more. And once my phone finally brought me to the new page, there it was—my result.

I had spent my whole life trying to prove to myself and the world that I could become somebody; and now, in my hands, I was about to read what one of the best institutions in the world had to say to me. So as my heart started to race, exactly as it would if I was about to see the river when I had a flush-draw and had made a $20,000 bluff, I saw it. I saw my decision.

All I could do was stare at my phone. Everything around me wasn't real for a minute. Suddenly nothing mattered anymore; at least for those ten seconds, while I watched my phone load, that was the only thing that was real—everything else disappeared.

And as I stared at my phone and read my decision, I didn't know whether to smile, laugh out loud, or cry. So I did them all.

ACKNOWLEDGMENTS

Charles Marquez doesn't believe in luck "or any of that crap," and neither do I. But, in the conventional sense of the word, I am probably the luckiest guy in the world, and I am also beyond blessed to have the people I have in my life. And there are lots of people to thank for this book.

First, thank you to my whole family for always supporting me. I couldn't imagine my life without you guys—specially, Bella.

Thank you, Dad, for finding the time to read my drafts and encouraging me to keep writing. You are the smartest person I know and having your small touch as an artist is a privilege. I appreciate how you have high expectations for me, and I work hard to make you proud by trying to reach those expectations. You are my role model.

Thank you, Mom, for always being my number-one fan; you are the only person I didn't want reading any of the book before it was published, as I wanted you to see it when it was real. Thank you for being as excited as I am about this. Thank you for helping with the photo shoot! This project is for you. I worked endlessly for two years making this, trying to make it beautiful; and my definition of beauty starts with you.

Thank you, Ulrich, for being my brother. You were also one of the first people to read this book, and I hope I can one day receive your approval in my writing. Who knew you would be the one gambling now. I wish you way more than luck.

Second, thank you to my amazing friends. My amazing childhood friends from Weston, my great friends at Chapel Hill, and every other friend who is constantly pushing me to be better. There are too many people to name, but thank you to every friend who has always supported me and been kind to me. I love you guys. Thank you to all who read some part of the book and suggested changes. I know I annoyed almost all of you guys and sent hundreds of "help" e-mails, and I appreciate everyone who replied.

Thank you to friends and acquaintances who inspired any characters, plots, or events from the book. Both good and bad. Thank you to the girls who inspired the Macoa character. You know who you are. Just look in your purse. Or you don't know who you are. Isn't that ironic?

Thank you to all my poker friends; I hope some can recall the specific hands I mention in the book. Thank you to all those who have supported my poker aspirations. Specifically, thank you to those who came and watched me play sometimes and really went through the journey with me. In addition, thank you to all my friends who constantly were excited for me and truly supported me. You know who you are. You guys are part of me.

When it comes to writing the book, thank you to everyone who helped in anyway. Thank you to all those who did heavy lifting when it came to editing. Nati, Spidey, Jessica, Kenneth and Ilana, you guys rock! If there are any grammatical errors, I will publish this book again with a different ISBN number and remove you guys from the acknowledgements.

Thank you, Tyler, for mentioning me in your book and answering all my questions. Thank you, Allen, for helping me in every sense of the word, for the advice and for the guidance. Thank you for the editing, thank you for your help with the promos, the cover design, and connecting me with the people who made this book special. Thank you for being a great friend. Thank you for your special touch and professional work. You're a good man. Thank you, Nicolette, for reading the book and giving me great tips and insight. I appreciate your patience despite me sending you updated versions with mistakes you had already commented on. Oops. Thank you, Robin for being the best editor. Wherever you are out there, you're amazing.

Thank you, Chevy, for the great pictures! The photo shoot was an awesome experience; we made it work! Thank you for your professional work. I hope you liked the boba. Thank you, Nadège, for the amazing work with formatting! Thank you for the quick turnaround and I apologize for the 40 emails is less than a week!

A big thank you to all my writing professors at UNC and writing classmates for making me a better writer. I have learned so much about writing and life in those classes which I am eternally thankful for. I am truly fortunate to learn from you guys and gals.

Lastly, thank you, Charlie. It's funny how a theme in this book is the false idea of luck being real in life. But I am nothing short of lucky to have you in my life, as I know I don't deserve your friendship. Thank you for always supporting me in all my endeavors. Thank you for simply being a great friend. Thank you for always being the first to offer any help whether it's professional, financial, or emotional. Thank you, so much, for making this world a better place. You are truly, honestly, a great individual and I am proud of everything you've accomplished. You were the first person I ever showed a piece of this book to when I had only a page written, and you encouraged me to keep going. I appreciate you more than you know. There've been times when I've doubted myself, and you've doubted yourself, but look how far we've made it.

ABOUT THE AUTHOR

Marek Garcia is a writer, investor, and student at the University of North Carolina at Chapel Hill. Marek, a business major is focusing his studies on investment management and pursuing a career in banking. In his hometown, Weston, FL, he is best known for his humor and dedication in leaving a mark in everything he has his name attached to, both professionally and personally. Marek claims he was "really good at poker but even better at losing money," and has now shifted his focus on a career in finance. He is a big soccer fan, his favorite team being Pumas UNAM from Mexico City, and tries to keep active and live a healthy lifestyle. When he isn't working he likes to find new places to eat, go on adventures, and create tasty drinks for his friends and family. Most importantly, Marek loves his dog Bella more than anything in this world.